FLY BYE

C.W. FARNSWORTH

FLY BYE

Editing and Proofreading:

Jovana Shirley, Unforeseen Editing

Tiffany Persaud, Burden of Proofreading

Cover Design:

Kim Wilson, KiWi Cover Design

ALSO BY C.W. FARNSWORTH

Four Months, Three Words

Kiss Now, Lie Later

The Hard Way Home

First Flight, Final Fall

Come Break My Heart Again

The Easy Way Out (The Hard Way Home Book 2)

Famous Last Words

Winning Mr. Wrong

Back Where We Began

Like I Never Said

Fake Empire

Heartbreak for Two

Serve

For Now, Not Forever

Friday Night Lies

FLY BY

verb

To pass (someone or something) by flying

AUTHOR'S NOTE

I've done my best to represent the places and professions depicted in this book accurately. However, it is ultimately a work of fiction and I've taken some creative liberties that depart from total accuracy. For anyone with extensive knowledge of these locations or careers, I hope the adjustments don't detract from the overall reading experience.

CONTENTS

SYNOPSIS

The first time I saw Grayson Phillips, I fell. Tripped, to be specific. His seven-year-old self saved me from scraped knees and sentenced me to a fate of pining after my brother's best friend for years.

People change. Childish crushes fade. I'm an adult now, a doctor with more important things to worry about. I gave up on the boy next door ever loving me a long time ago.

Or so I thought…until he returns to our hometown on leave from the Air Force. For the first time, not everything between us feels one-sided. That doesn't make it matter. He'll take off soon —literally.

I'm a fly by to him. Nothing more than a passing interest. A distraction.

I know getting involved with him will mean saying goodbye to my heart.

I know I should say no.

I know I'll say yes.

FLY BYE

C.W. FARNSWORTH

CHAPTER ONE

I fell the first time I saw him.

Literally.

Pitch forward, face inches away from the pavement, scary stomach lurch fell. The sort of unexpected motion that leaves your palms sweaty and your heart pounding long after you're back upright.

My best friend, Sloane's, babysitter returned me home after picking our five-year-old selves up from the first day of Charleston Zoo's summer camp. And there he was—a scrawny stranger playing basketball by the garage with my older brother, Noah, as movers unloaded furniture from two yellow vans parked in front of the house next door. I tripped on one of the scooters Noah often left lying on the asphalt driveway and was saved from the unfortunate fate of two skinned knees—the worst non-life-threatening injury besides a stubbed toe, in my opinion—by quick reflexes.

I looked up into the green eyes of my seven-year-old savior, and I was *done.*

Bye, heart. It was nice knowing you.

Following that fateful afternoon, my feelings for Grayson Phillips went through cyclical phases. Awed, annoyed, attempts at apathy. Five months older than Noah, he was a couple of grades ahead of me in school. A small separation that felt gaping, especially when the two of them moved on to middle school and then high school.

As we grew older, Noah became less childish and more protective. He'd invite—even encourage—me to hang out with him and his friends. I spent plenty of time around Gray from the day he moved in next door until he moved out when I was sixteen. The more time I spent around Gray, the better I became at acting indifferent toward him. I adamantly denied having a crush on Gray to all of my friends, even Sloane, especially once it became very evident he was interested in girls, just not *me*.

It probably would have been a more convincing lie if not for the fact that Gray was the guy *every* girl had a crush on.

The last time I saw him was almost four years ago—he was back in Charleston on break from the Air Force Academy in Colorado, and I was home from Boston, visiting my parents. Noah and I ended up at a local bar to catch up with a bunch of people from high school. Gray showed up as I was ordering a drink and proceeded to *loudly* ask if little Evie Collins was old enough to consume alcohol. Never mind that I was only six weeks past twenty-one at the time. He followed it up with a joke about my bangs, which I now acknowledge were a mistake. He left after forty-five minutes—*not* that I counted—with Miranda Hendrix, my junior year biology partner.

That was the extent of our interaction.

I *thought* I was finally indifferent to his existence. The acrobatics in my stomach as I flick my gaze between the phone in my hand and the mirror I attached to the back of my bedroom door this morning say otherwise. I'm overreacting. *Slightly*. Okay, a lot. I'm close with my brother and ecstatic about being able to see him more than once a year, which became the norm. His worst offense today is the six-worded text I've spent the past ten minutes staring at.

Noah: *Running late. Picking up Gray first.*

There's a *slim* possibility Noah isn't referring to the Gray who's been his best friend since the Phillips family moved in next door. Noah started work at a new architecture firm a month ago; he could have made a new friend. My older brother could become best buddies with a brick wall.

And Gray isn't that unusual of a name.

But it's *him*. It has to be him. And it shouldn't matter he's in Charleston instead of deployed who knows where. I'm an adult now, not a starry-eyed kid. A *doctor*. Who cares if the only guy I've ever *really* wanted has never shown any interest in me? I gave up on the fantasy of having a fairy-tale romance with Gray a long time ago. My younger self envisioned it all—candy-heart deliveries in homeroom, going to homecoming together, making out under the bleachers, trips to the beach. I could picture it happening so clearly, watch it like a movie in my mind. And it all *did* happen…just not with him.

I've dated other guys. One of them turned into a serious relationship. Unfortunately, I've yet to encounter a single guy who has ever elicited a tenth of the emotion in me Gray Phillips does by simply *existing*.

Growing up, I was the girl who arrived home ten minutes before curfew. Who was the designated drunk driver for most of high school. Who took every advanced placement science course Charleston East High offered so I was ensured a spot in Boston University's uber-competitive seven-year medical school graduation program. At twenty-five, I have a bachelor's degree and already took the Hippocratic oath.

I'm accomplished. I've done everything right. I've always been the girl who does *everything* right.

But one text mentioning *his* name, and I'm reassessing my entire outfit. It's infuriating. Pathetic. I'm back to being the twelve-year-old girl who biked two miles to peruse Charleston Surf's flipper collection just because Gray worked there his freshman year. It could be considered sweet, I guess.

Or stalking.

I yank off the green T-shirt dress I was wearing and swap it for a pink cotton one that's tight in the torso but flares at the waist.

"Evie! You ready?" Sloane calls.

If she's ready, then I've taken even longer than I thought. Sloane is notorious for her tardiness. In high school, our shared friend group used to tell her we were meeting an hour earlier than we actually were. Half the time, she was still late.

I cast one final glance at my reflection. I got my hair cut yesterday. Now, the blonde strands fall just past my shoulders. I let it dry naturally, so there's a slight wave to the texture. My blue eyes look wide, excited. The sleek lines of the pink dress make me look put together. Poised. Professional. Like I'm headed to a polo match or a lawn party. I take a deep breath and open my bedroom door before I decide against this outfit too. Most of my wardrobe is still in boxes. I don't have any other option that won't involve hacking at tape and flying fabric.

Sloane, my best friend and roommate, is lounging against the couch in the living room, scrolling on her phone. I'd bet my meager savings she's on a dating app.

She glances up and eyes my appearance. "You changed."

"Yeah. Did you like the green dress better?" I literally can't remember the last time I wore anything besides scrubs or yoga pants. I'm out of practice on the whole dressing-up thing.

Sloane's head tilts to the left as she studies me. "No, the pink is cute." She stands. "Is Noah almost here?"

"No, he's running late." I don't say why. "Let's just Uber."

One brown eyebrow arches. "You were *just* complaining about how broke you are last night."

"I *am* broke. But I'm also earning money for the first time ever, not just sinking further into debt."

Sloane rolls her eyes. "Please. You'll pay off your med school loans in no time. Doctors make a ton. The Phillipses are filthy rich."

"Dr. Phillips runs the *whole hospital*, Sloane. I'm a first-year resident. Two very different pay grades."

"Whatever. Dr. Phillips loves you. You'll be promoted in no time."

I smile. "That's not at all how it works."

Sloane is no longer listening to me, back on her phone and pulling up what I'm guessing is the Uber app. "Jimmy will be here in two minutes," she announces, heading toward the door.

"Great." I double-check I have everything I need in my bag, triple-checking for the two boxes of candles, then follow her out onto the porch and down the stairs.

We've lived here for just over a week. I moved back to the South from Boston as soon as I graduated from medical school. Sloane left her job as an administrative assistant at a fashion magazine in New York City to return to Charleston and start work as a paralegal at a private law firm. After one week, both of our jobs are still exciting and nerve-racking—and in my case, exhausting.

My first shifts as an honest-to-God doctor were fueled by pure adrenaline. It was mildly—and by mildly, I mean, paralyzingly— terrifying to realize that years of flash cards and tests and clinicals resulted in the responsibility of having people's *lives* in my hands.

Knowing that would be the case was very different than actually meeting patients relying on me to diagnose and treat them correctly.

I found my first few days overwhelming. Sloane found hers underwhelming. I'm not sure if she regrets moving back—not yet, at least—but I'm grateful she did. The two of us grew up practically attached at the hip. It wouldn't feel like home without her here.

June sunshine filters down from the sky as we wait for Jimmy to arrive. It's only eleven a.m. The sun hasn't risen directly overhead, but it's already burning bright and full. I acclimated more to the Northeast climate than I realized because the heat is harsher than I expected.

I study the exterior of our new home from the curb. We lucked out, finding this place. The bungalow is newly renovated but still has the charm the bazillions of cookie-cutter apartments we looked at sorely lacked. Its only downside is that the bus routes ensure it takes me half an hour to make it to work. Once I have a car, that will get cut down to fifteen. The brick exterior and front porch make up for it for now. There's also a patio in the backyard, perfect for enjoying the summer nights. Sloane and I strung up lights out there last night. Despite the fact that less than half of our belongings have been unpacked, it feels like home.

Jimmy pulls up in a silver Prius less than a minute later. I text Noah back as we start down the street.

Evie: *We'll just meet you there.*

I slip my phone back into my bag and then stare out the window at the colorful buildings of Charleston as they flash by.

"What do you think?" A photo of a blond man standing next to a surfboard is waved in front of my face, blocking the scenery. "He's cute, right?"

I squint at the screen. "That's an old photo."

"What?" Sloane pulls it back and peers at it. "How do you know?"

"That's at Folly Beach. They built that huge hotel up behind it, remember? The construction started right before I moved to Boston."

"Dammit. You're right. How'd I miss that?"

"Probably because you were more focused on his abs than the swimming pool atop old sea turtle habitats."

Sloane rolls her eyes, then swipes right. "Well, maybe he has an eight-pack now."

"Or he's over thirty," I say before I go back to staring out the window.

Under thirty and employed are Sloane's two requirements when it comes to men. She views online dating as the highest form of entertainment. She's tried to get me to sign up for it countless times by telling me it's the only way to meet someone these days, but I guess unrequited feelings didn't completely destroy the hopeless romantic in me. I'm still clinging to the fantasy of meeting a decent guy without the aid of computer code and carefully curated photos.

The Prius stops outside my childhood home ten minutes later. It's a white-shingled ranch my parents bought when they got married. They've hung on to it as the value of the neighborhood skyrocketed, resulting in the surrounding properties being torn down and larger homes being built in the sought-after location close to Edgefield Park. My parents' place has two bathrooms and three bedrooms. The Phillipses' house next door comically towers over it with its three stories, screened porch, upper balcony, and four-car garage. The only feature my parents' house has that theirs doesn't is a pool.

Our lot is large—mostly thanks to the fact that the house's square footage is a small fraction of the neighbors'—and my mom is an avid swimmer. The installation was a fifteenth wedding anniversary gift to her from my dad. I wonder what he has planned for their thirtieth, which is what we're celebrating today.

Sloane and I walk up the driveway and toward the backyard. Excitement fizzes in my stomach at the number of cars and the commotion coming from the backyard. I haven't been home since Christmas, and that was a short visit. Even worse than the excitement is the anticipation.

It doesn't matter if he's here.

I'm not great at lying to myself. But I have perfected bored nonchalance when it comes to Gray. Even Sloane has stopped winking at me when his name comes up, and she can read me like a book most of the time.

The backyard is overflowing with people. It's a perfect summer day—clear, sunny, and not too hot. Long tables line the patio, covered with dishes of food. My father is standing at the giant gas grill, which is his pride and joy, flipping burgers. My mother is in her element, placing tiny paper umbrellas in glasses of lemonade between replenishing appetizers. Most of the party attendees are friends of my parents, close to them in age, but the whole neighborhood was invited. There are a few couples here with younger kids, most of who are splashing around in the pool.

I head for my mom first. Sloane follows.

"Hey, Mom. Happy anniversary."

"Evie!" My mom's smile rivals the sun's wattage as she hugs me tightly. She smells the same as always—like lemon and eucalyptus with a faint hint of chlorine.

I think my parents were worried I'd stay north after graduation. They've both made their relief that I decided to return to Charleston to complete my residency obvious.

"Happy anniversary, Mrs. C," Sloane says, hugging my mom

8

after me. She's the youngest of eight and spent more time at my house than at her own growing up.

"Thank you, Sloane." My mom beams. "I'm so happy you're both here. Help yourself to some food."

Sloane grabs a plate and starts filling it.

"I'm going to go say hi to Dad first," I announce.

He's still standing by the grill, proudly wearing *The Grillfather* apron Noah and I got him years ago, as he talks with Henry Phillips. Our next-door neighbor, my dad's best friend, Gray Phillips's father…and the chief of the hospital where I started my residency a few days ago. Which makes him my boss's boss's boss, basically.

"Hey, Dad," I say when I reach him.

My dad hugs me to his side with a squeeze while simultaneously flipping sizzling meat. "Leigh-Leigh! You made it!"

I cringe at the childhood nickname. "I live ten minutes away now, Dad. Of course I made it."

My dad chuckles. "I'm sure you had better ways to spend your Saturday."

Not really. My social life is sadly lacking. The only reason Sloane hasn't successfully dragged me out to a bar yet is because we've been too busy with our new jobs and unpacking.

I turn to greet Henry. "Hi, Dr. Phillips."

He's insisted I call him Henry since I was little, but the dynamic between us has changed. I sat in a sea of awed faces during orientation as he welcomed us all to Charleston General Hospital. I personally witnessed his mere presence in an examination room make an experienced surgeon's hands tremble.

He chuckles. "Save the formalities for the hospital, Dr. Collins." He winks.

Even after years of hard work to earn the title, it still feels weird to hear it.

"How have your first few days been?"

Overwhelming. Chaotic. Stressful. "Good."

Henry smiles knowingly. "Parts get easier. I've heard nothing but good things about your work so far."

I flush, forever unable to take a compliment gracefully.

Henry's eyes flit away from my face to look behind me. "You're here." His tone changes. I know what that means before I turn around to look.

Gray Phillips closes the final couple of feet that separate us, appearing at my side to face our fathers. "Don't sound so excited, Pops. I might think you're happy I made it home in one piece."

My father and I both shift uncomfortably. Gray and Henry have always had a strained relationship. They butt heads at every possible opportunity. Henry likes to be in control of situations, to command them. It's what makes him a fantastic chief. And it's a trait he passed along to his son.

"You signed up for it, Grayson."

Henry held out hope for years that Gray would follow his footsteps to Duke and its medical school, right up until Gray announced he was headed to the Air Force Academy in Colorado instead. Gray hadn't even told anyone he applied. It was the talk of Charleston East High School—not to mention, our neighborhood—for weeks.

"Damn right, I did." Gray looks away from his father to mine. "Good to see you, Adam."

"You too, Gray. Nice to have you back."

"Yeah. Thanks."

Out of all other options to greet, his gaze slides to...me. Last choice, like always. Aside from the occasional teasing comment, Gray usually treats me the way people who don't like animals treat their friends' pets—with polite indifference.

"Hey, Everleigh."

My teeth grind together. I *hate* being called by my full name. Which he knows. With the exception of my parents and Noah, who occasionally call me Leigh-Leigh, I go by Evie everywhere.

"If you're going to be so formal, *Grayson*, you should call me Dr. Collins."

I don't know what his official title in the Air Force is, or I would use that. Noah mentioned he was the youngest something or other, which doesn't surprise me at all. Gray is a born leader. He oozes charisma when he wants to, and he *uses* it.

Gray studies me, the picture of amused indifference. If the sniping with his father bothered him, there's no trace of it visible on his handsome face now. His green eyes scan my features. Aside from my lack of bangs, I don't think I look that different from the last time he saw me, even though it's been three and a half years.

"Noah mentioned you finally graduated. Well done."

Angry heat crawls across my skin as I absorb his tone. It suggests I took more than the four years that it usually takes to graduate medical school, not a year less, thanks to Boston's unique program. That I was behind the curve when, actually, I finished at the top of my class. He also manages to make it sound like he's congratulating me for winning a middle school science fair.

My dad and Henry have turned back to the grill. I should take the opportunity to leave as well.

Instead, I ask, "How long are you back for?"

"Three weeks." Gray appears relaxed as he leans against the railing of the deck, but for some reason, it suddenly seems like he's on edge about something.

"Big plans?"

"Nope. You want to hang out?"

I stare at him. He's fucking with me. I know he is, and the

amused twinkle in his eye—the only thing that hasn't changed from his seven-year-old self—confirms it. Still, my stomach flips at the suggestion.

"I'm busy."

"Uh-huh. I regret not becoming a doctor less and less every day."

I glance at our dads, who are fiddling with the grill settings and paying no attention to us. "You considered it?"

"Not really."

Gray leans down and snags a can of seltzer out of the cooler next to the stairs. The lines of muscle in his forearms tense and shift. I could list each tendon off by name. Instead, I take the opportunity to ogle the rest of his body. I have no idea what sort of physical training airmen go through. Whatever it is, it must be intense because Gray is *ripped*. *Flip a tire* in shape.

He's wearing navy shorts and a light blue button-down. Both look tailor-made to his tall frame. At five-nine, I'm used to guys being roughly my height or shorter. It's not a problem with Charleston East's former star shooting guard—the one guy I'd like to have *some* sort of advantage over.

He tilts the sparkling water up to take a long sip. His Adam's apple bobs as he swallows, and his dark brown hair flops to the side, revealing freckles on his forehead. It must have been sunny wherever he was located for his last deployment.

I don't usually have any trouble coming up with small talk. Especially when I'm nervous—that's often when I'm chattiest. Unfortunately, the last few minutes have confirmed that Gray Phillips still throws me off-kilter. Despite the fact that I've known him for most of my life, I've never acquired any form of immunity to his presence. If anything, time has weakened my defenses.

"Hey, Evie." Noah appears and breaks the awkward tension hovering between me and Gray.

12

Well, *I* find the silence awkward. Gray is just standing a few feet away, casually sipping like he's posing for La Croix's spring marketing campaign.

"Hey." I give my brother a hug and am enveloped by the scent of bergamot. Noah has used the same brand of aftershave ever since he was old enough to. Probably before then, actually.

Noah glances between me and Gray, likely wondering why we're standing next to each other. I know Noah wasn't oblivious to my South Carolina-sized crush on the boy next door, growing up—just was nice enough not to say anything. He knew he had nothing to worry about when it came to his best friend and me.

"You getting settled into the new place okay?" he asks.

"Yeah," I reply. "You and Emmett were lifesavers. I owe you each a beer. Or six."

Noah smiles. He and his friend Emmett Baker helped me and Sloane move a seemingly endless stream of boxes into our new place last week with minimal grumbling. Despite the fact that she and I each lived in tiny places with multiple roommates in New York and Boston, respectively, Sloane and I managed to accumulate a surprising amount of stuff.

"Did you remember to get the cakes?"

Noah snaps his fingers. "Shit. I knew there was—" He laughs at the horrified expression I feel my face twist into. "Kidding. Yeah, I got them."

I punch his shoulder and have to hide my grimace as my fist encounters solid muscle. Unlike me, my brother works out on a regular basis.

"I'm getting food," Gray announces abruptly before shoving off the railing and heading for the buffet.

I'm grateful I no longer need to act like I forgot he was standing nearby. I'm less enthused about how his departure is setting me up for a healthy helping of some brotherly concern.

13

As soon as Gray is gone, Noah's gaze turns worried.

Called it.

"You sure you're doing okay, Evie?"

"Yes," I state emphatically. I soften my voice when he continues to stare at me with obvious uncertainty. "I'm fine, Noah. Really."

"It's a lot. The move, the new job, Logan…" Noah scrutinizes me closely as he lists each life change off, lingering on the last one.

I sigh in response. Noah is taking my breakup with Logan Fitzgerald harder than I am. I ended our ten-month relationship a week before we graduated. Logan had sat beside me on the first day of orientation; we became fast friends from there. I knew he wanted more than platonic for a long time before I gave it a shot. Just like I knew he wanted to stay in Boston for his residency, and I knew I wanted to return to Charleston. A long-distance relationship with a guy who had always felt more like a friend wasn't appealing to me.

"It's not like I'm in a strange place with strangers, Noah. And Logan…I'm over it."

"You just broke up."

"Exactly. We weren't…it wasn't really a hard decision," I admit. It sounds callous, but it also happens to be the truth. I don't know what it feels like to be in love. But I'm pretty sure I know what it feels like not to be.

Noah reads the sincerity on my face. Surprise mixes with relief. "Okay."

I give him a spontaneous hug. "Thanks for looking out for me."

He smiles with a mixture of pride and affection that makes me feel ten feet tall. "Always."

"How's work?" I ask, eager to shift the attention off me.

That question leads to ten minutes of feigned interest in the mall project Noah is working on developing. I love my brother a lot. Yet I have absolutely *no* interest in blueprints or zoning laws or steel shortages. I nod along until our mom herds us toward the burgers that have just come off the grill.

I spend the next hour catching up with family friends and neighbors I haven't seen in months, some in years. My trips back home over the last seven years were sporadic. It wasn't a short journey—especially for someone who hates flying—and there's a very good reason most people take eight years to graduate from college and medical school. Squeezing that into seven years was a challenging feat that required no shortage of sacrifices. I came home as often as I reasonably could, but those visits were mostly limited to catching up with close friends and family.

Noah reappears by my side as Mrs. Hanson, who lives at the end of the street, updates me on the horrific—according to her, at least—construction surrounding the condos going in along Hastings Cove.

"Time to get the cakes ready," he tells me.

I smile at Mrs. Hanson. "Daughter duty calls."

She waves me away with a smile.

"Didn't you say your new firm designed the Hastings Cove condos?" I whisper as we head for the deck stairs.

"Yeah. Why?"

"I just wouldn't mention that to Mrs. Hanson, is all."

Noah chuckles under his breath. Our elderly neighbor is known for her long-winded opinions.

My parents' kitchen hasn't changed at since childhood. White cabinets line the walls, offsetting the cheery yellow walls that took three tries to paint. My mom decided the first color attempt was too "egg yolk," and the second looked like "white paint that

15

went bad." The large wooden table where I used to eat breakfast and finish school assignments sits in the center of the room.

The cakes—a buttercream concoction from a local bakery that forms an elaborately decorated *3* and *0*—are sitting on the marble counter next to the sink. I fish the two packs of candles out of my bag and start sticking them in the cakes while Noah leans against the fridge.

"Crap. There are only twenty-eight," I say, shaking the paper container. No more candles magically appear.

Noah shrugs. "No one will count."

"You know Mom will notice." There's a good reason Noah and I both ended up in detail-oriented professions. I squint at the back of one package. "They say they have fifteen each!"

Hinges squeak as the deck door opens again.

Noah straightens. "You bring any candles, man?"

"Oh, yeah. I never leave the house without them."

I startle at the sound of Gray's voice, spinning to watch him rinse his hands off in the sink.

"Cake crisis?"

Noah jerks his chin toward me. "She's missing two."

I love how *our* parents' cakes have suddenly become *my* problem.

"Sure sounds like a national emergency to me," Gray drawls.

Inspiration strikes. "Would your mom have any?" I ask Gray.

His mom, Juliet, loves entertaining as much as mine.

"Stranger things have happened," he replies, drying his hands on the towel draped over the oven handle.

"Can you check?"

Gray blanches at the request. "For *candles*?" His tone makes it clear there's nothing stupider one could search for.

I don't deign that with a response. He knows the answer.

Gray lets out a long-suffering sigh; like this request is *by far* the most inconvenient one that's ever been made of him. "I wouldn't even know where to look."

Noah groans. "Just let Evie in the house, Phillips. Everyone is going to be wondering what the hell is happening with the cakes."

"Tell them we're baking them," I suggest.

Noah rolls his eyes.

Gray heads for the front door. "Come on, Everleigh."

I huff as I follow him out onto the front lawn. "You know I *hate* being called that."

"You know there are other things I could be doing than searching for *candles* with you, right?"

I focus on the rocking chairs on the Phillipses' front porch rather than retorting. Gray types the code into the keypad by the front door, then opens it. I step inside the house next door for the first time in over a year. My gaze roves over the walnut floor, white walls, and neutral furnishings. Timeless and elegant.

"I love this house."

Instead of the caustic answer I'm expecting, Gray says, "Yeah, me too."

"Is that why you never moved?"

Despite his distant relationship with his father, Gray has kept this city as his home base instead of moving elsewhere. Although, I guess he *did* choose a career that requires him to be who knows where for lengthy stretches of time.

"Nah. Just easier not to."

I snort. "Yeah, you hate challenges." It would take me a long time to list all the stupid things I know he and Noah did growing up.

Gray crosses his arms and leans against the banister of the staircase. "I got you inside. Get the candles."

I roll my eyes at his bossiness but head into the formal dining room. There's a massive hutch I'm betting holds my best chance of candles. Sure enough, the third drawer down contains an assortment of them. I grab two, identical to the ones currently on the cakes—then a third just in case—and walk back into the entryway.

"Got them."

Gray nods, then heads out the front door. I don't miss the glance at the third cubby I know used to hold his basketball equipment. I wonder when the last time *he* was back here was. Longer than me, I'd bet.

We're both silent on the short walk back over to my parents' house. Noah is waiting in the kitchen, right where we left him. He heaves an overly dramatic sigh of relief when I wave the extra candles around like sparklers.

I add one candle to the *3* cake and one to the *0* cake. "Okay, they're ready."

An off-key, hastily modified version of "Happy Birthday" begins as Noah and I step out onto the back deck. Noah holds the *3* while I carry the *0*.

"Happy anniversary to you. Happy anniversary to you. Happy anniversary, dear Laurie and Adam. Happy anniversary to you!"

Noah and I set the two number cakes down in front of our beaming parents.

"Happy birthday, Laurie," my father jokes. "You don't look a day over twenty-nine."

My mom giggles. Noah and I exchange a grossed-out look. I love my parents. I love that they're still so in love. I just have no interest in witnessing it—I saw plenty growing up.

"You guys can blow the candles out now," Noah suggests with a smirk as we all watch them make googly eyes at each other.

They finally do, so the cakes get distributed among the onlookers.

"Guess it's present time then." My father pulls a white envelope out of the pocket of his khakis. He hands it to my mom. Based on his *I did good* smile, it's not a gift card.

She pulls a slip of paper out and scans it. "Italy?"

My dad smiles. "I booked the ten-day cruise we've been talking about for years. We leave on Monday—and before you start freaking out, I already settled everything with work. We've just got to rope one of the kids into watering the plants and cat-sitting."

Not me, Noah mouths at me. He hates the white, fluffy Ragdoll.

I sigh, knowing who that leaves. "Fine."

Sloane sighs dramatically next to me. "*Oh no.* Over a *week* without being woken up at four fifteen a.m. by 'You Belong with Me'? However will I go on?"

I stick my tongue out at her. "That song is classic T. Swift."

"It's the *time* I have an issue with, not the song."

I turn to my parents. "I can stay here and look after everything while you're gone." Their house is ten minutes closer to the hospital anyway.

They both look thrilled, which makes it worth it. My father whispers something in my mother's ear that makes her laugh as she leans against him.

It feels good to be home.

CHAPTER TWO

Sloane waits until six p.m. to inform me she told Emmett we'd go to Malone's—our local bar of choice—to settle our debts from moving. I don't have any issue with thanking him and Noah for lugging our possessions around. I *do* have an issue with going out with Gray Phillips—who I'm certain will be there too—but I can't say so without undoing years of denial, so I have no choice but to agree to the outing.

For the second time today, I spend too long deciding on what to wear. I also put on heels, which I hardly ever wear. They pinch my toes, but they also make my legs look miles long. Sloane gives me an approving nod before we leave the house.

When we walk into the bar, it's already packed. Malone's doesn't run the tightest of ships when it comes to enforcing the drinking age, meaning the dark stone walls are hardly visible past the crowds. Not only with college students home for the summer, but also with young professionals reliving the nostalgia of coming here and hoping not to get carded.

A long bar dominates the center of the room with a chalkboard menu that displays tonight's specialty cocktails. We shuffle between the crowded barstools and the circular leather booths that line the walls.

"There are the guys." Sloane makes a beeline toward the back of the bar.

I take a deep breath, then follow her over to the booth, where Noah, Emmett, Gray, and the fourth member of their usual crew, Harrison, are all sitting. Gray and Emmett have their backs to us, but Noah spots us right away and smiles. He and Harrison move further into the booth, so Sloane and I can sit. I sink down onto the buttery leather immediately, grateful to be off my feet.

My seat is directly across from Gray, who's typing something on his phone. My throbbing toes remind me I'm wearing these death traps because of *him*—because I want to appear older, wiser, and closer to his towering height—and it pisses me off for multiple reasons. Mainly because he didn't even notice.

I know almost everything about the human heart. Its anatomy, its flaws, its cadence.

I can't figure out how to fix mine. To make it stop beating faster for the one guy it shouldn't.

A waitress appears by our booth. "Hey, y'all. What can I get for you?"

She's pretty. Young and blonde and cheery. All four guys perk up, but *her* gaze is on Gray. Unfortunately, he's the sort of attractive that is every girl's type, that stands out in all the right ways.

Gray looks up from his phone and grins, a slow, lazy one that takes its time unfurling across his face. "What do you recommend?"

She cocks a hip. "What do you like?"

For fuck's sake. "I'd like a whiskey sour, please."

Reluctantly, the waitress peels her eyes away from Gray's perfect bone structure to jot down my order. Sloane chimes in with her request, and the rest of the guys do the same.

"Got any plans while you're back, Gray?" Noah asks once she's left to fetch our drinks.

Gray looks at me, and for one wild second, I think he's going to bring up his invitation to me to hang out. The one I'm *almost* certain wasn't genuine. "Your *little* sister just got in the way of one."

Nope, he's talking about getting laid. As if he'll have trouble finding another willing female to take home tonight.

I snort. "I'm *thirsty*. She was here to take our drink order. And if that was the extent of your game...you've got bigger problems than me interrupting, Phillips."

Gray leans back and spreads one arm across the back of the booth. He's still wearing the same light-blue button-down from the party. The move stretches the cotton material taut across his chest, teasing at what lies beneath. I have his full attention, and it comes with a heady, thrilling rush of significance.

"The extent? That wasn't even the start, Collins."

He says my last name with the same taunting lilt I spoke his in. I roll my eyes, acting unaffected by the erratic pounding of my heart. It *almost* feels like he's flirting with me, which is an event worthy of a national holiday.

The first Saturday in June is now Gray Phillips Flirts with Evie Collins Day.

The parade I was planning is canceled when Gray gets lost in the waitress's cleavage. Or at least, that's what it looks like when she returns with our drinks and selectively bends over to deliver them.

I look away and sip my cocktail, hoping she didn't spit in it. The whiskey hits my tongue with a smoky burn that sears my stomach and slowly trickles into my bloodstream. I down it quickly, mostly for something to do while I people-watch. The

22

guys are discussing sports, and Sloane is messaging her surfer guy. I feel light and loose by the time the glass is empty.

"Come on." I nudge Sloane's arm. "Let's go dance."

She perks up immediately, giving me a delighted smile. "Yeah?"

"Yeah." I'm usually the one suggesting we head home early. Not that we wade into the pool of wandering hands and sloppy lines that often exist on a bar's dance floor.

"Later, boys." She slides out of the booth, and I'm right behind her.

I don't know the name of the song playing, but it has a steady, sultry beat that's easy to move in time to. I focus on the rhythmic pulse, letting the glimmer of warmth in my veins guide my movements. I only allow myself one glance at Gray. He's deep in conversation with Emmett.

"Now's your chance," Sloane tells me between songs.

"My chance for what? To show off my shopping cart?"

She snorts at the mention of my trademark dance move. "No. Your chance with Gray Phillips."

I tense and learn it's difficult to dance when your body feels like it's been encased in plaster. "I don't want a chance with him."

Sloane gives me her patented *I don't believe you* look. "I don't believe you. You've had a thing for him since we were kids."

"I had a thing for him *when* we were kids," I correct.

"Same difference. You need a rebound after Logan. Gray is *hot*, and he's only home for a little while. I think it would be good for you. Like a summer fling."

I scoff. Thankfully, the pounding bass of a Lady Gaga song saves me from any more of a response. I'm no longer loose and pliant. I can't return to my easy, relaxed state after Sloane's suggestion.

I'm attracted to Gray. He's no stranger to short, emotionless flings. If I actually made a move, what would he do? We're both single. Both adults. Maybe I need to shatter the fantasy once and for all. Knock him off the pedestal I placed him on the day we met.

But I know myself. I might be confident in certain areas of my life, but love and romance are not one of them. I never know the perfect outfit to wear on a first date or the right thing to say or the proper etiquette for texting. And like it or not—I *don't* like it— Gray Phillips has always been *that guy* for me. The one who throws my world off-center and reorients it around himself. If I were to gather the confidence to seduce a guy, it wouldn't be him —the man who makes me forget basic facts by being in the same room.

Is his effect on me healthy? No.

Reasonable? Also no.

But that's the elusive, infuriating thing about love—it can't be controlled. You can't channel it where you want it to go. It chooses its own path.

I'm not in love with Gray. I used to think I was. But it means something different now than when I used to doodle his name in the margins of my notebooks. It's a heavier word with weighted meaning. It doesn't mean those juvenile feelings have faded away, though.

"I'm going to the restroom," I tell Sloane.

As I hobble off the dance floor in my heels, she nods, already heading for the group of guys who have been watching us for the past ten minutes. I wish I had a quarter of her self-confidence.

The hallway leading to the restrooms is empty and smells faintly of harsh antiseptic. Better than other scents, I guess. Although it does remind me of work.

I lean back against the cool stone wall opposite the restroom door, seriously contemplating kicking off my heels. A questionable stain on the floor makes me second-guess that option. I sigh and tilt my head up to study the white plaster ceiling as I wait for the red above the handle to turn to green. The thick wall I'm leaning against muffles the commotion on the other side. Away from the activity and noise, I feel warm. Relaxed. A little sleepy.

Footsteps sound to my left. I'm annoyed by the irritating tap that signals an interruption from the moment I was having, making prolonged eye contact with the ceiling. The restroom door before me stays shut, meaning I'll probably have to make small talk. At the very least, it'll be weird if I just keep staring straight up. I roll my head to the side for a glimpse of who's approaching.

My heart takes off at a gallop.

"Had your fill of dancing?"

Awareness skates down my spine and spreads through my senses as Gray stops beside me, adopting a similar pose against the wall.

I shrug like I'm too nonchalant to care he saw where I went. "Just needed a break."

"Breaks are good."

The air around me feels weighted and heavy, filled with possibilities. I can't recall the last time Gray and I were alone together. Paired with Sloane's suggestion and the fact that he looks more comfortable to lean against than this wall, I'm the closest I've ever been to crossing a line I never thought I would—unless he crossed it first.

"Probably been a while since you've been to a bar, huh?"

He tilts his head to smirk at me. Lazy heat traverses my veins.

"Sure. At least twenty-two hours."

Riiight. "I figured you just got home."

"Been back since Wednesday." His green eyes flick down to my heels and back up so fast that I almost missed the glance. It was far from a heated perusal, but he definitely looked. "Last time *you* went out?"

I can't even remember, but I'm not admitting that to Gray. "I go out."

"I didn't say you don't."

"Your face did."

He chuckles. The sound slides over me like the burn of whiskey—smooth, languid, and potent.

Amusement disappears as he assesses me, focusing on my face. "You look different."

"It's been years." I don't specify I've kept track of how many. Don't mention the bangs, either.

"Yeah, it has, huh?"

"You seem different too."

"*I* never had bangs."

Dammit, that is *what he was talking about.*

"I said, you *seem* different, not that you *look* different."

Although he does, especially up close like this. The line of his jaw looks sharper, his eyes appear greener, and his hair is long enough to run fingers through. You know, *hypothetically.* That's *definitely* not what I'm imagining doing right now.

"Are you happy to be home?"

He doesn't answer right away, just shifts positions against the wall beside me. "No. Not really."

"Why not?"

The restroom door opens. If Gray wasn't standing beside me, I'd think, *Finally.* Since he is, I'm tempted to shove the two girls stumbling out right back inside to prolong this moment. Both girls gawk at Gray before walking back down the hallway. The general consensus among the female population seems to be that Grayson Phillips is the sort of gorgeous that makes bad decisions seem like the best ideas you've ever had. For once, Mr. Flirty barely spares

26

them a glance. His gaze stays focused on me, and it's one of the most thrilling things I've ever experienced.

Sloane's voice echoes in my head. *"Now's your chance."*

"Being here..." He pauses. Studies me. Weighs something. "It's just boring."

That's not what he was going to say. We both know it. I feel like I failed a test without being asked a single question. Fell short without knowing where the finish line was.

"Oh." I flounder for something else to add. I thought he might mention his ongoing rift with his dad. Thought we might discuss something of significance.

Gray straightens abruptly. "Go ahead." He nods toward the empty restroom.

I don't move. "Are you—"

"Or I'll go." That's what he says. *Conversation over*, is what he means.

"Go ahead."

He hesitates. For a few seconds, I think he might change his mind. Then, he walks into the restroom, and I realize he was just giving me another chance to go ahead.

I let out all the air in my lungs with a long exhale. There's a hum under my skin that wasn't there until I saw who was walking down the hallway, and it hasn't abated now that he's gone.

Gray opens the restroom door a few minutes later. "All yours."

I nod, unsure of what I might say if I open my mouth. His face is guarded. I can't tell what he's thinking, what he wants. But my feelings toward Gray have never been about what *he* wants from *me*. They're about what *I* want from *him*. So, when he steps out of the restroom, I do the stupidest, most impulsive thing I've ever done in my life.

I close the gap and kiss him.

27

Really kiss him.

It's the furthest thing from a slow inching toward someone. That moment where you hesitate, where you gauge the other person's reaction and try to remember when you last brushed your teeth? I erase it. I toss *should haves* and *might haves* and *maybes* up in the air, light them on fire, and kiss Grayson Phillips.

My childhood idol.

My middle school crush.

My teenage fantasy.

And to my complete and utter shock, *he kisses me back*. I didn't think he ever would. But I didn't think *I* would ever kiss *him* either.

Am I dreaming? If so, I'd better have forgotten to set my alarm.

Chemistry combusts. The kiss turns greedy. Dirty. Hands are wandering. Tongues tangling.

My brain completely shuts off, too overwhelmed to process everything that's happening. I'm a slave to sensation, barely registering we're moving until the restroom door slams shut, sealing us in the smaller space. I'm right up against another hard wall, and this time, I'm being pressed by a body that feels deliciously warm and distinctively male. He pins me against the back of the restroom door as he continues to kiss me.

I can't pull in enough air, can't breathe anything but him. My heart races, and blood rushes. I feel like I'm drowning. Everything is muffled, except for burning need. Not for oxygen —for *him*.

Can a kiss *make you feel this way? Apparently.*

My legs are on solid ground. I can feel the pinch of the heels that I no longer regret wearing because they're making his mouth more accessible. But I'm also floating, flying, and falling. My surroundings are a blur, and my mind is a mess.

I can taste the smoky burn of tequila on his tongue. He smells like expensive cologne and sweat. One hand lifts the hem of my dress to slide between my legs, and I forget where we are. Who I am. Everything I thought I knew about lust and desire and arousal flees like pappi on a windy day.

Is there a moment more powerful than having a wish fulfilled? Mine isn't altruistic or commendable or worthy of winning a Nobel Peace Prize. It's selfish and silly and senseless. But it's mine, and I've protected it. I haven't let the rationality that governs the rest of my life reach how much I hoped to one day experience a moment where Gray treated me as anything more than his best friend's little sister. I think this qualifies.

Fantasies don't have to make sense. They often don't—that's the point. And they rarely become reality. Yet somehow, I'm living mine now.

I dig my fingers into his thick hair the same way I was imagining in the hallway, running the tips of my fingernails lightly along his scalp.

"Fuck," Gray rasps. The low, masculine rumble ignites new heat that fizzles in my stomach. It sinks lower when he slips one finger inside me, then two. "You're so tight. Like you've never taken a cock."

My body responds to his filthy words and confident movements, coating his fingers with evidence of how I'm responding to his touch. Words I don't mean to say follow; my tongue loosened by heady sensation and the lingering buzz of alcohol in my blood. "I haven't."

It takes a few seconds for those two words to register. As soon as they do, Gray freezes. Drops his hand. Moves away. "You're a *virgin*?" He says the question like lack of promiscuity is a contagious disease.

I jut my chin out defiantly. "So what if I am?"

"Shit." He takes another step away, shaking his head and gripping the back of his neck with one hand. "I almost deflowered little Evie Collins." He says the words to himself, punctuated with a small *what the hell were you thinking* shake of the head.

I'm embarrassed *and* pissed. I step away from the door and yank down my dress so fast that I'm surprised it doesn't rip. "You didn't seem to think I was so *little* when you had your *fingers* in me a minute ago."

He snorts and turns toward the sink. Forget whiplash. I feel like I was just spun in circles and then shoved out an airplane.

After he washes his hands, Gray turns back around. There's a smirk on his face and a teasing glint in his eyes. "Did Boston convert you to Catholicism? Or were you just too busy studying?"

"You're *such* an ass."

"You knew that when you kissed me."

I pick my dignity up from the dirty floor. "Temporary lapse in judgment. I'm drunk"—more on him than anything else—"and you're decent-looking, I guess." *Heartbreakingly handsome* would also apply. "You can go now."

Gray doesn't move. "Weren't you with that guy in Boston for, like, a *year?*"

Under other circumstances, the fact that he's paid any attention to my love life would send a stupid thrill through me. But I know where he's going with this, and it eradicates any excitement.

"None of your business."

He crosses his arms. "Felt like my *business* a minute ago."

I snort. He waits. Silence drags until I crack, caving like a poorly stacked house of cards.

"We were together for ten months, if you want to get super specific."

"*Ten months.* And you never…"

30

"Nope." I pop the *P* for emphasis.

"Jesus. Was he gay?"

I scoff. "No. He was a *gentleman.* I think he's dating a chef from Cambridge now. She owns her own restaurant."

Seeing that photo proudly posted on social media didn't bother me half as much as the waitress flirting with Gray did.

"So, he could get it up?"

"*Get. Out.*"

"I hope you—"

"The only thing I'm *hoping* for is that this is the last time I see you until you ship back out to the middle of fucking nowhere," I snap.

"Felt more like you were *hoping* I'd be the first one to fuck you when you were dripping on my fingers."

I flush, both from anger and the crude description. He has a dirty mouth, and if I said I hated it, I'd be a liar. "Unless you want Noah to know exactly how *you* know that, you'll never mention this again."

Unease flickers on his face at the threat, and I almost take it back. Grayson Phillips might not care about much in this world, but he values his friendship with my brother. He knows how protective Noah is of me. And if we want to get technical, I kissed *him* first and have no business blackmailing him. But embarrassment and lust make people say stupid things, and I'm flooded with plenty of both at the moment.

"Now, *get out.*"

He leaves without another word.

I place my hands on either side of the porcelain sink and stare at myself in the mirror, taking deep breaths in an attempt to calm myself.

He *kissed* me.

Touched me.

I'd dreamed of that happening for years. Disappointment is winning out over other emotions. Because for seconds—a thrilling, uncountable number of them—I thought it might actually happen. That *we* might actually happen.

Stupid, stupid, stupid, I chastise myself.

It'd never happened before; why would it happen now? It's unhealthy, ridiculous, and futile, allowing Gray to have this much of an effect on me. But if I knew how to turn it off, I would have years ago. And if his rejection isn't enough to curb my attraction for good, I don't know what will.

I use the restroom and wash my hands. Three women are waiting in the hallway when I open the door. They all give me annoyed looks before one rushes in. I guess my emotional turmoil took longer than I thought. Or they saw Gray leave and think we made a mess of the restroom. I've had plenty of opportunities to lose my virginity in a bar restroom before. This is the only time I would have gone through with it.

I hurry back to the booth, worried Noah or Sloane might have noticed how long I was gone for. But everyone is busy drinking and joking when I slip back into my empty spot. There's no sign of Gray.

Sloane glances over when I take a seat beside her. Her face is flushed from dancing. "Everything okay? You were gone for a while."

"Fine." I force a smile. "Long line. Like always."

She nods.

"Had your fill of dancing?" Without meaning to, I echo Gray's earlier question and immediately wish I could shove it back into my mouth. It's an unwelcome reminder of what just took place.

Sloane swirls the amber liquid in her glass and sighs. "Yeah. Those guys watching us were less promising than Todd."

"Todd?"

She sips some whiskey, then nods to her phone. "Surfboard guy."

I roll my eyes, and Sloane smiles. Of course his name is Todd.

For a split second, I consider telling her about Gray. Not *now* —because Sloane has never been one to react subtly and Noah is sitting a few feet away. But then I spot Gray leaning against the bar, talking to the blonde waitress. She rubs his arm as she leans forward to whisper to him. He doesn't move away; he says something back.

Emmett's spotted them too. He shakes his head with a grin. "Phillips is going to get that poor girl fired. He can't wait to get laid until the end of her shift?"

Harrison chuckles. "Poor girl? She's all over him."

I rub at a puddle of condensation on the table and study my empty glass like it's a work of art. Jealousy unfurls in my stomach, along with distaste and disgust. Noah and Sloane are watching the flirtfest unfold now too. I have nothing else to focus on.

"We're never going to get refills," Harrison grumbles.

"I'm kinda worried about him," Emmett states. "He's been... intense ever since he got back on Wednesday. Surfing at the crack of dawn. Drinking. He brought two girls home last night. Haven't seen him do that since college."

"Dude." Noah nods toward me and Sloane meaningfully.

Emmett and Harrison shut up. I don't even care if that means they think we can't handle hearing about sex.

I wish they'd stopped talking sooner. I definitely could have gone without knowing Gray had a threesome recently. The hottest moment of my life probably doesn't even rank in the top hundred of his.

Even though I should probably regret kissing him, I don't. It doesn't even have anything to do with Gray. I took a risk, put myself out there. I wanted to kiss him, and I did. What followed doesn't have to ruin that satisfaction of successfully crossing the line separating my comfort zone and things I never thought I'd do.

Sloane smirks. "That's sweet that you're censoring yourselves, but I've heard worse. And your sister is a doctor. She practically looks at dicks for a living, Noah."

I roll my eyes as Emmett and Harrison laugh. "I'm going to be a cardiologist, not a urologist, Sloane."

She sucks down the rest of her drink. "Same difference."

"There's definitely *a* difference," I reply.

"Do you think something happened?" Harrison asks after a pause. "On his deployment?"

Emmett shrugs. "He hasn't said anything—not that he would. You know how he is."

"He must see all sorts of shit, right?" Harrison questions.

"Sup, boys?" Gray chooses this moment to reappear, dropping his tall frame down onto the leather of the curved booth. Right next to me.

There's more space on this side, but it still feels like a deliberate move. Or maybe he's just drunk. He smells like tequila. His arm brushes mine as he settles against the leather. I jerk away like I've been burned by an iron. "Boys" feels like a dig at me— although I can't figure out what *he* could possibly feel entitled to be mad at *me* about.

"The *boys* were just updating us on your sex life, Gray," Sloane says.

I keep my gaze on the table but smile when I hear her emphasis.

"Sounds like you've been busy," she adds.

34

"Were they?" He says the words in an easy drawl but with an underlying tang of annoyance.

No one else seems to catch the undercurrent.

"It's not boring at the loft when you're in town, Phillips— that's for damn sure." Emmett drains the end of his drink and stretches. "I've got to head out."

"It's barely eleven," Gray states. "When did you become such a responsible lightweight, Baker?"

"When I co-founded a business that requires me to get up at the ass crack of dawn on Sundays," Emmett replies. "Not all of us are on a vacation, man." Emmett's tone is teasing.

"*Vacation*. Right." Gray's is not. Bitterness lurks beneath sarcasm.

I'm not the only one who catches it this time. Sloane's eyebrows rise. Noah taps the side of his beer bottle.

"Can I catch a ride, Emmett?" I ask.

"Yeah. Of course," he replies.

"You're leaving?" Sloane pouts, but she doesn't sound surprised.

"I'm exhausted," I tell her. Which she knows. She's heard me stumble around the apartment in the early mornings all week.

"I thought you were off again tomorrow?"

"I am. I've got a ton to do, though. Unpacking boxes. Packing to stay at my parents'. That bookcase arrived earlier. I have to start looking for a car and—"

"Okay, okay." Sloane waves her hand. "Get out of here. Listening to you stress is stressing *me* out."

I laugh. "Okay. Should I worry if you don't make it home tonight?"

"*No*. If I do, it'll mean the photo was more than five years old. Thirty is still a hard limit for me."

"Text me?"

"Yeah." Sloane gives me her best mock glare. "And next weekend, we're finding you a guy, got it? I liked Logan, but I kind of got the feeling he didn't know what he was doing in bed."

"Jesus," Noah groans. Because he—like everyone else at this table, with one very new exception—thinks I would know how Logan is in bed.

I act like she didn't say anything. "Enjoy the rest of your night, guys," I say, then turn toward said exception. He doesn't move. "You're blocking me in."

Gray holds my gaze. The longer it lasts, the faster my pulse pounds. Being near him is a vigorous cardiac workout. There's something unsettled in his expression, like he's searching for the right way to say something but can't summon the words. Or can't say them in front of my brother and his friends. Our silent stare-off lasts a few more seconds before he finally moves. I swallow a groan as my bruised feet protest standing. I stumble as I slide out of the booth, wobbling in the heels. Gray grabs my elbow, steadying me. His touch hits my nervous system like a shot of adrenaline.

"Look at Phillips, being a gentleman," Emmett teases.

"First time for everything," Gray replies. But he's not looking at Emmett.

He's looking at me.

"You ready, Evie?" Emmett asks.

"Ready." I yank my arm away from Gray's hot touch and follow Emmett out of the bar.

CHAPTER THREE

On Monday morning, I wake up at 4:13 a.m. I look away from the three numbers burning my retinas to stare at the abstract shapes that are all my eyes can make out in the dark, debating whether I get up now or remain under the warm covers for two more minutes. The opening chords of "You Belong with Me" start chiming before I've decided. I have to vigorously tap the screen three times to shut off the alarm.

I sit up, rub my face, and turn on the lamp beside my bed. It used to sit atop a cardboard box labeled *Books*. Now, it's on a three-legged stool that was meant for the living room. Sloane and I spent more time lounging around, watching television yesterday than unpacking. My parents leave for Italy this morning, so I'll be sleeping in my childhood bedroom for the next week and a half.

My shin collides with the suitcase on the floor as I roll out of bed. I swallow a curse and stand, rubbing the stinging skin. A clean pair of scrubs are draped over the chair in the corner, serving as my temporary closet. I shed the oversize shirt I slept in, grab a sports bra off the floor, and change before tiptoeing into the bathroom across the hall.

I run through the routine so deeply ingrained that I don't have to think about it—convenient since I'm usually half-asleep—then return to my room to grab the suitcase. I pull on a fleece jacket and make sure my phone and the keys to the car my parents dropped off yesterday are in the pocket. I've been taking the bus to work in the mornings, but since my dad doesn't need his ten-year-old Subaru while gallivanting around Italy, I've been granted temporary custody of it—along with the cat. Guess which one I'm more excited about. If I wasn't so paranoid about being late, I could have slept in for an extra ten minutes.

Cool, damp air greets me when I step outside. There's not even the faintest glimmer of light in the sky. The roll of the suitcase wheels against the concrete is the only sound on the street as I walk over to the silver Forester. The lights flash as I unlock it.

The drive to Charleston General passes quickly. It's an easy trip, one I don't have to think much about. Unsurprisingly, there's no traffic this early in the morning. Once I'm awake, I don't mind being up at this hour. There's something special about witnessing the world when most people don't. The stillness makes you appreciate everything more. The soft glow of streetlights illuminates the line of palm trees along the road and the cheerful colors of the buildings I pass. They fly by like a rainbow—coral, sky blue, periwinkle, a light yellow that's similar to my parents' lemon-cream kitchen, tangerine. I half-listen to a celebrity gossip podcast as I drive.

When I arrive at the hospital, I park in the garage reserved for employees for the first time. Ahead of schedule, thanks to the car, I pass the bus stop that usually marks my arrival at work and walk across the street into Charleston Coffee Traders. They're open twenty-four hours, catering to the long shifts, late nights, and early mornings that are the norm for hospital staff.

My phone buzzes as I get in line behind two EMTs. I'm

surprised anyone is texting me this early. Traitorous excitement spikes, then plummets when I look at the screen.

Logan: *Hey.*

Logan: *Heading into work.*

Logan: *Can we talk soon?*

I chew on my bottom lip as I debate on how to respond. I *want* to be friends with Logan. It wasn't just a line I used when we broke up a few weeks ago. But I'm wary of what that might lead to—mindful of how we progressed from friends to more before. I don't know for sure if he's moved on. He might just be friends with the chef, and I don't know how to ask for sure. I don't want to hurt him any more than I already have.

It's my turn to order before I decide how to reply. I pay for a large vanilla latte and type three different responses while I wait for the barista to make my drink. I send the texts right as my coffee appears.

Evie: *Me too.*

Evie: *Things are super hectic.*

Evie: *Yes, want to hear all about Mass Gen.*

I'm embarrassed it took me five minutes to come up with that. I shake off the uncomfortable interaction and shove my phone back into my pocket as I cross the street. The bright glare of fluorescent lights and acrid scent of chemical cleaners hit me as soon as I walk through the sliding doors and pass the elevator bank on my way to the locker rooms. By the time I reach my locker, I've finished half my coffee.

I hang my jacket up, clip my badge to the front of my scrubs, and head for the stairwell to climb to the cardiac wing. It's five flights, but I embrace the burn. The discomfort makes it harder to think about how I was hoping that text was from a different guy.

I'm so tired that I'm having trouble seeing straight. Hours of poring over patient charts and MRIs for the past two hours didn't help. My vision blurs as I wash and dry my hands and wipe my face with the damp paper towel.

"Evie?"

I blink away the boulders resting on my eyelids and glance to the left. Rose Adams, another first-year resident specializing in internal medicine, is standing at the sink next to mine as she twists her red hair up into a messy bun.

"Yeah?"

"Want to come with us?"

"Come where?"

Her lips twist up in a silent tease because I haven't been paying attention to the conversation taking place in the locker room. "Some pizza place nearby." She shrugs. "Chris said he knows of a good place."

I'm tempted to beg off. I haven't slept well the past two nights —my brain has been too busy replaying a certain interaction on repeat. I never told Sloane what happened with Gray, just listened to the recap of her night with Todd.

Everyone else just finished the same long shift that I did, though. And I don't want to be known as the responsible, studious girl I was in med school and college. Graduating and beginning my residency is supposed to be a fresh start.

"Yeah, sure. That sounds good." The chicken salad sandwich I wolfed down feels like a distant memory.

Rose smiles. "Great. Do you need a ride? Stephanie said she

has room."

"No, I have a car today, thanks. Just text me the address, and I'll meet you guys there."

We all exchanged cell and pager numbers the first day of residency in case of any emergencies.

She nods. "Okay."

Most of the other residents have changed into street clothes, but I didn't pack any in my bag earlier. I was planning to go straight home and shower. I've got clean outfits in my suitcase in the car, but my desire to go get them and then come back in here to change is pretty much nonexistent. I brush my teeth, use the bathroom, and head outside, still wearing my blue scrubs.

The air is cool, and the sun is sinking down. A whole day gone that I barely got a glimpse of.

You wanted this, Evie. More than wanted—I worked my ass off to get here.

I knew the long hours would test me and the sad outcomes would haunt me. I don't have any regrets about my choice of profession. It's just an adjustment. A steep curve with no flatness in sight.

I'm home, but it doesn't fully feel like it. The last time I lived in Charleston, I was eighteen. Focused on preparing for college and my summer job. Filled with minimal responsibilities and lofty dreams.

My phone buzzes as I enter the garage. Rose texted me the address for the pizza place. I've never been there before, but I know how to get there. I also have two unread texts from Logan, which I ignore. I call Noah instead.

He answers on the third ring. "Hey, Leigh-Leigh."

I groan. "Notice how I never call you No-No?"

Noah laughs. "Oh, wait. Hang on a sec."

The second turns into two minutes. I cross the lot and climb in the Subaru before he's back on the line.

"Sorry. Emmett was calling to see if I was watching the game tonight."

"It's fine. I'm actually calling to ask a favor…"

"Uh-huh. I figured you weren't calling to pretend to be interested in my job again."

I roll my eyes, and it's just as satisfying as if he were able to see it. "I'm going to get pizza with some of the other residents. It's some new place on Mulberry. Mom and Dad's is fifteen minutes out of the way…"

He sighs. "The cat?"

"Mom said she left *detailed* instructions on the fridge."

"Okay. I'll head over there now."

"Really?"

"Really," he confirms. "Have fun. You deserve it."

"Thanks, Noah. Seriously. Between this and moving, you're making a promising run for Brother of the Year."

He chuckles. "Yeah. You're welcome."

It's a ten-minute drive to the pizza place. I luck out with a street parking spot and head inside. The air is saturated with the scent of roasted garlic, oregano, and tomato sauce. Most of the other residents have already arrived. I'm not the only one still in scrubs, which makes the group easy to spot. Across all the specialties, Charleston General's residency program has a couple hundred doctors. About a quarter are first-years, more often referred to as interns. All the faces at the table are familiar, but the only person here I've exchanged more than a few words with is Rose, since we share the same chief resident and attending.

"Evie!" Rose celebrates my arrival as soon as I start toward the table.

I take a seat between her and Ben Harland, one of the neuro interns. He's cute, with blond hair and brown eyes. He's nice too, immediately asking about how my shift was. It's perfectly reasonable to talk about work—it's what we have in common. But that was one of the things that bugged me about my relationship with Logan—sometimes our choice of career felt like *all* we had in common. I shove thoughts of my ex away as I answer his question. At least I don't have to worry about Ben's eyes glazing over as I talk about the coronary angiography I got to watch earlier. I'm only a week into the three-year internal medicine residency I have to complete before I'll be able to sub-specialize and start a cardiology fellowship. But I'll grasp every opportunity I can get until then.

Stephanie Williams is on Ben's other side. She's petite, with a blonde bob and tortoiseshell glasses. Her locker is next to mine, so we make small talk most mornings. Across from me is Chris Aarons. He's the *class clown with unexpected depth* type. A jokester most of the time, but I saw him retain complete composure when he had to do an emergency intubation in the ER last week. He's earned a reputation for more than his sense of humor too. Tuesday's lunch was spent gossiping about his relationship status.

The atmosphere is light and the pizza is tasty. The mood reminds me of outings in Boston. I was part of a tight-knit group there, and I miss the rapport. Medicine is a team sport in many ways, especially at a teaching hospital. Different specialties collaborate to treat patients. Doctors seek out opinions from peers on techniques and treatments. It's more than a paycheck; it's a job you bring home with you. One that demands full attention and a draining schedule. It's rare to find people in other professions who fully understand that.

Once we're all finished eating, Chris suggests heading to the bar across the street for a beer. Ben falls into step beside me as we walk along the sidewalk, telling me about the stray cat he unwillingly inherited with his new apartment. He admits he already bought it a litter box, which makes me think he might be exaggerating the *unwilling* part. I don't tease him about it; it's sweet.

As soon as we walk inside the bar, I break off from the group to head to the restroom. I have a tendency to neglect hydrating at work, so I ended up downing two glasses of water at dinner.

This bar's dark color scheme reminds me of Malone's. Old wood comprises most of it. The restroom is white plaster and faded linoleum. The walnut paneling, decorated with old sports team pennants and a few dartboards, looks stark in comparison.

Rose and Ben are standing by one of the dartboards, already with drinks in hand. I'm a little worried consuming alcohol will immediately put me to sleep, but I figure I can just sip on something until I head out.

I make my way over to the varnished slab of wood serving as a bar top. It's barely eight p.m. on a Monday, and the place is far from packed. Aside from the other interns I came with and the odd couple, the only other group here is a gathering of guys at the opposite end from where I'm standing. I scan them, simply for something to do as I wait for the bartender to finish serving them and come down here.

I blink twice when I spot a familiar face.

Freeze.

Stare.

Shit.

Gray Phillips is lounging on one of the stools along the bar, talking with a dark-haired man with a full sleeve of tattoos who is wearing a backward baseball cap with *USAF* embroidered above the brim. Before I can look away, Gray's gaze collides with mine. Surprise flashes across his face before I drop my head and play with a stray straw wrapper someone left behind. I'm tempted to abandon the drink I don't even want, but my stubborn pride keeps me rooted in place.

"Hi."

I stiffen at the sound of the familiar voice but say nothing; just continue fiddling with the white paper.

"*Evie.*"

"Assholes get served at the other end of the bar."

"Would an asshole apologize?"

"You *haven't* apologized," I point out.

Gray chuckles. "I'm sorry about Saturday night, okay?" Any amusement has disappeared. He sounds...genuine.

"If I say okay, will you leave?"

"Maybe."

I finally look over at him, and it's a mistake. His attention is on me. *Fully.* I soak his appearance in, even though I know I shouldn't notice. Shouldn't care. The hair that I now know is soft. Lips that I now know are demanding. Hands that I now know feel like sin.

"Okay."

One corner of his mouth curves upward. My stomach flips.

"I believe you now."

"About what?"

"That you go out."

"I didn't really want to come, actually," I confess. "Long, exhausting day." I'm surprised by how easily that confession flies off my tongue. I used to curate the glimpses of my life Gray saw —leaving tests I got As on out on the kitchen table when I knew he was coming over and asking my parents for permission to go out with guys when he was in earshot. I didn't mention the twenty minutes it took me to find the pathology lab or the patient I gave discharge paperwork to instead of the correct intake form to any of the other interns, just the cardiac procedure.

Gray doesn't tease me. Instead, he asks, "Do you want to talk about it?" in a tone that suggests he'd listen to my answer.

"Nope. I want the other interns to think I'm reasonably sociable and then go sleep for about twenty hours straight." I study him. "What are *you* doing here?"

"Just catching up with some guys I haven't seen in a while."

I glance at the man he was talking with before, then the rest of the group. "Guys from the Academy?"

"Yeah."

I'm still annoyed—and embarrassed—about what happened in Malone's restroom. Yet I stupidly keep the conversation going. "You planning to spend your whole leave in bars?"

"It's led to some good moments."

"Glad you had fun with the waitress."

"That's not what—" He sighs and runs a hand through his hair, mussing the strands. "I *am* sorry, Evie."

"Just how I like my apologies—two days old."

He starts to smile before he rubs his jaw to cover it. "Haven't seen you this mad since Suzie Jacobson beat you out for class president."

"I'm *not* mad," I say with heavy annoyance.

Gray doesn't hide his smile this time. "You left with Emmett before I could talk to you alone. And honestly, I had no idea what to text you. The only reason I even *have* your number is because you're Noah's little sister. I didn't think—"

The bartender appears in front of us. "What can I get you guys?"

"Uh…" Truthfully, I don't want anything alcoholic. The one drink at Malone's hit me like a bulldozer. "Do you have seltzer?"

The woman's brow furrows. "You want water?"

"Uh, yes. Please."

She sighs. "Coming right up."

I can feel Gray's eyes on me as she moves away to fill a glass. I focus on shredding the straw wrapper into thin ribbons of white.

"Wanna get out of here?"

If I already had my drink, I would be spitting it out. He's wearing a small half-smile, but he also looks *serious*.

"I thought you weren't interested."

"I never said that."

"You didn't stick around either."

"You asked me to leave."

Okay, fine, he has me there.

"You were halfway out the door as soon as you found out I'm...you know."

"Intact?" Another smirk.

Asshole. "Yeah...you can go *now*."

But he doesn't. He steps closer, caging me against the bar top. One hand captures the end of my ponytail and tugs, tilting my head back as his body presses against mine. My traitorous heart stops, then starts pounding out a rapid staccato. Warmth rushes to my cheeks as I hold his gaze.

"I can be a guy in a bar. And you can be a girl in a bar. And I could ask you if you want me to kiss you. Do *more* than kiss you." Suggestion drips from the words like warm honey.

What the hell happened to all the oxygen in here? It's evaporated.

"Why did you kiss me, Evie?" His voice is soft. Hypnotic. It commands an answer, and I have an awful inclination to comply.

"I—I wanted to."

"Do you want *me* to kiss *you*?"

I barely nod before his lips crash against mine. This is different than our first kiss. There's heat and urgency, but it's languid and measured. Like this might not be the main event, but the buildup to it. A marathon, not a sprint.

His tongue glides against mine. His teeth graze my bottom lip. I feel like I just downed a dozen espresso shots.

I've never felt more awake.

More alive.

I moan as I kiss him back, sliding my fingers into his hair and tugging the strands the same way he pulled mine. He presses closer, letting me feel the evidence of how this is affecting him. Letting me know *I'm* affecting him.

I'm not sure of anything—except that I need him to keep kissing me. Need to keep kissing him. More than food or water or oxygen or anything deemed essential. I never understood the power of lust until I tasted Gray's lips.

He pulls away first, tracing my bottom lip with his thumb. His eyes are heated, his expression earnest. "I don't want Noah to know."

It's not a question, more of a condition. Which means...he's really serious about this.

"Me neither. My sex life is none of his business." I'm not sure how Noah would react, and I have no desire to find out.

Gray nods. "And...it's just sex. I know we have history because of Noah, but I'm not the happy-ending guy, Evie."

"I know." I'm aware he considers an emotional connection to be a burden.

He studies me, testing my sincerity. "How come you've never had sex?"

"Does it matter?"

"Not really. But I'm curious."

The bartender sets down my seltzer.

I thank her and pay before answering. "Honestly? I wasn't ready in high school. Then, I moved to Boston, and I was in a new city with strangers, constantly feeling overwhelmed and afraid of failing. I worked my ass off to graduate at the top of my class. Studied all the time, barely went out. The only guys I spent time with were in the program with me. Hooking up with any of them…it would have been awkward when it ended. We shared classes, were in study groups together. Maybe it would have been different if I had been super into one of them, but I wasn't."

"What about the guy you dated?"

"Logan?"

He nods.

"We were friends from the start. He made some…I knew he wanted more. I finally agreed to go out with him last year. I think he felt like he'd pushed me into that, so he didn't push for anything else. There were a couple of times it almost happened… but it didn't. It wasn't that I *didn't* want to, I just didn't *want to* very much either."

"But you want to with me." It's not really a question, but he pauses like he's waiting for a response.

"Yes. It doesn't have to mean something. I just don't want it to be meaning*less.*"

He contemplates that for a minute. "You ready to go now?"

Nervous anticipation dances in my stomach. I should stay longer. I didn't say a word to the group I came with before coming over to the bar, expecting this to be a short stop. But I won't be able to focus on anything, knowing what's to come later. "Yes."

Gray nods and steps away. "I'll meet you in front."

I grab my seltzer from the counter, down a healthy portion of it, and head toward the other interns. It's a minor miracle I make it all the way over there. My head is spinning. From desire, from shock, from nerves.

I approach Rose, who's talking with Stephanie. Ben and Chris are playing darts.

"Hey, guys. Sorry. I got held up at the bar."

Rose smirks and takes a sip of her drink. "We saw. He's hot."

I shift awkwardly. I've never left a bar with a guy I didn't arrive with before. "Yeah... I'm actually going to head out."

Stephanie's eyes focus behind me, then widen. "With *him*?"

I follow her gaze to Gray, who's talking with the group of guys he was sitting with. The three of us watch as he saunters toward the door and outside.

"Uh, yeah."

"*Damn*, Dr. Collins. You work fast."

My insides squirm uncomfortably, but I don't get into the *brother's best friend, childhood crush* of it all. I've known Rose and Stephanie for roughly a week. It normally takes a lot longer than that for me to warm up to someone, much less share intimate details about my life.

"Yeah, thanks. And thanks for inviting me. This was fun. I'll see you guys tomorrow?"

Stephanie nods and smiles.

Rose smirks. "Have fun."

I take a final sip of my seltzer and head for the door. Gray is standing outside, leaning against the green siding. The sun is setting, spreading fiery streaks of tangerine and mauve across the blue. He isn't on his phone. His eyes are on the sky. I study his strong profile in the soft glow.

"Have you ever flown at sunset?"

Gray doesn't startle when I speak, confirming he heard my approach. He clears his throat. Once, then twice. "Couple of times."

"It must be something."

"Yeah, it is." He shoves away from the wall.

"Did you drive?"

"No. Got a ride with one of the guys earlier. You?"

"Yeah. I'm using my parents' car this week." I elaborate to his puzzled expression, "I'm staying at their house. I'm taking care of the cat while they're in Italy...remember?"

He stares at me, obviously *not* remembering how that came about on the party Saturday. "So, you're staying at your parents' house. Which is…"

"Next door to *your* parents' house. Correct."

He blows out a sigh. "Too weird. What about your apartment? Will Sloane be home?"

"Probably. Your place?"

"Emmett was going out tonight. He might be back by now."

"We could…risk it? If he's there, I'll just say I gave you a ride home."

Gray studies me for a minute before he nods. "Want me to drive?"

"Are you good to?"

"I haven't had anything to drink," he replies.

That's good to know—for multiple reasons. I pass him the keys as we cross the street.

Neither of us speaks on the drive. The radio hums in the background, but I have no idea what song is playing.

I'm nervous. Maybe he's second-guessing.

It's a short trip. Apparently, he and Emmett live in one of the trendy lofts downtown. It's a nicer place than I was expecting. The Phillipses are well-off, but I'd be surprised if Gray is taking money from his parents. I have no idea what the Air Force pays. Emmett founded a gym with a friend from college, which opened a few months ago. Noah said it's doing well, but I doubt he's rolling in cash.

I don't ask any questions. Don't say a single word as he parks the Subaru in the garage and we take the elevator up to the third floor. The hallway smells fresh, like someone just opened a window that's letting in the evening breeze. We walk along dark hardwood floors that contrast with cream-colored walls.

Gray pulls a key out of the pocket of his jeans and unlocks the first door on the right side of the hall. I have an *oh shit, this is really happening* moment.

The apartment is empty and silent when we walk inside. Gray flicks on a few lights before he shuts the door, illuminating the layout. The kitchen is to the right. I assume the two doors lining the hallway to the left are the bedrooms.

"Nice place."

"Emmett did most of the decorating," is his response.

I was referring more to the building itself. The hardwood floors and exposed brick wall and picture-frame windows. It's obvious I'm looking at a bachelor pad. The walls are bare, and there's not a throw pillow in sight. A leather sectional couch takes up most of the central space across from a huge flat screen television sitting on a stand with a lot of gaming equipment below it.

"Most of? What did you contribute?"

"The toaster."

I smile. "Impressive."

Gray jerks his chin to the left. "My room is down here."

I follow him down a short hallway and into the room on the right. His room is messier than I expected, though it's got nothing on mine. I thought the space would reflect the fact that he's been home for less than a week. Instead, wrinkled clothes dot the floor. There are a few empty water bottles on the dresser. His bed is unmade.

I stare at the tangled sheets. "It's so...clean."

Gray snorts and picks a couple of T-shirts up off the floor. "I wasn't expecting company."

"*Right.*" Sarcasm saturates my tone.

He tosses the shirts in the hamper, then focuses his attention back on me. "Really. I usually go to their place. Easier to leave than kick someone out."

"Well, I guess you never claimed to be a gentleman."

He smirks. I inhale.

Now, I *do* wish I'd ordered a real drink at the bar. Falling asleep is the furthest thing on my mind. Every nerve in my body is strung taut, waiting to respond to the slightest cue. I feel jittery and reactive.

And if I'd had any idea how this night might end, I *definitely* would have gotten clothes from my suitcase and changed out of my scrubs. Not to mention, I'm wearing a Nike sports bra and bikini-style cotton underwear beneath them. No sexy lace or anything gravity-defying.

Gray watches me fiddle with the hem of my mass-produced shirt. "If you've changed your mind, we—"

"No." I drop my hands and curl my fingers into defiant fists. "I haven't changed my mind. I just...need you to talk me through this. Logistically, you know? Tell me what I should do...first."

I've never planned a hookup out like this. It's always just happened in the moment. There's less than ten feet between us, but it feels like an unbreachable distance.

He looks at me for at least a minute. "Take off your clothes and get on the bed."

I kick off my sneakers and untie the drawstring of my pants. The soft, loose material droops and falls, pooling at my feet with an audible *whoosh*. I kick the fabric away and then pull my shirt off, exposing my utter lack of lingerie.

In my bra and underwear, I walk over to his bed and take a seat on the mattress to watch Gray pull his jeans and T-shirt off.

Before I lose my nerve or my train of thought, I ask, "You're not doing this because you feel bad for me, right?"

Gray arches a brow as his clothes hit the hardwood floor, clearly not expecting the question. "What?"

"I don't want a pity fuck or a favor. *You* can change your mind."

He appears amused. I'm not sure if that's a good or bad thing.

"I don't do things I don't want to do, Evie."

"You've never shown any interest in me."

"You're Noah's sister."

"I'm still his sister."

"Tonight, you're also a girl from a bar."

He approaches me purposefully, crowding my space until I lean back. The cool cotton sheets warm instantly beneath my back. Gray follows, pressing me against a soft surface this time instead of a hard wall. All of a sudden, there's a lot of his naked skin touching a lot of my naked skin. He braces his hands on either side of my head, holding most of his weight. Still, I can feel him everywhere. Warmth pools between my legs.

I pull in a shaky breath. "Does it bother you that I'm...intact?"

He grins when I borrow his word choice. "Honestly?"

"Lie to me, please." *Why does anyone bother asking that?*

He gifts me with a rare, full grin. "It's hot, knowing no other guy has been inside you." Whatever expression I'm wearing amuses him more. "I've never been with a virgin though, so tell me if it's too much. Okay?"

"Okay." I whisper the word. I'm nervous. I'm also excited. Aroused.

Gray dips his head and kisses me. It's just as overwhelming as the last two times. He's a drug, one that overcomes everything else. I can't think. Can barely breathe. All that feels concrete is the soft glide of his tongue against mine. I make a soft, breathy whimper that doesn't even *sound* like me.

My hands slide down his back. His whole body tenses when I reach the waistband of his boxer briefs. I slip my fingers inside and wrap my hand around his hard length. His jaw tightens, and his eyes close as I grip the smooth, hot skin, moving my hand down to the base and then back to the flared head.

Gray's cock bobs free of his black boxers. A small gasp I don't intend to let out is the only sound in the silent room as I give him a slow, gentle tug. This part, I've done before. It's just often been rushed, sometimes sloppy. The haze of alcohol has often coated my movements. It's never been like this. I've never touched someone so deliberately. No guy has ever watched me touch him so intimately, the way Gray is doing right now. It's erotic. Intense. I can feel the way my body is throbbing with anticipation, imagining how it will feel inside of me. I'm holding the evidence of how it's affecting him.

Trepidation mixes with expectancy as I memorize how masculine and thick and long he is.

Holy fuck. Gray Phillips grew up all right.

"I'm well aware this sounds like a line, but are you sure you'll *fit?*"

He chuckles as he slips one hand under the elastic confines of my sports bra, cupping my bare breast. "I'm up to the challenge."

This easygoing, lighthearted side of Gray is one I've only caught glimpses of since he hit puberty. Most of the times we've interacted in the past decade, he's been moody and serious.

He tugs the stretchy fabric up and over my head. Fresh warmth sears my flushed skin, sinking into the flesh like a fever.

"Fuck, Evie." His voice sounds like the scrape of sandpaper, low and rough.

His boxers get kicked off, and my underwear disappears. And just like that, we're both completely naked. There's nothing but heated appreciation in his gaze, and it eases a little of the anxiety balled up in my chest about any comparisons to other women he's been with.

The uncertainty and anxiety that have always appeared every

other time I've neared this step are absent. I'm apprehensive, but I want this. *Badly.* There are no stop signs, only green lights.

And it's so, so close. Right in front of me.

Gray's lips meet mine again, thoroughly distracting me with his talented tongue. I part my legs automatically, letting him settle between them. His fingers tighten on my thighs as his cock bobs against my center. I hiss. One hand moves to the wetness between my thighs. I thought the whiskey I'd imbibed before the last time he touched me there was the reason it felt so fantastic, but he takes the opportunity to prove me wrong. I'm stone-cold sober and hurtling toward nirvana. A mindless haze spreads.

"Fuck." He groans the word with a gritty edge, feeling how wet I am. How much I want him. "You're so responsive."

I grind against his erection in response.

He kisses me—wet, sloppy, and filthy. His tongue traces down the side of my neck, licking and nipping the sensitive skin. I'll have hickeys, and I don't care. Gray pauses to tease my nipples into hard points, then trails down the center of my stomach. He hesitates at the curve of my hip, ghosting his lips along the ridge of the bone and down.

I moan, more turned on than I've ever been in my life. There's no awkward fumbling or unsure movements, but the knowledge it's *Gray* touching me is what amplifies everything he's doing.

There's something about a fantasy taking place that coats everything in a fog. It happened in that bar restroom. And it's happening now, as the guy who's starred in many a dirty dream slides his tongue between my thighs.

It feels so *good.* I come in minutes, and the rush of relief is so satisfying that I can't find room for any embarrassment about how I'm grinding against him or panting his name or begging for more. I lie, sprawled on the sheets, like a towel that's just been thoroughly wrung out, as Gray leans over to his bedside table and pulls out a foil square. I don't move as I watch him grab his erection at the base and roll the condom on. The bliss still searing through my veins makes way for some apprehension.

"It might hurt," Gray warns as he settles back between my legs.

I nod, nerves hitting me in full force as my heartbeat flutters. "I know."

He leans down and kisses me, sliding one hand into my hair and likely destroying my ponytail. My body relaxes into it but immediately tenses when I feel him begin to ease inside me. It doesn't hurt—yet—but it feels strange. My reflex is to flinch away from the intrusion. I force myself to stay still. Gray's finger rubs the nub of nerves right above his dick. Fresh sparks of pleasure flare, and it helps distract me from the foreign sensation. He slides in another inch, then two. Pain overtakes pleasure as I start to feel full. So full that it stings.

Every person gets one first. There's no redo, no takebacks. There's no uncertainty or regret anywhere in me. It could hurt like hell for the next twenty minutes, and I'd still do this all over again.

He thrusts deeper, and the burn intensifies. I bite my bottom lip—*hard*.

"Are you almost in?"

Gray stills. I suck in a couple of rapid breaths.

"Um...no." He sounds apologetic...and a little proud.

I roll my eyes. "Get it over with. Just—"

He moves, and it feels like I'm being split open. I whimper as I stretch. As I feel him—everywhere. Forget touching his dick. This is intimate on a whole other level. He's in me. Above me. Around me. And then he's no longer moving, letting me get used to him.

The room is silent, aside from the sound of our breathing.

"I'm good," I say after a minute. "You can, you know, move."

I'm adjusting. Rather than strange, he feels good.

"Are you sure?"

I clench around him in response.

"*Fuck.*"

That erotic rasp makes me moan. Then, he's kissing me. Kneading my breasts. Caressing my clit. I lose the capability of forming whole sentences. Single words. I make sounds I hope convey, *Keep doing everything you're doing.*

I'm shocked to feel the beginnings of an orgasm.

Sweat beads as our skin rubs and slaps. I pant out his name, intermingled with, "Please," and, "Harder," and, "More."

After the sharp pain, the sweet pleasure feels unbearable. I'm chasing it and running away from it. And then I fall, feeling my inner muscles tighten around the foreign fullness filling me. My nails dig into his back. Gray keeps thrusting, prolonging my pleasure until he finds his own.

He pulls out and collapses beside me.

"Wow," I say once I'm able to speak. *Is it always like that?* I think but don't ask.

Gray chuckles, then leans over and grabs a tissue to wrap around the used condom. "I'm going to get a drink. You want anything?"

"Um, no, I'm good."

An "Okay," and I'm in the bed alone.

I just acclimated to his presence—in me, near me—and suddenly, it's missing.

You knew what this was. Gray isn't a happy ending.

I had one of those—the potential for one at least—and I walked away. Back here. I got what I wanted.

Maybe that's why this feels like a letdown, not a victory.

I shove away my messy emotions, roll over, and splay out on the sheets like a starfish—spent and satisfied.

So, that's sex.

Voices wake me. I blink, trying to orient myself in the strange surroundings. The room is dark. I roll onto my back. The twinge between my legs breaks through the fog of sleep.

I fell asleep in Gray Phillips's bed after having sex with him.

If only my younger self could see me now. She'd be so proud. For a while, that was the only item on my bucket list.

More details trickle in. I'm in bed alone. And naked.

I strain to hear what the distant voices are saying, but all I can make out is the timbre. It's enough to recognize them though, since they're both familiar ones. Gray and Emmett.

Will he tell Emmett about me? I doubt it, since he didn't want to go anywhere we might be seen together. Didn't want Noah to know. I don't think he planned for me to sleep here either. I must have fallen asleep before he came back to his room.

Footsteps sound.

"Yeah. Night, man." Gray's voice is louder. Closer.

I turn back onto my side, trying to keep my breathing deep and even. The door opens and closes. The bed dips as he climbs back into it. I keep my eyes closed.

I'm not sure if I fall back asleep before I become aware of light. I crack one eye open, then both. The sun hasn't risen. Gray is lying beside me, typing on his phone. I read the messages appearing on the screen, just inches from my face.

"What are you doing?"

He startles, not realizing I'm awake. "Nothing. Go back to sleep."

"You're arranging a hookup?" I say it like a question, but it's not one. I'm looking at the evidence.

His jaw flexes as the accusation in my voice registers. "Don't ask questions you don't want the answers to, Evie."

Shock stills me for a minute. I know Gray has slept—sleeps—around. I didn't expect this.

"*Wow.* I thought I'd seen you at maximum asshole. Con-fuck-ing-grats on outdoing yourself, Gray."

At first, his only response is a sigh. "You knew what this was. I'm not a *rose petals on the sheets* kind of guy."

I laugh, but it's not a happy sound. "No. You're the kind of guy *who plans your next hookup while the last one is still in your bed.*"

"*She* texted *me*, okay? Look, if you don't believe me." He tosses his phone on the sheets and runs a hand through his hair. "She lives in the building. She would've just shown up here if I hadn't replied."

I stare at him, which seems to freak him out a little bit. Uncertainty flickers across the face that belongs to my biggest weakness. Then, I turn the lamp on, toss the covers off, and climb out of bed. We're both naked, but I don't let myself look at his body.

There are a few drops of blood on the sheets, which I *do* look at. In other circumstances, I'd be embarrassed by the sight. If this had happened with Logan, I'd have offered to wash them.

I hope Gray can't get the stain out. That he has to go buy OxiClean and washes them with hot water.

His gaze flickers to the crimson spots as well, then back to me as I pull on my bra and underwear before I start hunting for my shoes.

"What are you doing?" His voice is wary, like he's dealing with a live bomb. He has no idea.

"Leaving."

"It's the middle of the night."

"So?" I locate my pants and sit on the edge of the bed to pull them on.

"Evie." He exhales. "You're overreacting."

"No." I stand and yank on my shirt. "I'm *reacting*."

Gray climbs out of bed and pulls on his boxers before walking over to me. "Don't act like we've been dating since preschool and this was some magical moment. Listen, I've—you knew this was…" He scrubs a hand across his face. "This was a mistake."

Just what every girl wants to hear after losing her virginity to the guy she's lusted after since preadolescence.

"This was a mistake."

I straighten to my full five feet nine inches and pin him with a harsh glare. "No. *You* listen. You might fuck every girl with perky boobs and a weakness for green eyes, but I don't treat sex with the same level of emotion as a handshake. I *trusted* you, Gray. I've known you since I was *five*. Yeah, I knew what this was. I gave up on you falling in love with me a long time ago. And, yeah, I set this *mistake* in motion. I wasn't expecting rose petals or a magical moment. All I expected was some respect afterward, and you couldn't even manage that. So, *fuck you*, Grayson Michael Phillips." I shove his chest and yank on my shirt. "And don't you *dare* say that *I already did*."

I grab my sneakers, spin, and head for the door. I think Gray might say my name, but I can't hear a word over the loud rush of anger and heartbreak. My blood pounds in my ears as I jerk the apartment door open and slam it behind me for good measure.

Hard.

CHAPTER FOUR

Words blur before my eyes as I shovel tomato soup into my mouth.

After leaving Gray's loft, I drove to my parents' to feed the cat a very early breakfast and then came straight to the hospital. The first time anyone has shown up two hours early for the five a.m. shift, I'm sure. I tossed and turned for an hour in the on-call room, then decided to catch up on my charts.

It's one p.m. now, and my bloodstream is mostly caffeine. I've never been more physically or emotionally drained.

I set the research article I was trying to read aside and unlock my phone. I like a meme Sloane sent and reply to an email from my mom, letting me and Noah know they arrived safely in Florence, before opening the unread messages Logan sent yesterday.

Logan: *Sounds good.*

Logan: *Also...your graduation gift arrived*

Logan: *Let me know where to send it.*

I let out a huff of disbelief at the realization I dumped this sweet, considerate guy and am wildly attracted to the living embodiment of the phrase *catch flights, not feelings.*

My mom once told me she almost fainted on her first date with my dad—because she was so nervous that she kept forgetting to breathe. When she said it, I thought that was the stupidest thing I'd ever heard. Romantic, sure, but irrational. How can one person have so much of an effect on you that they affect an essential reflex? Now, I get it. When he's near, Gray consumes oxygen like a fire. Like he consumes *me.*

I always breathed just fine around Logan.

I debate on what to reply, glad he's not pushing for a time to talk. Aside from our respective residencies, I'm not sure what we would discuss. So much of our relationship and friendship were centered around school. Studying, applying to internships, conducting research, guest lectures, clinicals. The list goes on and on. I also don't know what I'd say if he asked if I was seeing anyone. I'm not, technically. If we'd never dated, I might have told him a vague version of what happened last night. I even mentioned Gray to him once before, back in our second year. We got drunk on cheap vodka, and I confessed I'd been hung up on one guy forever. By that point, I was adamant about harboring only attraction for Gray. I said it mostly as a deterrent—because I thought Logan might try to kiss me.

Evie: *Logan!*

Evie: *You did NOT need to get me anything else.*

We all exchanged joke gifts at graduation. Custom pens, stethoscope name tags, and *#1 Doctor* socks were some of the highlights.

Three dots appear immediately, which surprises me. He must be on his lunch break as well.

Logan: *Don't worry; it's not a "girlfriend" gift.*

Logan: *Kind of a joke, but I think you'll use it.*

Logan: *And it was custom, so I can't return it.*

Logan: *Thought it got lost in the mail but just took a while to get forwarded to my new address.*

Evie: *You moved?*

Logan: *Yeah.*

Logan: *I'm in Back Bay now.*

Damn. Mass General must pay its residents well.

I send him a wide-eyed emoji, which he likes, and then my address.

Evie: *Thank you!*

Evie: *I'm sure I'll love it.*

"Wow. This soup is so bad." Rose plops down in the seat opposite me with a bowl of the same tomato soup I've been mindlessly eating.

"It looked better than the chili," I respond.

I don't trust any meat served in the cafeteria. Hospitals aren't known for their gourmet cuisine.

"True." Rose circles my face with her spoon. "You look exhausted."

"I am. Didn't get much sleep."

"Guy from the bar keep you up?" She wags her eyebrows at me.

In the short time I've known her, I've heard a lot about Rose's sex life. She's a sharer, and she has never seemed to care that I don't reply in kind. I'm not sure if she's realized it's because I don't have any stories to share. Or didn't, rather.

"Yeah."

Rose's eyes light up. "Details! Was it good?"

The sex? "Yes." *The emotional aftermath? No.* Not that I have anything to compare the first to.

"Ugh, I'm so jealous. He was *hot*." Rose drops her spoon and reties her ponytail. "Do you think you'll hook up with him again?"

Hell no. "Uh, I doubt it."

"Why not? You should—oh, hello, soldier."

Fuck.

Charleston General has the top physical therapy program in the country and often treats members of the military from the joint base or nearby Fort Jackson. Men and women in uniform aren't a rarity here, but I have a bad feeling—mostly based on Rose's delighted smile—before I turn around to see Gray walking into the cafeteria.

"Shit," I mutter.

Rose gives me a proud grin. "Damn, Evie. He's even hotter than I remember. I'd let that boy keep me up *all night.*"

"Don't look," I hiss at her. "I don't want him coming over here."

It's too late though. I can already hear the heavy thud of approaching footsteps.

"Can I talk to you, Evie?"

My grip on the spoon tightens as I deliberately keep my eyes on Rose. "I'm actually busy, doing *absolutely anything else.*"

Rose, the traitor, smiles and sticks a hand out. I guess I should have told her the full story. "Nice to meet you. I'm Rose."

"Gray," he replies, shaking it.

She looks at me and raises both eyebrows. I stare stubbornly at my red soup.

"Everleigh Claire Collins."

I threw his full name at him when I left, and he's tossing it right back with a not-so-subtle *I know you too.* I'll never be able to avoid him forever. This conversation will have to take place sometime. But still, I don't move. It feels too raw, too fresh.

"I'll drag you out of here if I have to," Gray warns.

I'm not sure I believe him, but I stand up anyway. Rose has already figured out there's more to the story than a drunken hookup—if her curious eyes bouncing between us are any indication—and she's my only friend at work. I don't want her figuring out we have history or that he's the chief's son. I'm sure there are already whispers about how I'm the only resident Chief Phillips knows by name. "There's an empty on-call room or two," she teases. "To talk or…" Her voice trails off suggestively.

"I'll see you later, Rose." I give her a hard look that makes it clear the suggestion was not appreciated, then risk a glance at Gray.

He looks amused. I gather up the article I was reading and toss the mostly empty container of soup in the trash.

"Come on," I mutter, walking toward the doors.

Gray falls into step beside me. "You told her about last night."

I don't deny it.

"What did you tell her?"

"That you were a lousy lay."

"Compared to who?" His voice is lofty, cocky. *Possessive.*

It simultaneously pisses me off and turns me on.

I say nothing as I lead the way down the hall and into an empty on-call room. I shut the door behind us and lean back against it, arms crossed. "You wanted to talk. So, *talk*, Gray."

"I'm sorry."

I'm taken off guard by his apology, which is a sad testament to his effect on me. Anyone else, and I never would have talked to them again. I still would have expected an apology, though. The thought didn't occur to me with him. I didn't think I'd see him again before he left. As much as I hate how he callously pointed it out, I *did* know I was one hookup in a long line for him. And that the list would keep growing.

I nod once in acknowledgment.

"Are you...okay?" He asks the question like it's one he's never spoken before. Maybe it's not.

"Yep. Great."

He steps forward and tilts my chin up, so I have no choice but to meet his gaze. Those green eyes burrow into me. I clutch the magazine tighter to my chest, using it as a flimsy shield.

"I mean it, Evie. Are you okay?"

"I'm fine. Just...sore." I wince. That wasn't something I meant to share with him. It's just something I'm suddenly aware of as my body responds to how close his is.

Gray's expression softens, then shifts to an emotion I can't discern. "Do you regret it?" The question hurls at me abruptly.

And...here it is. My chance to hurt him back. To take revenge for years of disappointment and second-guessing—for last night. An opportunity to hurt the guy who isn't affected by anyone, much less me.

I can't do it.

Because I *don't* regret it. I wish it had ended differently. But I wouldn't change it.

"No."

He nods. Something that looks a lot like relief flashes across his face until he schools it into the indifference he usually wears like a mask.

"Do you think it was a mistake?"

"No." His answer is swift. "I shouldn't have said that. I was— I'm sorry, Evie. Really. I was an ass."

I don't dispute it. He came, he apologized, and now he's silent. The quiet allows for too many thoughts, so I break it. "Why are you wearing your uniform?"

I've never seen him in it before, and, yeah...he wears it well. It dregs up memories I'm trying very hard to repress.

Gray glances down at the camouflage print that has *Phillips* and *U.S. Air Force* stitched on the front. "I had a meeting at the base this morning."

"Oh." All of a sudden, I'm at a loss for what else to say to him. Our expected interactions—brief and surface level—don't look like this. Things have shifted between us—irrevocably. "I won't tell Noah."

His brow furrows like crumpled paper, forming twin lines between his eyes.

"That's why you're here, apologizing, right? I played the *best friend's little sister* card last time something happened between us, and now, you're feeling guilty and worried I'll tell him. I won't, okay? He'll never know."

Gray nods. "Okay." Then, he steps forward and kisses me, which I was not expecting. At all. It's barely more than a light graze, yet it leaves a sear of sensation behind. "Noah isn't why I'm here though."

He smirks at what I'm guessing is a lustful, confused expression, then reaches for the handle by my hip. I shift to the side so he can open the door. Noise and activity spill in from the hallway. He walks out, and I trail behind, trying to figure out what to do or say now. Some stupid, idiotic part of me wants to prolong this somehow.

"Gray?"

We both turn to see Henry walking toward us.

Fuck.

"Dad."

Henry glances at me. "Dr. Collins."

"Chief."

Gray makes a small, amused sound in his throat at the formal greetings. That draws his father's attention back to him.

"What are you doing here, Grayson?"

Although I doubt Gray expected to run into his father on this visit, he takes the question in stride. "Thought I'd see what sort of job you're doing, running this place. I know how much you love constructive criticism."

Henry's jaw tightens. So does Gray's.

They look a lot alike, especially in this moment.

"Chief?"

I straighten as my boss's boss approaches. Dr. Watson is the head of the Cardiac Unit. He's in his late forties with a perpetual cheerfulness that's rare to retain in a profession that sees a lot of sad endings.

"Sorry, John. I was just headed upstairs for the meeting," Henry says, glancing away from Gray.

Dr. Watson looks to me. "Dr. Collins."

"Dr. Watson." I nod respectfully.

"And who's this?" Dr. Watson is looking at Gray.

"This is my son, Grayson," Henry answers.

Dr. Watson holds out a hand, which Gray shakes. "Nice to meet you. Navy?" He's squinting at Gray's uniform, trying to make out the stitched letters.

"Air Force."

"Thank you for your service."

Gray smiles and nods. Henry looks more uncomfortable than I've ever seen him. I wonder if he's ever said anything similar to Gray. Ever acknowledged the fact that while his son took a different path than he wanted him to, it's still an admirable one.

My pager goes off. I glance at Gray and state the obvious. "I have to go."

He nods.

I don't know what else to say. *Thanks for coming? See you around? Sorry for leaving you with your dad?*

I settle on a small smile before I spin and sprint in the direction of the stairwell.

CHAPTER FIVE

The Subaru's engine clicks off. I stare at my parents' home. Climbing out of the car sounds like a lot of effort, so I just sit here and look at the house where I grew up.

When did I grow up? I feel like a great-aunt at a family reunion. I blinked, and I'm twenty-five. In some ways, I'm further than I thought I might be. In others, I'm way behind.

I sigh and climb out of the car because I know Skye will be meowing. Taking care of her for the past few days has disabused me of any notion about getting a pet of my own. I work too much to spend time with a living animal that expects an owner who will do more than sleep.

"Evie!"

I pause halfway up the driveway and glance over to see Juliet Phillips crossing the thin strip of grass that separates my parents' property from the mansion next door.

"Hi, Juliet." I give her a tired smile.

"I was worried I'd missed you! Will you come over for dinner tonight? I made way too much."

I contemplate the convenient offer. "Did my mom put you up to this? Tell you I can't cook?"

Juliet laughs. "No. I feel bad you have to stay here because of my silly allergies. You just started your own life here. The least I can do is feed you a home-cooked meal. Take a night off from reheating." She winks. "Henry tells me things have been hectic at the hospital."

"They have been," I agree.

"So… is that a yes?"

"That's a yes." I wasn't exactly looking forward to heating up another frozen pizza.

"Great! Come on over whenever you're ready." Juliet smiles, then heads back for the house that towers over the one I'm looking at.

I walk inside, feed the hungry cat, and then climb into the shower. Hot water pounds over me, washing away the remnants of a long day. I turn it to tepid as my skin turns pink before starting to shampoo and soap.

I rinse, towel off, pull on a dress, and comb through my hair. Skye has curled up on the couch, content now that she's been fed. I grab a bottle of wine from the rack above the fridge, lock the front door, and walk over to the Phillipses'.

Henry opens the door on the first knock. "Evie!"

I smile. "Hi, Henry." The last few times I've seen him have been at work. It's strange to see him in jeans and a T-shirt instead of a tie and a white coat.

"Come on in." He steps aside and holds the door open.

The mouthwatering aroma of fried chicken floods my nose as soon as I walk inside. "Wow. It smells amazing."

"Juliet always pulls out all the stops for special guests."

"Guests?" I assumed it would just be the three of us.

But I round the corner, and there he is. Leaning against the kitchen island, sipping a beer. My steps stutter. The smirk on Gray's face tells me he noticed. I hope his parents didn't.

"Evie!" Juliet rushes over to give me a hug. "You're here!"

"You said to come over whenever," I remind her.

She laughs. "I did."

I hold the wine out. "For you. From my parents."

Another laugh. "Thank you. Have you talked to them lately?"

"This morning. The time difference works out well for my drive into work. I usually catch them before lunch."

Juliet moves to the cabinet and pulls out a serving plate. "They're enjoying themselves?"

"Mom was seasick the first day, but other than that, I'm a little worried they'll move to a vineyard and I'll be stuck with the cat forever."

"I'm so glad they're enjoying themselves." Juliet smiles. "Everything is ready. Are you hungry?"

"Starved. The hospital cafeteria leaves a lot to be desired."

Henry chuckles at that.

Crap.

As chief, he technically oversees the entire hospital's operations, including the food served in the cafeteria and to patients.

"I mean—"

"I'm not your boss tonight, Evie." He winks. "The catering service is something I've been meaning to bring up to the board anyway."

"I'm hungry." Gray shoves away from the island. "Dinner's ready?"

Juliet immediately jumps into action. "Yes. You all head into the dining room. I'll bring everything out in a minute."

Gray leaves the kitchen without another word. I trail behind with Henry, who's telling me about his garden. I'm close with Henry and Juliet. They're like a second set of parents—have been

72

since they moved in next door two decades ago. Unlike Gray, I came home for every break and holiday I could manage to after I left for college. Growing up didn't sever the bond I have with them. In Henry's case, it strengthened it. I basically followed in his footsteps.

I never thought that it might be uncomfortable to eat dinner in their dining room.

Never thought I might have sex with their son.

Gray appears indifferent as Henry and I join him at the table that could comfortably seat twelve. Henry is still talking about the begonias he planted out back. I nod along like I know anything about botany. Juliet appears with a big salad and a plate of fried chicken, and we all dig into dinner.

We cover all the small talk. Where my new apartment is. How the cat is doing. Who might have bought the Zimmermans' house down the street.

Gray is silent through all of it, and I wonder how much of my invitation tonight was as a buffer. I knew they weren't perfect, but I assumed the Phillipses were just as shiny and happy on the inside as they appeared from the outside. I've witnessed enough interactions between Henry and Gray to know their relationship is strained, but I didn't fully realize the state of his disconnect with Juliet as well.

The air is heavy and uncomfortable when conversation pauses —weighted with awkwardness I'm contributing to. I have no idea how I feel about Gray right now, so I'm far from a neutral media-tor. I haven't seen or spoken to him since he showed up at the hospital three days ago.

And then Juliet asks Gray what he did today.

"I surfed," he says.

None of us miss Henry's quiet scoff.

"Not really any waves this morning, so I mainly just sat there.

Doing nothing." The last two words are emphasized with the reminders of past conflict and purposeful accusation.

If this were a sitcom, it would be my cue to look around with exaggerated confusion and ask, *Did I miss something here?*

The Phillipses' large dining room suddenly feels tiny. Tension swirls in the air-conditioned air and expands.

"That sounds nice, sweetheart." Juliet makes a valiant effort to break it.

"You ever going to do *something*, son?" Henry asks. "You could be making a difference, just like Evie."

I *really* wish I could be left out of this conversation. For lots of reasons.

"Noah landed the Danbury contract today," I blurt.

He texted me the news earlier. The new development going up downtown was a coveted contract for his architecture firm, one he wasn't expecting to play a part in.

"That's fantastic!" Juliet exclaims.

"Yep." I nod, then glance at Gray. It was the first thing that popped in my head to say. Too late, I realize my attempt at distraction could be interpreted as a dig or an agreement with what Henry is saying. "He's really excited."

"Tell him congratulations from us," Henry adds.

Gray stiffens beside me.

"I will," I reply weakly.

We finish dinner.

"Why don't you two head out onto the porch?" Juliet suggests when all our plates are empty. "I made a pie for dessert. We should eat out there and enjoy the weather while it lasts."

I agree, since Gray hasn't said more than four sentences all night and is showing no signs of becoming more verbose anytime soon. "Sure, sounds good."

Juliet and Henry disappear into the kitchen. I stand and walk out onto the screened porch, leaving Gray sitting alone at the table. The screened porch is about half the size of the formal dining room. One end holds a couple of wooden rocking chairs while the rest of the space is taken up by wicker table and chairs. String lights cast a soft glow. I walk over to the periphery and stare out into the dark night. I can't see anything past the screen.

"Pretty impressive they didn't run out of compliments for you the whole dinner. My parents are usually stingy with them."

I turn to watch Gray approach me with his hands shoved in his pockets. My first thought is that *his* opinion means more to me than his parents', but I don't share that truth.

Instead, I make an observation. "So are you."

He stops a few feet away, his gaze dark and intense. It sends shivers up my spine.

"Fishing for one?"

Forget fishing. I'd need a stick of dynamite and a shovel to unearth a compliment from Gray Phillips. I've never heard him compliment *anyone* about *anything*.

I snort at the suggestion. "My hopes are nice and low; don't worry."

He moves closer. Every inch that disappears between us increases my anticipation. There's nothing resembling an appropriate distance between us. My spine presses into the wood that separates the sections of screen. The night air felt cool at first. Now, I'm flushed.

"If you want, I'll give you compliments. All"—his lips brush my ear—"night"—ghost across my jaw—"long." Press against my lips.

I moan into his mouth without meaning to.

"Do you want that, Evie?" He says my name like he never has before—with hidden meaning and heated familiarity.

I frantically search for my self-respect. "I thought we were a onetime thing."

"We could be an *as many times as we can until I leave* thing." He drops that sentence like it's a simple statement with an easy answer.

This should be a hard, fast, and firm *no*. I already rode this emotional roller coaster. Got the T-shirt and the turmoil. Once can be a mistake. Even though he took it back, it probably *was* one. I'm the type of person who learns from her mistakes. Who thinks logically and follows reason.

Gray reads the hesitation on my face. "Look, I lied to Emmett that night. Told him I was back at the loft and was alone. He ran into Rachel and told her that. That's why she texted me. It won't happen again, I swear."

He wants *this*, I realize. *Wants* me.

And rather than remember the aftermath—the embarrassment, the rejection, the anger—my body is focused on how it felt when he touched me. Kissed me. Was inside me. If it felt like *that* the first time, I want to know what it will be like the second.

Third.

Fourth.

Fifth.

Before I can say anything, Gray moves away, hearing what I didn't—approaching footsteps. I sink into one of the wicker chairs just as Juliet rounds the corner, holding two plates of pie.

"It's peach," she tells me as she hands me a plate.

"It looks amazing," I reply. "Thank you."

"Gray." Juliet holds the other plate out to him.

"Thanks, Mom." He takes the seat next to me.

Henry appears with two more plates. We eat pie and enjoy the cool, peaceful evening.

Henry and Juliet talk about their trip to visit Juliet's parents in

Connecticut in a couple of months—just like they do every year. Juliet talks about her book club. Henry, his new golf clubs.

I ask questions and steal looks at Gray. He appears bored, just like he told me in the hallway of Malone's. He mostly focuses on picking apart his dessert. But his brief glances at his parents say a lot. Gray doesn't want what they have. He views a quiet life as constricting, not comfortable. We might have had similar upbringings, but that doesn't make us similar people. I always imagined my future would include a family life, like the one I grew up with. Modest house, supportive husband, and kids.

But if Gray makes good on his words earlier, I know what will happen. I want him more than I'm looking for a happy ending. I'm young and working hundred-hour weeks. Fun should be my focus, not finding a life partner. Especially fun with a firm expiration date.

"You're sure everything next door has been manageable?" Juliet asks. "I feel bad I can't help out."

I'm quick to assure her it has been. "I'm closer to the hospital. And it's nice to be living back home. It feels familiar after being in Boston for so long."

"Well, we're sure glad to have you back in town. Wish this kid would follow your lead." Juliet looks at Gray meaningfully.

He sets down his empty plate and mimes checking items off a list. "Disapproval. Check. Pie. Check. Guilt trip. Check. That means the evening is over, right?"

I keep my eyes cast down as I play with my fork, pushing all the stray crumbs on my plate together until they form a small pile in the center.

Juliet sighs, stands, and starts collecting plates. "I've got lots of leftovers, Evie. Will you take some home?"

"Sure, I'd love to." I jump up to help her carry the dishes into the kitchen.

Juliet refuses my attempts to load the dishwasher. She fills four Pyrex containers with chicken and pie despite my protests that it's far too much.

"Thank you *so* much for coming tonight, Evie." She smiles at me. "I'm sorry about…well, dragging you into this."

Strain and sadness tug at the curves of her mouth as she confirms my suspicions that I was invited as a buffer. I don't think I eased tensions all that much.

"I had fun," I lie.

Juliet shakes her head. "You sweet girl. Thank you for lying." She snaps the lid on the last container and sets it on the other three.

Gray enters the kitchen as I'm struggling to pick up the tall stack of containers. Without a word, he takes all of them from me. "Night, Mom. Thanks for dinner."

I cast him an incredulous look.

"Good night…" Juliet looks just as taken aback by Gray's behavior.

"I've got them," I tell him.

Gray acts like I didn't say anything. "Night, Dad."

"Good night, Gray," Henry replies gruffly.

Gray heads for the door.

"Thank you so much for dinner." I smile at Juliet and Henry, then hurry after him.

When I enter the front hallway, he's standing with the door wide open. I walk past him without a word, onto the front porch. The soft *click* of the door closing is the only sound in the still night.

We walk in silence to my parents' front door. I fish the key out of my pocket, unlock the door, and flick the light on.

Gray chuckles. "I like what you've done with the place."

I study him, not expecting the sudden shift in attitude. Five minutes ago, he was sullen and somber. Now, the annoyance that hung around him like a cloud at dinner has evaporated. I don't ask any questions. He's Noah's best friend, not mine. Sleeping together once doesn't change that. Not to mention, I'm pretty sure mentioning his parents will just piss him off.

I kick aside a pair of sneakers to clear a path. One lands on the dirty scrubs I was too tired to take off at work and too eager to shed so I could shower, while the other knocks over the half-empty water bottle I left on the floor for some reason. "Cleaner than your place."

"I like the mess. When I wake up in the middle of the night, I'll know it's probably not because we just got bombed."

"Oh." I don't know what else to say to the raw admission; I've never heard Gray talk about what his deployments are like, and I'm unsure how to react.

He heads in the direction of the kitchen before I can decide on what else to say. Decide *if* I should say anything.

"Does pie have to be refrigerated?"

I follow, grabbing my breakfast dishes off the table and setting them in the sink. "No idea. Just put it in there."

I turn on the faucet and watch water fill the empty glass and bowl. The refrigerator door shuts.

I take a deep breath, shut off the tap, and spin around. "I want."

"Huh?" Gray glances up.

He's bent down, scratching Skye's furry head. The white cat purrs as she weaves around his ankles. Warmer greeting than I've ever gotten.

"Earlier, you said if I wanted to, we could, you know, have sex again. I want to."

A smirk spreads across his face as he straightens. My pulse pounds wildly as he walks toward me.

"I thought I was a lousy lay?"

"Consider this a chance to redeem yourself."

"Lucky me," he murmurs. But he's not being sarcastic. He sounds serious.

His lips meet mine, and the kiss starts off slow and teasing. Quick nips. A hint of tongue. Then, it deepens. His hands slip beneath my shirt. I grind against his thigh.

Somehow—thankfully—the sound of the front door opening breaks through the Gray haze I was engulfed in. I can't go anywhere; I'm pressed against the counter. But Gray hears it too. He moves away as I stiffen, letting me pull my shirt down.

When Noah walks into the kitchen seconds later, closely followed by Harrison and Emmett, Gray is leaning against the counter across from me with his arms crossed. The rapid pound of my heart vibrates through my whole body. Gray appears completely indifferent. He's even better at masking his emotions than I realized.

"Evie!" Noah beams when he sees me.

I've only seen my brother drunk enough for it to be obvious a handful of times. This is one of them.

He walks over to wrap his arms around me.

"Hey. Congrats on Danbury, Noah."

"Thanks, sis." He squeezes me, then laughs. "Still can't believe they gave it to me. I've got the least experience out of anyone at the firm."

"Doesn't matter. Obviously, they wanted the best."

Noah's face softens as the sincerity in my voice registers. We bicker plenty, but we're incredibly close. I didn't realize just how much I missed living nearby my brother and parents until I moved back. Technology can't replicate all the tiny moments that can only be shared in person.

Noah glances at Gray. "Hey, man. I've been calling you. What are you doing here?"

I hold my breath, but there's no suspicion in Noah's voice, just confusion.

"My mom roped Evie into coming over for dinner," Gray replies. "I just helped carry the leftovers over here."

"Juliet cooked? Sweet!" Emmett makes a beeline for the fridge.

Noah nods, then looks to me. "I hope it's okay we're here. We went out for dinner—"

"Drinks," Harrison interjects, smiling wryly.

"*Drinks*. And we thought it'd be fun to play some pool basketball before heading downtown later."

"Pool was Emmett's idea," Harrison adds.

"Yeah, of course it's okay."

"I wasn't sure if you'd even be here with your crazy-ass work schedule."

"Yep. I've even got tomorrow off."

"You should come downtown," Noah offers. "Drinks on me. We're celebrating, and I owe you for taking care of the hairball."

"Rain check?" I request. "I'm really looking forward to getting more than a few hours of sleep, and the *hairball* starts meowing at seven sharp."

Noah laughs. "Yeah. Sure. Come out and play with us at least."

"'Kay. Just let me go change. You guys brought suits?"

"I left a few here."

I nod, then walk out of the kitchen.

As I head down the hallway, I hear Harrison ask, "You staying, Phillips?"

"Yeah," Gray responds.

I blame that one-worded answer for why it takes me ten minutes to decide between the three bathing suit options I have here. One is a sporty one-piece from my high school swim team. One is a red halter-style from a spring break trip in college. The last is a navy set with a scalloped edge. I try on all three and rule out the one-piece. The red is the most revealing. That leaves the navy. I change into that and then see half of the bottoms is pilled. No wonder I left it behind.

"Evie! You coming?" Noah calls.

"Be right there," I shout back.

Red it is. I risk a final glance in the mirror before I leave my room. It's not that I don't think I look good. And I'd be lying if I said I'm not curious what Gray's reaction might be. He's seen me in a bikini before, but not since high school. Definitely not since he saw me wearing nothing at all.

The guys have made even more of a mess of the kitchen. The leftovers from Juliet are almost all gone, and they also broke into the alcohol stash. I pour a glass of what smells like a margarita and take a long sip before I pad out, barefoot, onto the back deck. Emmett and Noah are setting up the hoops in the pool. Harrison and Gray are sorting through the bin of floats and noodles. Looking for a ball to use, I'm guessing.

"You'll probably have better luck finding one in the garage."

They both look up when I speak. Harrison's eyes widen before he quickly glances back down. Gray doesn't visibly react at all. But he doesn't look away either. And his gaze isn't staying on my face. I feel his eyes rove over me like a physical touch. Goose bumps form. I wonder if he's thinking about what we might be doing right now if Noah, Emmett, and Harrison hadn't shown up. That's what *I'm* thinking about.

"I'll check the garage." Harrison heads that way.

I hope it'll leave me and Gray alone for a minute. We weren't just interrupted—we were interrupted by my brother, who happens to be his best friend. I'm not sure how Noah might react to me getting involved with one of his best friends. It's not a conversation we've ever had. I have no idea if Gray might rethink things between us following the reminder I'm *not* just a girl from a bar.

Emmett and Noah come over to us before Gray or I can say a word.

Emmett lets out a low whistle. "Ever given a patient a heart attack *because* you showed up, Dr. Collins?"

Noah punches his arm, but it's a good-natured one. His brow furrows as he looks at me. "*That's* what you chose to play pool *basketball* in?"

"I didn't exactly have a lot of options. Most of my clothes are still packed. And since I'm *here*, taking care of *everything*, I haven't had the chance to unpack them."

Noah rolls his eyes. "Yeah, yeah."

"Got one." Harrison jogs back from the garage with a ball in hand.

I down the rest of my drink and dive into the pool. The water temperature is warmer than the air. I swim a few lengths, enjoying the cool sluice as I glide through the water. The way it offsets the warm rush of alcohol in my veins. Eventually, I flip onto my back and just float, staring up at the dark, star-scattered sky. Splashes alert me to the fact the guys have all jumped in as well.

"You ready, Evie?" Emmett calls.

"Uh-huh." I stop floating and swim over to the center of the pool.

"Me and Gray versus you all?" Harrison suggests.

"How'd you come up with those teams, Ledger?" Emmett asks, rolling his eyes.

It's well-established that Gray's team ends up being the winning one.

"We should make it fair. I'll play against you all," Gray suggests, smirking.

"Let Ledger protect his fragile little ego," Noah replies. "Him and Phillips versus us."

We start playing. I mostly tread water. I wouldn't say I'm uncoordinated, but I wouldn't call myself athletic either. When I lived in Boston, I'd jog along the Charles River on an occasional basis. I prefer swimming to running, but this is the first time I've been in my parents' pool since I moved home. Noah and his friends aren't only athletic; they're all competitive. Elbows are being thrown around with insults.

Noah eventually calls me out on my laziness. "Pull a little weight, Evie. They're killing us!"

I look at Gray. It's good the rest of the guys are drunk because I don't think I've been all that subtle about the number of glances I've snuck his way tonight. Gray grins at me as he spins the ball on one finger. If we were alone, I'd stick my tongue out at him. But as oblivious as everyone else seems, I'm not going to press my luck. I settle for an eye roll instead.

When Emmett passes to me next, I attempt a basket, swimming toward the hoop with the ball tucked in one elbow. I'm not expecting for it to go in, which it doesn't. I'm also not expecting for Gray to guard me, which he does. Rather than snag the ball out of midair, like he's done to thwart most of Noah's and Emmett's attempts, he makes contact. There are no rules to pool basketball. It's a *get the ball through the hoop by any means necessary* sort of sport. The water does nothing to muffle the sensation as his palm presses against my stomach.

The ball drops onto the surface of the water several feet from the net.

"Evie!" Noah shouts. "Seriously?"

"That was a fucking foul, Phillips," Emmett adds.

Neither of them seems concerned by the only thing *I'm* concerned with—Gray is still touching me. And his hand has dipped lower, grazing the edge of my bikini bottoms. Flirting with danger in more ways than one, considering Noah is about ten feet away from us. It might be too dark to see what's happening below the water, but it's obvious how close we are. Emmett, Noah, and Harrison are all too busy arguing about what constitutes an illegal play to notice.

One of Gray's fingers dip beneath the hem. I inhale sharply, wondering how far he's possibly planning to take this. I get the answer seconds later when he pulls his hand away.

"You look good in red," he whispers, then glides away. "Let's call it," Gray shouts.

"Yeah, fine. Let's go downtown," Emmett says.

I swim to the edge of the pool and pull myself out. My mom keeps a stack of towels in a bin out here. I lift the lid, grab one out, and wrap it around myself. "I'm going to shower, Noah. Congrats again. Have fun downtown, guys."

"Thanks, Evie," Noah calls after me. It mixes with the good-byes from the other guys.

I smile at them as a group—not focusing on anyone in partic-ular—and head inside. I strip off the wet swimwear in my room and walk into the adjoining bathroom.

Minutes later, I'm standing under a steaming stream of water. I already showered after work earlier, so I focus on rinsing the chlorine out of my hair and off my skin and then shut the water off.

There's a knock on the door as I step out of the shower.

I grab my towel off the hook and wrap it around my body. "Yeah?"

I'm expecting it to be Noah.

But the voice that says, "It's me," definitely does *not* belong to my brother.

There's something oddly intimate about hearing Gray say, "It's me," not, *It's Gray*. It alludes to a level of familiarity I guess we've reached.

I walk over to the bathroom door and open it. He's braced against the side of the doorframe with one arm, wearing nothing except for black swim trunks.

"Hi."

"Hi." I glance behind him, at my empty room and shut door.

"They all left."

"Oh. You didn't want to go?"

He shakes his head. "No. Moved my car around the block and came back."

"Whatever bar they went to probably has a hot waitress or two."

One corner of his mouth hikes up. "Probably. Do you still want to?"

Apparently, Noah's appearance didn't change a damn thing. I tell myself the relief is because I'm eager to experience sex again and short on other options on who to have it with. There's not a single guy from high school I'd call up for a booty call. The only other men I know in Charleston are ones I work with. Getting involved with colleagues gets messy, fast.

I drop my gaze deliberately, tracing the ridges and valleys of Gray's abdomen. First with my eyes and then with my fingers. The distance between us quickly shrinks. Gray tilts my chin up and stares down at me. My breathing turns ragged. Oxygen is becoming scarce. My whole body is tingling with anticipation. He doesn't kiss me, just stares. I realize he's waiting for me to answer.

"Yeah," I whisper.

His mouth touches mine. Tingles turn into thrills. I wonder if the rush of kissing Gray will get old before this ends. I've never responded like this to anyone else. There were guys I was attracted to, guys I was excited about kissing. But I've never craved anyone's touch like this before. Wanted it so badly that everything else fades away like an old photograph.

The fluffy towel slips away and falls to the floor, leaving me naked. Gray slides his hands down my bare back and lifts me up against his body. I wind my legs around him. He starts walking, heading in the direction of my bed.

Once we're lying on it, I expect Gray to escalate things right away. But he doesn't do anything more than kiss me. We kiss and kiss and kiss until I've memorized exactly how it feels. Every groove, every flick, every taste.

It's messy. Slow. Wild.

I grow impatient first. I start by rubbing against his body. He's hard; I can feel his erection pressing against me through the thin fabric of his swim trunks. But he just keeps kissing me. I pull a hand out of his hair and run it down his chest and stomach, tugging down the damp material of his trunks until his cock is exposed.

"I want *this*," I whisper to him, moving my hand up and down his length.

He groans into my mouth.

"I'll be right back," he tells me, then stands and disappears.

I listen to his steps echo down the hallway. They fade, stop, then start to return, growing louder until he appears back in the doorway. Gloriously naked. I watch as he rolls the condom on. Spread my legs as he approaches. Hiss as he finally gives me what I want.

It doesn't hurt when he slides inside me this time, but the stretch still feels strange.

"Fuck," Gray growls. "Fuck." He repeats the throaty sound. His features tighten as he stops moving, fully sheathed inside me. "You good?" He raises a hand and brushes a drop of water off my cheek.

"Yeah." I nod. "Move."

He smirks. "No *please*? You're normally so polite."

"If you make me come, I'll say thank you."

I feel his chest rumble with amusement as he withdraws, then thrusts back inside of me. After a few strokes, I gain some confidence. I start meeting his movements, falling into a rhythm. It surprises me—how quickly the pleasure appears and how fast it spreads.

Gray notices. He starts filling me faster as his hand slips between our bodies and starts caressing my clit. His mouth lands on my neck, sucking at the sensitive skin. And just like that, I'm over the cliff, free-falling into ecstasy as the pleasure bursts. He keeps pumping, prolonging my orgasm and chasing his own. I feel him jerk inside me when he does.

We're both breathing heavily. My limbs feel like jelly.

Gray pulls away. I don't move as he stands and walks into the bathroom. I tell myself I won't care what happens next. It doesn't matter if he leaves right away.

He reappears seconds later. I watch him deliberate for a moment before he lies back down beside me. I'm not sure what to do now. I was already tired from a long workweek. After the swimming and sex, I could fall asleep, standing up.

I roll, wiggle, and shift until I'm lying horizontal on the bed with my head on the pillow. I pull the sheets over myself. I've never slept naked before, but it feels nice—the soft cotton against my bare skin.

Gray hesitates again, but then the covers move. His leg brushes mine as he slides under them beside me. Before I can think it through, I muster my last ounce of energy and flip over, so I'm facing him. Touching him. I doubt he's expecting to snuggle, but he doesn't flinch or move away.

"Thank you," I mutter.

I fall asleep to the sound of his laughter.

CHAPTER SIX

I wake up in a bed I've woken up in a thousand times before. More than that, actually. My parents swapped out a double for this queen when I was ten. The blue walls and white curtains have decorated the room for over a decade. The scratch of Skye's paws as she tries to claw her way through the door is also familiar.

But something's different. The covers feel warmer. The mattress seems smaller.

I roll over, and the answer is staring me in the face. In the form of a very bare, very muscular, very *male* back.

Yeah, that's new.

There's nothing stopping me from staring at him, so I do. At the tan line just above the edge of the tangled sheets that cover him from the waist down. At the strong lines of muscle leading to his bunched shoulders. At the brown hair peeking out from underneath the pillow concealing the rest of his head.

Gray Phillips is in my bed. With me.

Gray Phillips is in my bed.

With me.

Holy.

Shit.

Even if I woke up to men in my bed on a regular basis, this would be a shock. Since I don't, this feels like a *pinch me* moment. I squeeze the skin inside my elbow. The flare of pain disappears in seconds. The guy beside me doesn't.

What do I do? Pretend to be asleep? Brush my teeth? Get dressed?

I hadn't expected last night to end the way it did. I definitely hadn't expected for him to spend the night. I would have faced this dilemma the first time we slept together, but *certain* events had happened.

Before I can decide what to do—much less do it—Skye lets out a loud howl. I glance at the alarm clock—7:02. It's her patented *why haven't you already fed me* yowl.

When I look back over, I'm staring at Gray's face, not his impressively formed back.

One green eye blinks at me. The other is still hidden in the folds of the pillow. "Morning." His voice is scratchy with sleep.

"Morning." Mine is quiet. Shy. "You're still here." Words that could be interpreted as rude, I guess. I'm just confused. Surprised. I don't think this is proper *one-night stand* etiquette.

"Yep." There's another yowl, and he props himself up on his elbows. "What the hell is that noise?"

"It's Skye's way of saying good morning."

"That little cat is making that sound?"

I laugh. "Yeah. I'll go feed her." I slide out of bed, trying to ignore the fact that I can feel his eyes on me. I pick up the towel that spent the night on the floor, wrap it around myself, and walk into the bathroom.

My eyes widen when I look at my appearance in the mirror above the sink. I look...well, I look like I was thoroughly fucked. My hair is messy, my lips are swollen, and there's a hickey on my neck. I wet my toothbrush and squirt some toothpaste on the bristles. I start brushing with my right hand as I work on fixing my hair with my left.

This feels normal. I'm usually rushed in the mornings, hurrying to get to the hospital. I relax some, melting into a routine. Until things shift from expected into unexpected again.

Gray walks into the bathroom. I stop brushing. Unlike me, he didn't bother to put anything on. He's still completely naked. I choke a little, the sharp tang of mint burning the back of my throat.

I can't look him in the eye. I'm looking lower.

He's hard. *Is it because it's morning, or is it because of me?*

He's looking at me like it's me.

The bathroom attached to my childhood bedroom is small. I still had to fight Noah for the room with the en suite. The other full bathroom is twice the size, but it requires walking down the hallway. This bathroom has never felt tinier than it does right now.

He approaches me deliberately. I've always admired that about Gray. He doesn't shirk away from what he wants. When he chose the Air Force Academy over Duke, he wore a USAF baseball cap every single day for months. Noah was upset—they'd talked about attending Duke together for years. His basketball teammates were disappointed—he would have had a spot on Duke's highly competitive team. And Henry—well, I'm not really sure there's a word to describe a man who's had a dream shattered. Was it fair of him to pin all that on Gray? Probably not, but he did anyway.

Gray still wore the hat.

"Cat stopped screaming," he tells me.

"She'll start back up again soon. She's just regrouping."

Gray smirks, then takes the toothbrush from me, adds more

toothpaste, and sticks it in his mouth. He watches me as he brushes and spits. A little toothpaste remains on his lip. Slowly, I reach out and wipe it off.

His hands land on my hips. And suddenly I'm not leaning against the counter. I'm sitting on it. Gray watches me closely as he reaches for the knot holding the towel up and then jerks it open.

"You *really* don't like this towel, huh?" My voice sounds breathy. Eager.

"I *really* like pulling it off of you." He steps closer so that he's standing between my legs. His bare skin brushes against mine.

"Is *this* why you spent the night?"

He considers my question, then says, "I've never had sex in a bathroom."

I study him. "Never?"

"Never," he confirms.

"So…this would be your first time?"

Gray smirks. "Sure."

I run my hands up the back I was just admiring. "I heard there's a first time for everything."

A dimple pops out, creasing his cheek like a comma.

Impulsively, I lean forward and lick it.

"I've heard that too."

Then, he's kissing me—a kiss I feel everywhere. *He's* everywhere.

With a muttered curse, he pulls away. "Hang on. I need to grab a condom."

"Wait! I have one—I think." I move my leg to the side and lean over, pulling out one of the drawers just below the marble edge. In the very back is the box of Band-Aids I'm looking for. I open it and shake three condoms out.

Gray laughs. "How long have those been there?"

"High school. Sloane and I went out to buy them." I squint at the small letters. "Do you think they're expired?"

"Definitely."

"Damn it." I toss them back in the drawer.

Gray walks back into the bedroom, still chuckling. But when he returns with a foil package in hand, he looks serious.

"Who were they for?"

"Huh?"

He's rolling the condom on, and it's a distracting sight.

"The condoms. Who were they for?"

"Oh. Um…" The only guy I fantasized about having sex with back in high school was…him. "No one. Obviously. I never used them."

Something in Gray's expression makes me think he knows the real answer. I don't think he was oblivious to my feelings for him when we were younger. It's just something we never discussed. And it's definitely not something I want to discuss right now. Thankfully, he doesn't seem to either. He thrusts inside of me—deeper and faster than I expected, even though I *was* expecting it. There's no pause this time. No asking if I'm okay. It's rough and fast and greedy and desperate, and I love every second of it.

I'll never be able to look at this bathroom counter the same way again.

"What about this one?"

"A *minivan*? Seriously?"

Gray shrugs. "You said under ten thousand."

"I need a car to drive myself to and from work. I'm not transporting six kids to soccer practice."

"Yet."

I eye him. "What does *that* mean?"

"Don't you want kids?"

"I don't know," I reply, flustered. "I mean, probably. Maybe. Why? Do *you*?"

It feels extremely weird to be discussing kids with the guy I'm currently sleeping with. Or that I've *slept* with—a total of three times, to be specific—since I'm not sure if it's going to happen again. Family planning didn't come up between sex on the bathroom counter and him offering to come car shopping with me over breakfast. I've never discussed marriage with a guy, let alone kids. I didn't even know Logan's Starbucks order.

"Nah, I don't think so."

"Why not?"

"I'm similar to my dad in a lot of ways."

I wait, but he doesn't add anything else. "Yeah, I know."

"So…I'd worry that I'd be like him *as* a dad."

"Oh." That's my response when I don't know what my response should be.

Gray's expression turns wry. "I know you think my dad is—"

"I think your dad is a good person," I interrupt. "I think he's smart. I think he's accomplished. He's a great boss. Well…my boss's boss's boss technically. But he's not *my* dad. I don't know what it's like to have him as a dad. I can respect him as a doctor and my chief and the guy who judged the school science fair because I asked him to and still think that it's shitty that he removed the Duke Dad sticker from his car and never replaced it with an Air Force one."

Gray stares at me. "I broke his heart. His father and grandfather both went to Duke. Became doctors. I got in…I could've gone, and I think that's the worst part for him. I got in, and I walked away."

"Why did you?"

He shrugs. "I realized I'd never meet his expectations. I decided it was better to stop trying, especially when it wasn't what *I* wanted."

"Why the Air Force?"

"It's a rush. A high. The work I do...it's important. I'm *good* at it. And I thought..." He lets out a dry laugh. "I thought my dad would get over it. Might respect it. Nine years later, he's still holding a grudge."

"Have you tried talking to him?"

"And say what? Ask him to respect the decision I made nearly a decade ago? He *knows*, Evie. He knows I'm too stubborn to bury the hatchet first, and even if I wasn't? What do *I* have to apologize for? Choosing my own path? He should respect that, not resent it."

I nod. "You're right."

Gray's face shows surprise. He obviously thought I would defend his dad.

"And you shouldn't assume I'll take someone else's side over yours. Because honestly? Most of the time, I'll take yours." The words *are* honest—*too* honest.

I respect Gray. My attraction to him has never been superficial. I've always thought he was the best-looking guy in the room. But I more admire the characteristics you have to know him to see. I might not see him as a brother, but I'd defend him as viciously as I would Noah. Even against another man I respect.

"I'm sorry about dinner last night. I was pissed she invited you like some sort of referee."

"I didn't realize how...tense things were."

"Yeah, well..." Gray shrugs. "It is what it is."

"Are you interested in test-driving this one, Evie?"

I startle at the sound of Steve's, the car salesman who's been helping us, voice. I look away from Gray's intense gaze, and it all sinks back in slowly. The rows of cars. The dealership building in the background. Steve and his slicked-back hair, hovering.

What the hell? I came here for a car, and this seems to be the only option. "Yeah, sure."

Steve beams and pulls out a key. "Excellent!" He looks at Gray. "Will you be accompanying her?"

Gray makes a face but agrees. "Yeah, why not?"

"I just need to make a copy of your license, miss."

I pull it out of my wallet and hand it to him.

"Thank you. I'll be right back!"

As soon as Steve disappears, Gray speaks as if we weren't in the midst of an intense conversation before he interrupted. "So, now, you *are* considering the mom-mobile?"

"You suggested it!"

"You said ten thousand was the top of your budget. This is the only car they have under ten thousand, so…"

I sigh. "I know." Who knew Hondas were so expensive? Not this millennial.

Gray eyes me like he's trying to decide whether to say something. "Last I checked, doctors don't make pennies."

"Residents don't make much. And I have a lot of debt from school."

"Wouldn't your parents—"

I cut him off. "I don't want to ask my parents for money."

He nods as Steve returns with my license.

"Here you go!"

"Thanks." I take it from him before climbing into the driver's seat. Gray takes the passenger side.

"Damn. This has comfy seats," he comments, reclining the chair way back.

I roll my eyes as I flip through the radio stations, trying to find a song I like. When I glance over at Gray, he's looking at me, no longer admiring the seats. There's a small smile on his face. "What?"

"Nothing," he replies.

I shift into drive and pull out of the lot.

"You can probably drive over the speed limit. No self-respecting cop would pull a minivan over; just assume you're rushing to the hospital to have your third kid."

"Gray!"

He just laughs. A reluctant grin tugs at my lips as I drive a few more blocks and then turn around to return to the lot.

"Should I get it? It's way too big, but I *really* need a car. I'm going to have to go back to taking the bus once my parents get back from Italy."

"Remember Jay Harper from high school?"

"Um, no?"

"He was on the basketball team with me."

"What gave you the impression I memorized the high school's boys' basketball roster?"

"You came to some of the games."

"Not because of Jay Harper, obviously. I have no idea who he is."

Gray lets out a combination of a laugh and a sigh. "Well, he went to high school with us. Now, he has a dealership just down the road. A new branch of his dad's place. You should look there before buying this. It's close by."

"Why didn't you say that from the start?"

"You said you wanted to come here," he reminds me. "I'm just along for the ride. Literally."

Steve is excited when we return the minivan without a scratch and full of praise for the reclining seats. He's far less pleased when I mention I'll have to think it over, handing me two copies of his business card, one "just in case" I lose the first.

Gray wasn't downplaying the distance to the other dealership. It takes about three minutes to drive there. If I'd turned left instead of right on the test drive, we would have gone right past it.

I eye the rows of shiny cars with some trepidation. If the minivan was in my budget, I doubt any of these are. Gray is right; I could probably afford to get something nicer. But the only impulsive thing I've ever done in my life is...him. Gray grew up with money. My parents made smart financial decisions, but we never had extra money lying around. I invested in a high-paying career that would pay off my debt—eventually. But right now, I have a lot of it.

"Gray!" A guy who looks to be in his mid-twenties—Jay, I'm assuming—strolls toward us. "Man, it's good to see you!"

"Hey, Jay," Gray responds, doing that *hug and back slap* thing guys do.

"You're not here to trade the Jeep in already, are you?"

"Nah, it still runs great." He nods toward me. "You remember Evie Collins?"

Jay's eyes widen as he looks at me, then glances at Gray. I feel like I might be missing something.

"Yes—yeah, of course. How have you been, Evie?"

"Not bad. You?"

"Good. You're back in town?"

"Yeah, I just moved back to Charleston. Which is why we're here. I need a car."

Jay smiles. "Well, you've come to the right place." He looks at Gray again. "Are you two..."

"No! He just gave me a ride."

Gray smirks behind Jay's back.

"A ride here," I clarify.

I stick my tongue out at Gray when Jay turns away to study the row of cars, oblivious to the subtext.

"What are you looking for?" Jay asks me.

"Just a car to commute in. So, good gas mileage would be a plus, I guess." I have nothing else to add to the list. My automotive knowledge could barely fill a pamphlet.

"Oh, where are you commuting to?"

"Charleston General."

"Are you a nurse there?"

I decide I don't like Jay all that much after the quick assumption. "Doctor, actually."

"Wow. Impressive."

"Thanks."

We stop beside a cherry-red MINI Cooper.

"What do you think of this? You're in luck; it just got traded in yesterday. It got a full inspection already. It needs a few minor tune-ups, but it will be good to go in a week or so."

I love it, but I'm not about to say that. "It could work. How much?"

Jay flips through some papers he's holding. "We were going to list it at eleven thousand two hundred dollars. But I'd give you the friends and family discount—ten thousand five hundred."

I glance at Gray, who gives me an encouraging nod. "Can I drive it?"

"Yep. Of course. Let me just grab the keys."

I look back at Gray as soon as Jay disappears. "Seven hundred off for a stranger? This guy is legit, right?"

"You think I brought you to some black-market car lot?" He sounds more amused than offended.

"Of course not. I trust you." The words slip out without me

thinking about them, but they're true. Especially because I didn't have to think about them—at all. "I just…it's weird, right?"

"He had a thing for you in high school."

I look over my shoulder to make sure Jay isn't in sight. He's not. "He did?"

"Uh-huh."

"But…it's been *years*." Not that I'm not in a position to judge the length of other people's crushes. "He's never even talked to me."

Gray shrugs. "Noah warned him off."

"Did he warn other guys off?" *Did he warn* you *off?*

Another shrug. "Probably."

"Here you go." Jay reappears with keys. "I realized I forgot to copy your license."

"Oh." I start digging through my bag.

"Don't worry about it. I know where Phillips lives." Jay laughs; Gray and I don't.

"Okay." I give Jay a tight, small smile before taking the keys from him and approaching the red car. I open the door and turn to Gray. "You coming?"

He eyes the small car. "I'm not sure if I'll fit."

"I thought you said you were up to the challenge?"

Gray's eyes dart to me, shock mixing with the green. I smirk.

"I'll, uh, I'll be around when you get back." Jay seems to have caught on to the subtext in *this* conversation.

I feel Gray's gaze on me as I adjust the seat and start the engine. "What?"

"Nothing. Just…the minivan had better legroom."

I laugh.

An hour later, a warm breeze fans across my face, sending strands of my blonde hair flying. I fling my hand out the open window, letting the air rush between my fingers as the sun warms the skin. There's something about driving with the windows down on a summer day that soothes the soul.

It's never felt quite this perfect, though.

Maybe it's the Lana Del Rey song on the radio about being young and in love.

Maybe it's the guy sitting next to me.

I roll my head, so I'm looking at Gray instead of the scenery. The wind is tugging at his hair too; there's just less to grasp at. Tendons tense in his forearm as he turns the steering wheel of his Jeep. Rays of sunlight filter down from the blue sky, framing his profile.

He glances over and catches me staring at him. "What?"

I shake my head, hoping my cheeks were already flushed from the heat. "Nothing."

A brief, disbelieving hum is barely audible over the stereo. "I'm supposed to swing by the base. Do you mind if we stop before I drop you off?"

Excitement courses through me. "No, of course not. I'm just along for the ride."

Gray laughs under his breath as he merges onto the highway.

It takes ten minutes to reach the joint base. Traffic thickens around the airport, but Gray's Jeep is the only car that approaches the iron gate. I crane my neck to look past the fencing as Gray scans his badge and waves at the gate attendant.

"Wow," I say when we start to crawl ahead. "This place is massive."

The front gate gave no indication of the size and scale of the base. We pass a playground, a coffee shop, rows of townhouses, a chapel, tennis courts, basketball courts, a pool, and a barbershop. It's like a miniature city.

"Yeah. It's over three thousand acres."

"I had no idea." I feel like I should have, having grown up here. "How many members of the military work out of here?"

Gray flicks on his blinker and turns. "Eh, active? Probably at least ten thousand. A lot more if you count reserves and contractors. Not to mention retirees. The Naval Weapons Station holds a lot of manpower and so does the Coast Guard sector."

I bite back another *Wow*.

A massive warehouse-looking building appears on the right. Gray parks beside it.

"I've got to run inside for a minute. Feel free to look around. Anyone says anything to you, just tell them my name. Okay?"

"Okay."

I watch him stride toward the building in his white T-shirt and faded jeans, and then I open the Jeep door and climb out. Now that we've stopped moving, there's no breeze to counteract the temperature. Heat radiates off the asphalt, shimmering in the still air. I wander over to the shaded sidewalk, watching as a group of men jog by in camo pants and light-green T-shirts. Once they pass, I turn to the left and walk toward the building Gray entered. When I reach the front, I realize it's a hangar. At least ten aircraft fill the expansive space. They all look brand-new with gleaming paint and clean lines.

I stare at the massive machines, trying to imagine Gray flying one.

"Wanna go for another test drive?"

I spin to see Gray approaching me. "You mean…"

"Yeah. I've got to check a couple of things before we add these to the fleet."

"Um, I'm good. Thanks. I find flying in a passenger plane stressful enough. Never mind *that*." I wave a hand at the sleek, small aircraft.

Rather than tease me, his face softens. "You trust me, right?"

"Phillips!" a gray-haired man calls from a doorway in the corner, which I can see leads to a small office. "You're good to go in the Raptor. Take FY7K, okay?"

"Got it," Gray replies. To me, he says, "It's just a fly by, Evie."

"Is that code for something?"

"No." He smiles. "Just a quick pass. If anyone's watching the sky, we'll be gone before they realize we're there."

Sounds like him.

"Is that supposed to be comforting?"

"I'd ask for you if I had a heart attack."

"I'm not even a cardiologist yet."

He smirks. "Exactly. So, you coming?"

I take a deep breath. And then I give the answer I always seem to give him. "Yes."

A smile breaks across his face like the rising sun. "Let's go."

I know absolutely nothing about planes, but the one Gray is leading me toward looks like a menacing one. It's a dark shade of gray, with a combination of identifying letters and numbers painted on the side in black. The cockpit is tiny, and the wings are broad. The exterior is sleek and streamlined, but also dangerous-looking. I think that *before* I spot the missiles tucked under the wings.

Gray follows my gaze. "Don't worry; they're not activated yet."

"Once again, not comforting."

I make a decidedly ungraceful entrance into the small plane. The last time I was in an aircraft was when I came home for Christmas a year and a half ago. The interior of that plane was large and spacious in comparison to this. There are only two seats. I sink down into one, and Gray takes a seat beside me. He hands me a headset before he begins flipping switches and pressing buttons. The engine roars, and the radio crackles.

"I'm not going to have to do anything, am I?" I ask into the mouthpiece.

His voice comes through the headset a few seconds later. "Nah, I could get in trouble for that."

"But not for this?"

"Not unless we crash." He spots my expression and grins. "We're not going to crash, Evie."

"You promise?"

Gray stops fiddling with the controls. His right hand drops to my thigh. He squeezes. "I don't make promises I'm not certain I can keep. But I'm better at flying than you are at driving, if that makes you feel any better."

"I'm an *excellent* driver."

"Uh-huh." He shoots me a smile that makes my heart race for reasons unrelated to the fact that we're about to be thousands of feet above the ground. His hand moves back to the controls.

The plane starts moving. Slow at first as we roll away from the hangar and other aircraft. But then there's nothing in front of us but a long stretch of asphalt, marked with yellow and white lines. I know what that means, even before the scenery starts to blur by. The speed is stunning.

"This is my favorite part." His voice grounds me, even as we lift up off of it.

It's a rush. In seconds, Charleston is spread below us, and the sky surrounds us. Fluffy clouds float by like cotton candy. Streets that I know stretch miles long shrink to thin strips, separating buildings and neighborhoods. As impressive of a view as it is, I find myself mostly studying him. Watching him speak codes and flip switches and *fly*. Not many people can fly.

He catches me, just like he did in the car earlier. After studying him so intently, I could probably draw his profile from memory.

The small smile he was already wearing grows. "You good?"

Rather than answer, I say, "I'm glad you went to the Academy."

His expression turns serious. I wonder if anyone has ever said that to him before.

"I'm glad you came back to Charleston."

I smile at him before looking back out at the clouds.

CHAPTER SEVEN

I'm experiencing a lot of gratitude toward whoever invented sunglasses right about now. Eyes say a lot. A lot I don't want to say at the moment.

Sloane's phone goes off beside me, so I tear my hidden gaze away from the water. Or more specifically, one of the many people in the water. Sloane sits up, stretches, and smirks when I nod toward the tube of sunscreen. She flips over to expose her back to the rays and continues her *twenty minutes per side* regimen. Hopefully, she has aloe on hand.

I go back to reading. Or rather, to using the cover of my sunglasses and the pretense of a propped-up paperback to pretend I'm reading. In reality, I'm watching Gray surf. He's good. Then again, I've yet to find anything Gray is bad at.

Except communication maybe. But I'm not sure he's *bad* at it. Just not employing it.

I haven't seen or heard from him in nearly four days. Eighty-two hours, to get super specific. Not since he dropped me off after our trip to the base. I was high—on adrenaline, on excitement, on *him*. And then four days of silence. I don't know what that means.

Did he get bored? He initiated everything last time. The sex, the car shopping, the flight. He stayed. He offered to go with me. He invited me to the base.

If he were any other guy, I'd ask my best friend, who's conveniently lying right beside me. Sloane has far more experience with guys. My only relationship before Logan was with an English major in a band, and that only lasted for a few weeks. Of the two of us, Sloane has always been the bold, adventurous one, while I play it safe. She'd be proud of this development. She *suggested* it—although I'm confident she didn't think there was any chance I'd follow through. *I* didn't think I'd follow through.

But Gray is *not* any guy. So, I stay silent.

A part of me likes having a dirty secret for once in my life. I'm also worried Sloane will confirm what I suspect—if a guy is into you, he doesn't ignore you for days. He has my number; we've been in plenty of group chats together over the years. And we've stopped pretending we don't share a past, so he has no good reason not to use it.

Today is the first day both Sloane and I have had off since starting our new jobs. Since I'm sleeping at my parents' and working twelve-hour shifts, I've barely seen her. We got brunch this morning. It was light and fun and felt like old times. And then Noah called when I was halfway through my waffles, telling me he was going surfing with the guys and asking if I wanted to meet them at the beach. I couldn't ask if Gray was going to be here. Sloane was immediately on board. So, here I am—following the figure in the water I'm ninety-eight percent certain is him.

With a sigh, I give up on fake reading and drop my head onto the towel. Despite my anxiety about encountering Gray, it does feel nice to be back at the beach. I had summer classes for the past seven years. This is the first time I've been back home during warm weather months in a while.

Lying in the sand with Sloane makes me feel like I'm back in high school.

So does surreptitiously watching Gray.

The sun warms my skin, and the sound of surf pounding the sand serves as the distant soundtrack. Sloane and I didn't drag our stuff far—we're closer to the parking lot than the water. Maybe the guys won't see us.

That hope is dashed when Sloane sits up beside me and shouts Noah's name. I raise my head when she follows it with a laugh.

"Of course. Isn't that Miranda Hendrix? And Tanya Ford?"

I rise up on my elbows and squint toward where she's looking. Noah, Emmett, Harrison, and Gray are all standing about twenty feet away, each holding a surfboard. Two girls have stopped next to them, talking animatedly. Sure enough, I recognize them both from our year.

"Yep. Looks like them."

"*Great*," Sloane drawls. "They're all coming over here. Get ready for lots of giggling."

I sit up, then stand, not wanting to be at a height disadvantage. I tower over Miranda, who's a petite blonde. The top of her head barely reaches my chin when she gives me a hug. We were friendly in high school. Most of our interaction stemmed from a shared biology class. I wouldn't have any issue with her—if not for the fact that I'm pretty sure she slept with Gray the last time I saw the two of them together, and based on the way she's eyeing him, she'd like a repeat.

"It's so good to see you, Evie! I didn't realize you were in town."

"Yep." I smile. "Just moved back."

"We should go out sometime! Get a drink at least."

"Um, yeah, sure. My schedule is a little crazy, but that sounds nice."

"What have you been up to?"

"I just graduated medical school. I'm working at Charleston General now."

Miranda's eyes widen. "Wow. Guess biology actually paid off for you."

This time, my smile is genuine. "Yeah, I guess so."

Tanya approaches me and gives me a hug as well. "Evie!"

"Hi, Tanya. How are you?"

She shrugs a slim shoulder. "Can't complain."

There's an awkward moment as they both greet Sloane, who was selectively friendly in high school, whereas I felt the compulsion to be constantly cheery. After some fake pleasantries, Tanya and Miranda both turn back to the real reason they came over—the boys. Sloane rolls her eyes at me once they do. I smirk in response, but my amusement fades when I see Miranda's hand on Gray's arm.

Sloane sits back down on her towel. I follow her lead and decide to spread more sunscreen on my arms, simply for something to do.

"I'm running to the bathroom," Sloane tells me. "I'll be right back."

I nod, still focusing on rubbing in the sunscreen and not on eavesdropping on the conversation taking place a few feet away.

Noah leaves the huddle and sits down beside me a couple of minutes later. "Hey, sis."

"Hey."

He tweaks my ponytail, the same way he always did when we were kids. "Glad you came."

"I'm glad you invited me." I am.

Noah has always been great when it comes to including me. He never ignored me at parties or made me feel unwelcome around his friends. He's a good brother, and I'm probably a shitty sister for getting involved with his best friend.

"Me too. It barely feels like you moved back. I miss you."

"I know. My schedule will get better soon."

"Will it?"

I sigh. "No clue."

"Hey, Evie." Harrison drops down on my other side.

"Hey. How's it going?"

"Not bad. You?"

"Same. It's nice to be doing nothing. Long week."

"Yeah, I hear you." Harrison is an associate at a big law firm downtown. His hours are almost as hectic as mine.

"You bowing out, man?" Noah nods toward the group standing near us with a laugh.

Harrison rolls his eyes. "Yeah. Emmett will too, I bet. He said he just wants to surf all day. Gray's probably their best bet."

My arm is too oily to absorb any more sunscreen, but I keep rubbing away at the skin anyway.

"No way," Noah says a few seconds later.

"What?" Gray's voice. Close.

I keep my eyes cast down.

"Figured you'd be all over that."

There's a pause where Gray's reaction to Noah's comment happens silently.

Then, Harrison asks, "How was Colorado?"

I look up. Right at Gray, who is sitting in the sand a few feet away and already looking at me. His gaze slides over to Harrison as soon as we make eye contact.

"Fine. It was a short trip."

He was in Colorado?

"Is there footage of this ceremony?" Noah asks.

"Nah."

"I thought it was a big deal?" Harrison questions.

Gray shrugs. "Compared to what?"

"I don't know, man. Compared to something that would actually require you to talk about work."

Gray shakes his head before looking away, toward the water. I keep my gaze on him, drifting away from his face and down the impressive musculature of his body. Over the sculpted abdominal muscles and the deep V that drags my attention further south. There are plenty of attractive, half-naked guys on this beach. A couple came over to me and Sloane an hour ago. But I'm looking at Gray because I know he was obsessed with Spider-Man in third grade. I know he makes really good pancakes because he made some before we went car shopping. I know the state of his relationship with his father bothers him. I know how he looks when he comes. Those are the reasons I can't look away, not his six-pack.

I wish we were alone. Not only so I could ogle him, but also so I could ask him what his silence means. But before I look away, I notice the small gash on his shin.

"You're bleeding."

Gray looks at me, then down at the cut just below his knee. "Yeah. I hit a rock out there."

Without really thinking about it, I stand and approach him. Kneel down directly beside him and touch the skin just below the scrape. It's not that deep, but it'll scab and scar.

"Will I live?"

I glance at his face, just inches away. I can see every freckle on his forehead. The edge in his voice when he was talking to Noah and Harrison has smoothed. Flattened. Some switch has flipped. I can't tell if it was an act before or if it's an act now or if neither is genuine.

It bothers me.

It shouldn't.

"You should put something on it," I tell him.

"I'd feel better if a doctor did it." He manages to make the sentence sound normal while adding hidden meaning.

I narrow my eyes in response.

"There's a huge swell coming in." Emmett appears, gulps some water, then looks at me and Gray. I'm still crouched down beside his leg. "Sup, Evie?"

"Hey, Emmett."

"What happened?" He nods toward Gray's leg.

"Gray versus a rock. The rock escaped unharmed," Noah summarizes.

Gray flips him off.

Emmett laughs. "I'm headed back out."

"Me too." Harrison stands.

Noah shoves himself up last. "You coming, Phillips?"

"Maybe in a bit."

"Okay."

All three guys disappear, leaving me and Gray. Alone.

I sit back on my heels. "I can put some Neosporin on it."

He nods. I rifle through my bag and pull out the small plastic box.

"You travel with your own medical kit?" He sounds amused.

"Yep." I squeeze some ointment out of the tube, dab the cut, and then wipe my fingers on my towel. A laughable use of my medical skills, but better than nothing. I figure a Band-Aid will just litter the ocean if he decides to surf again, so I leave the wound uncovered.

"Thanks," he says quietly.

"Yep," I repeat.

I'm silent. He's silent. The waves are crashing and seagulls are cawing and people are laughing, but between us? There's *so much silence*.

"I got promoted. From second lieutenant to captain."

I look over; he's still staring straight ahead. "Congrats."

"Thanks."

"Was it a big deal?"

I don't know why I ask him the same question he basically just refused to answer. But then he does, and I realize why I asked it—because I wanted to know if he would answer *me*.

"I guess so. There was cake."

"Most big deals have cake."

He smiles, a small tug in one corner of his mouth that makes my stomach feel like it's getting turned inside out. "True."

"Your parents didn't go..." It's not a question. I'm still living next door. I know they didn't.

"I didn't tell them about it."

I lean back on my hands and search for a way to change the subject. "What's your favorite flavor of cake?" It's dawning on me, kind of slowly and also all at once, how I know all the big things about this guy that I've known for most of my life but not many of the little ones. That I know what his parents are like and what he does for a living and that he's really good at basketball, but I don't know his favorite color or his favorite movie or his favorite kind of cake.

Just how he looks naked.

"Of cake?"

I nod.

"Chocolate."

I wait, but he doesn't reciprocate the question. Instead, he's looking at me with his head tilted, like I'm a puzzle with pieces he's missing.

"Aren't you going to ask me mine? It's proper *cake flavor* etiquette."

Gray chuckles before he answers. "I don't need to. I already know your favorite flavor is carrot."

I stare at him.

"No red today?"

"What?" I'm still recovering from the revelation Gray Phillips knows my favorite flavor of cake when I spent a healthy portion of adolescence unsure if he knew I was even in the same room.

He leans over and trails one finger along the black string of my bikini, just above my left breast.

"Oh. No. I finally did some unpacking. That one didn't really...fit."

"I thought it fit."

Double meanings hang heavy as his fingers trail over my shoulder and down my arm. It's an innocent, small brush that feels anything but. His touch seeps away all my confidence about me being able to walk away from whatever this is between us if he isn't.

I know it will end when he leaves.

I just won't be the reason it stops before then.

I embrace the weakness rather than shy away from it as I lean into his touch.

"You free tonight, Dr. Collins?"

"To do what, *Captain* Phillips?"

He grins. "Me."

"I'm not that easy, Gray." I feel obligated to say it even though when it comes to him, I absolutely have been.

I expect a teasing comment, but Gray looks serious when he replies, "I don't think you're easy, Evie."

"I promised Sloane I'd go out with her tonight."

"Downtown?"

"Yeah."

I watch him closely. Watch his jaw tighten and relax. He doesn't like that I'm going out. I like that he doesn't like it.

"Fun."

I smirk. "Yeah. Was Colorado *fun*?"

He narrows his eyes, like he's not sure if he is ready to move on from the topic of tonight's plans. But there's nothing else to say, and we both know it. We're not dating. He doesn't have the right to have an opinion on any part of my life.

"Sheesh." Sloane suddenly appears beside me. "I feel like I accidentally ended up at a high school reunion. Just ran into Landon Jones *and* Macy Thompson." She leans past me. "Hey, Gray."

"Hi, Sloane."

Her gaze lingers on his abs, which makes me want to do something really irrational, like tell him to put on a shirt.

Sloane lies back down on the blanket next to me. "What happened to the rest of the guys?"

"They're surfing."

"'Kay. Wake me up when they're back. Or when it's five. I made reservations at Sakura for seven."

"Okay." I'm barely listening, far more focused on watching Gray as he untangles the ankle strap connected to his surfboard.

A few seconds later, he stands. My stomach fills with disappointment.

He looks at me, but he doesn't say a word before turning and walking toward the water. I bury my face in the towel and sigh.

I can't believe I'm wearing heels again. My feet aren't happy about the decision either. Sloane insisted they're super comfortable and they go perfectly with the blue dress I'm wearing. I believe her about the latter, but I'm calling bullshit on the former.

Sloane strides confidently inside our destination, a popular bar on King Street. I stumble behind her, feeling the raw fish, seaweed, and sake I had at dinner slosh around in my stomach. I would love to be curled up on the couch in sweatpants right now. But if I were, I know I'd be analyzing every word Gray said earlier for the thousandth time. This is healthier even if the air is so thick with cologne and vape smoke that I can barely breathe.

We squeeze in at the packed bar. Lines of liquor bottles sit on shelves with mirrored backgrounds, making them appear endless. Sloane debates between ordering a Moscow mule or a Paloma as I watch the bartenders rush about. I worked at a bar down the road from my apartment in Boston my first summer there until my school schedule became too hectic to manage both without losing my mind. It was fun, though. Shifts would pass quickly, and people would tip well.

A bartender appears. "What can I get you ladies?"

Sloane nods to me. "You go ahead."

"Gin and tonic, please," I order.

The guy nods, then turns to Sloane. She starts asking questions about one of the specialty cocktails. I hide a smile, suspecting her interest in the Double Standard has more to do with the fact that the bartender is young and attractive than the drink itself.

I fish my phone out of my clutch while they flirt and scroll through my new notifications. Photos from my mom, junk emails, and new messages from Noah, Logan, and two from...Gray Phillips. Instantly, butterflies appear. My palms start to sweat.

Sloane is still busy talking to the bartender. I unlock the

screen and tap on his name.

Gray: *Colorado wasn't fun.*

Gray: *It was lame.*

He sent it seven minutes ago. *Should I play it cool? Keep him guessing?*

Evie: *Charleston is boring, and Colorado was lame? Is there anywhere you like being?*

Three dots appear immediately. I reread what I sent.

Evie: *Don't make it dirty.*

Evie: *I'm not sexting you.*

Gray: *I was going to answer Vancouver.*

Gray: *Went there once.*

Gray: *Cool city.*

Evie: *I can't tell if you're kidding.*

Gray: *And I have a new appreciation for Malone's restroom.*

Evie: *Okay, now, I can tell.*

"He's hot, right?"

I startle at the sound of Sloane's voice. "Who?"

"The *bartender*, Evie."

"Oh. Yep."

Gray hasn't responded, so I click on Noah's name. He sent me one of the photos our mom sent earlier of her and my dad in front of the Colosseum, looking like total tourists. He added the two of us over their shoulders, appearing wildly out of place.

Noah: *Family Christmas card?*

I laugh and show it to Sloane. She requests she be added to the photo, which I pass along to Noah.

Gray still hasn't replied. I reread what I sent him last, debating if I should text him again. I check the message from Logan instead.

Logan: *You're welcome!*

Logan: *Glad it works.*

His graduation gift arrived this morning. It's a book seal that imprints a circular design, reading *From the Library of Dr. Evie Collins*. I have a huge book collection I accumulated in Boston and lugged south, which Logan knows. It's sweet and thoughtful and exactly like him. I sent him a photo of the seal pressed onto the title page of a novel earlier, thanking him and telling him how much I love it.

The bartender reappears with our drinks. Sloane hands me mine before striking up another conversation with him.

My phone lights up with a text from Gray, and I almost upend my cocktail in my haste to grab it. Sloane gives me a weird look before she continues talking. Because I'm acting strange, I hope, not because she saw the name on the screen.

Gray: *Are you having fun?*

I bite my bottom lip, trying to decide how to respond.

Evie: *Yes.*

Evie: *Would I have seen you this week if you hadn't been in Colorado?*

I regret the message as soon as I send it. *Why has no one come up with an Unsend option for texts yet?* The regret fades when I read his answer.

Gray: *Yes.*

Gray: *Will I see you tonight?*

Evie: *Yes.*

Gray: *Charleston is growing on me.*

Evie: *What about Colorado?*

Gray: *Nope. Still lame.*

"Come on. Let's grab a table," Sloane says.

I look up to see the bartender has disappeared.

"Sure you don't want to stay by the bar?" I wink.

She waves a napkin in my face. "He said to text him. He's off at midnight. Which means"—she hooks an elbow through mine and pulls me through the throng toward a high-top table in the back—"that we need to find *you* a guy for the night."

I slide onto a stool, and my toes breathe a sigh of relief. "Sloane, I appreciate it. Really, I do. It's just…" A heavy ball of guilt forms in my stomach, but I keep talking anyway. "I thought I was over Logan and ready to move on, but I'm not. I need more time."

Sloane blinks at me in surprise. Every time Logan has come up, I've insisted I'm fine. This is a rapid one-eighty.

"You said you're over him."

I nod. "I thought I was. But he's been texting me lately, and he sent me that gift, and I—I don't know. It made sense to end things with him, but it might have been a mistake."

"The book thing was thoughtful," Sloane agrees. "I think you should play the field some, though. Logan is the only guy you've really ever dated. Explore what's out there, you know?"

"Maybe." I shrug. "I'm just not ready to jump into something new."

"Okay." Sloane takes a sip of her drink and leans back on her stool. "We'll have a girls' night. And if Logan is really who you want, I'll be supportive. He still seems super into you. No way in hell I would send my ex a gift."

I smile, even as the guilt grows. I've kept things from Sloane over the course of our long friendship, but this is the first time I can recall ever lying to her outright, especially about something of importance.

Once Gray leaves, it won't matter, I tell myself. I'll move on —for real—and let Sloane push me out of my comfort zone.

"Thanks, S."

She smiles. "Of course. I just want you to be happy, Evie."

"I know. You too."

"Oh, I am." She winks. "Ready to dance?"

CHAPTER EIGHT

I climb out of the Uber and glance around the quiet, dark street. Sloane and I ended up in a more family-centric neighborhood. It's after midnight, and the only place with lights on is ours. I paw through my clutch until I find my house key and unlock the front door. I step inside and turn on more lights.

When Sloane mentioned to Noah that we were going out tonight, he offered to take care of Skye in the morning. I wasn't about to turn down the chance to sleep past seven—and unpack more than a few boxes. My new bedroom resembles a storage container at the moment.

I kick off my heels and pull my hair off my sweaty neck. Sloane and I danced for the past two hours straight, up until she left with her bartender beau, and I ordered a ride back here.

As I walk through the house, I flick on more lights. Sloane is neater than me, so the living room and kitchen are both clean. I pour myself a glass of water and text her.

Evie: *Just got home.*

Evie: *You good?*

In response, she sends a photo of the bartender making her a drink...shirtless and in what must be his kitchen. I laugh at it and then switch over to my thread with Gray. He hasn't sent anything since our exchange earlier. I type out my address, send it, and then toss my phone on the counter and head for the bathroom. After dancing in the bar for a couple of hours, I feel sweaty and gross.

I shower and shave all the necessary spots, stepping out of the stall right as the doorbell rings. My towel is missing from the hook. Sloane must have washed it. Considerate and *really* inconvenient right now. I dart down the hall, almost wiping out twice before I reach the hall closet and find a towel.

By the time I make it to the front door, my skin is still damp, and I'm out of breath. I peer through the peephole before I open the door.

Gray is leaning against the doorframe with one shoulder, looking like he's been standing out here for hours, not minutes. He takes in my wet hair and bare feet and heaving chest. I'm guessing most of his late-night hookups look a little more put together. A hint of amusement forms in the corners of his eyes and the curve of his lips.

"This your thing?"

"Huh?" I ask eloquently.

"Answering doors, wearing a towel. This is the second time it's happened."

"This is the second time I've *ever* answered a door, wearing a towel," I reply. "Guess it's just your lucky night."

"Yeah, it is."

He leans forward and kisses me before strolling inside, which I was not expecting. I shut the door and turn around to watch him take in the front hallway. There's not much to see, just a striped rug and the hall table Sloane brought from her old place. Framed prints lean against the wall, waiting to be hung up.

"Decorating is a work in progress," I explain as we walk down the hallway and past the kitchen. "My room is down here."

It feels strange having him here in my space. Even weirder than when he was in my childhood bedroom. Gray spent plenty of time at my house growing up. Not because of me, but still, he was there. This room is all me. The only reason he's *here* is me.

"Wow. You have a lot of books."

There's not much else to comment on in my bedroom. The walls are bare with the exception of a few pink sticky notes bearing scribbled reminders, and most of my other belongings are still packed away in brown boxes.

"I know. There was a used bookstore right by my place in Boston."

"You hauled these all the way from Boston?" Gray's eyebrows rise as he takes in the high stacks. I pulled a bunch out earlier to try my new seal on.

"Yeah. I've only read a few of them. I had so much reading to do for school that whenever I had any free time, it was pretty much the last thing I felt like doing."

"Huh." He looks around some more. "And…why are they all on the floor?"

I sigh. "I bought a bookcase, but I haven't had time to put it together."

He looks at me.

"I couldn't figure out how to put it together," I amend.

Gray laughs. "Where is it?"

"The closet."

He walks over and opens the door. I follow, peering under his arm at the scraps of wood that haven't moved since I dumped them in there the day the bookcase arrived from IKEA.

"The box didn't come with instructions. After spending

twenty minutes on hold, a nice woman named Susan said she would mail them to me. But I still haven't—"

Gray starts pulling pieces of the bookcase out of the closet.

"What are you doing?"

"Putting it together."

"You don't have to do that."

"I know." He takes a seat on the floor.

"Seriously. What are you doing?"

"I like a challenge, remember?" He flashes my favorite grin. Which leads to the realization that I *have* a favorite grin. That I know his different facial expressions *that well*.

"So… I should put clothes *on*?"

"Clothing is optional for construction."

I roll my eyes as I walk over to a box and pull out an old T-shirt of Noah's that I swiped in high school. It's oversize and soft, and it fits over the towel before I drop it. Not that there's anything Gray hasn't seen before.

Gray glances up as I walk back over to him. "Nice T-shirt."

I can't tell if he's being serious or teasing me.

"It's Noah's."

"No, it's not. It's mine. I went to Glen Ridge Basketball Camp. Noah must have borrowed it and never given it back."

"Oh. Do you want it back?" I ask and pray he says no. I had no attachment to this T-shirt until right this second, when I found out it was his.

He shakes his head with a small smirk.

I take a seat on the hard floor beside him, tucking my legs up underneath me. "Does it feel weird to you?"

"Does what feel weird?"

"What's happened between us lately. We've known each other for most of our lives, and now, we're…now, it's different. For

124

now." I add the last part quickly, so he knows I'm not harboring any delusions about where this might lead.

"No. It's the opposite of weird."

I tilt my head. "What *is* the opposite of weird?"

Gray shrugs as he starts assembling the base of the bookcase. "Not sure. Usual?"

"I don't think I want to be usual," I protest.

"It's not a bad thing," he counters.

"I guess not." I watch him work, deft movements shifting wood and sorting screws.

"Which one of these"—he gestures toward the stacks—"is your favorite book?"

I flip through the closest pile. "No idea. I told you, I haven't read most of them."

Gray chuckles and leans past me to grab one of them. "No way. You bought the sex books?"

My cheeks burn as I snatch my copy of *Fifty Shades of Grey* back from him. "Just the first one. I wanted to know what all the hype was about."

"Did you read it?"

"I started it," I admit.

"Got too graphic for you?" he teases.

I toss the book back. "If you're so interested, why don't *you* read it?"

He pages through the beginning, like he's actually going to. "*From the Library of Dr. Evie Collins?*"

I'm sure I'm blushing again. "It was a graduation gift. I just got it, and I'm trying it out."

"Didn't you graduate almost a month ago?"

"Uh, yeah." I play with the hem of my—well, Gray's—shirt. "It was from Logan. He moved, so it got lost in the mail. It just arrived today."

"Hmm." An innocuous sound that hints at a lot.

I fall right for it. "What?"

"I guarantee he's had it this whole time. He just wanted to figure out where you two stood first."

Male insight is welcome even if the only guy I'm really interested in analyzing is him.

"How do you know?"

"You broke up with him, right?"

"Yeah."

"He gave you time to miss him, and now he's testing the waters."

"I think he's dating someone. The chef, remember?" I hurriedly continue since the context of that conversation isn't one I want to dwell on. "We were friends before. He's just being... friendly." *I think.*

Gray scoffs. "If you say so. But I'm guessing he'll try to get back together with you."

"It's not going to happen," I tell him. Despite what I told Sloane earlier, I have no regrets about ending things with Logan. Not to mention, I'm more interested in analyzing the fact that *Gray* is analyzing things than his actual analysis.

"Did you love him?" Gray's not building my bookshelf anymore. He's completely focused on me.

These aren't things you talk about with a one-night stand, right? Or a three-night stand, which is what we're up to?

It's an immensely personal question. One I wouldn't ordinarily answer. But something about the way that he asked it—like he cares what the response might be—causes me to reply.

I shake my head. "No."

Based on the way his body relaxes, that's the answer he wanted. "Is that why you didn't sleep with him?"

"Maybe. But it was more... I don't know. I didn't want it to just be a physical thing. Not a fairy tale, but someone familiar. Someone I trusted. Someone I wanted enough not to freak out about it."

He assembles two shelves before he speaks again. "I'm sorry I was such an ass before, at Malone's. I was in a bad headspace, but still…it's no excuse. You deserved better. *Deserve* better."

"You already apologized. You don't need to again."

"Yes, I *do*." His face and voice are fierce. "Don't let people treat you that way, Evie."

"I *don't*, Gray. If anyone else had said those things to me, acted that way, I would have never talked to them again. Much less *slept* with them."

"Then, why…"

I crawl into his lap. He shifts to accommodate me, his hands sneaking under the cotton and settling on my hips. The simple touch sends shivers up my spine. Metal clanks as the screws on the floor scatter. I don't want to reply to him; I want the release my body has come to crave from his. Lust pools in my lower stomach as I grind against him, seeking friction.

"Don't ask questions you don't want answers to, Gray."

His eyes meet mine, blazing with questions and understanding. "This shirt looks good on you," he whispers before he kisses me.

The kiss is full of sensation. It's also brimming with emotion. I didn't know you could convey words with a kiss until right now —this exact second.

I know what a kiss means. *Something*. You don't kiss someone for no reason at all. You're chasing a feeling. You're not saying anything.

Except…Gray is saying a lot.

So am I.

With our hands. Our lips. Our moans and groans.

But we don't actually say anything at all.

I wake up to dim light. I blink a few times, experiencing an uncomfortable flash of déjà vu. The decision on whether to roll over or not becomes an internal battle.

"Don't let people treat you that way, Evie."

Maybe he's *trying* to push me away.

Slowly, I turn onto my back. My head moves even more gradually. Inch by inch, the view of the ceiling shifts to my wall. Shifts to the guy beside me in bed.

The light is coming from a lamp.

He's holding a book, not a phone.

I exhale, relieved.

Gray glances over. "Sorry. Did I wake you up?"

I shake my head, then squint at the cover of the paperback. Laugh.

He shrugs, not at all embarrassed. "I was curious. It has my name in the title."

Without really thinking about it, I move. I drape my arm over his stomach and rest a leg between his. "Did you learn anything?" My voice is sleepy. Anxiety has drained away, leaving contentment behind.

"Sure, if you want to experiment with safe words."

I laugh before I close my eyes. His chest rises and falls as he breathes. I can hear the swoosh of his heart. Rather than lull me to sleep, it keeps me awake. I like listening to the rhythmic, reassuring whoosh.

After a few minutes, I slide out of bed. Goose bumps rise as the air-conditioning hits my bare skin. "I'm getting some water. You want anything?"

"I'm good. Thanks."

I nod before walking into the hallway, turning lights back on as I go. My glass from earlier is still sitting out on the kitchen counter. I refill it and retrace my steps back to my bedroom. Rather than head straight for bed, I linger in the doorway.

Gray hasn't moved. He has one arm tucked behind his head, making his bicep bulge. Either he's actually absorbed in the book or he's a really good actor because he doesn't look up as I continue staring at him. The lamp by my bed illuminates the tanned skin of his bare chest and the brown hair I made a mess of with my fingers.

I might be drooling a little bit.

The glass of water gets set on a box, and then I climb back into bed.

He looks over as soon as the sheets shift. "You didn't want to take a picture?"

"Shut up," I grumble as I lie down and cross my arms.

Smug satisfaction radiates off him.

The paperback hits the comforter with a soft *thud*.

"You tired?"

"No," I admit. I should be exhausted; it's the middle of the night. "I have to go feed the cat at seven. My parents won't be back for a few more days."

His brow creases with confusion. "Why did you tell me to come here, then?"

"I figured you'd prefer it. You know…it's cleaner."

"Cleaner?" he echoes.

"Easier," I amend.

"Easier?"

"Stop repeating everything I say!"

129

"I'm trying to figure out *what* you're saying."

I sigh. "I know you said you don't think it's weird, but I do. Having sex with you in my childhood bedroom is weird for me. Having sex with me next door to the house you grew up in must be somewhat strange for you."

He's silent.

"You're barely in Charleston. I live here now. It'll be easier to…move on from this if there aren't reminders of you *everywhere*."

Although it's probably too late, I realize. He's invaded my work, the car I'll probably buy, Malone's, my parents' house, and now, my new home.

When he speaks, it's anticlimactic. "Okay."

"Okay?"

"Yeah. We can have sex wherever you want. I've already fucked you on a bathroom counter and the floor when there was a bed right here. Obviously, I'm not picky."

That wasn't exactly the point I was trying to get across, but it doesn't really matter. I can set as many boundaries as I want. Gray won't be any easier to forget.

He rolls, so he's above me—heavy, hot, and hard. I move to kiss him, but he dips his head before I can, skimming my jaw with a light brush that licks at my skin like an open flame.

"So fucking sexy," he murmurs into the crook of my neck. "You should never wear clothes. Except maybe scrubs."

"*Scrubs*? Scrubs are not sexy."

"On you? Yes, they are."

He moves away. I start to protest until I realize where he's headed. The journey down my chest is leisurely and teasing. He pauses at my breasts before kissing a line down the center of my stomach.

"Almost as bad as that red bikini." He swears, either at the memory or in response to the wetness between my legs.

I gasp his name at the first swipe of his tongue. Last time he did this, I was a mess of nerves. Now, there's nothing but anticipation as his mouth works me over with the same expert touch he does everything else. Callous palms part my thighs, keeping them spread as he licks and swirls at sensitive flesh, sending sparks of pleasure everywhere. My skin feels so hot that every touch sizzles. I thread my fingers through his hair and pull him closer as the pressure builds and builds and explodes.

I don't care to stay quiet. His name falls out of my mouth over and over again as waves of release wash over me.

Gray gives me no chance to recover before flipping me over. The crinkle of a wrapper is my only warning before he slides inside me in one slick stroke. It's not soft and slow and languid, but rough and deep and desperate. Faster than I thought possible, I'm coming again. Gray growls before his hips still and he jerks inside of me.

Harsh breathing is the only sound. He moves off of me and heads into the hallway, probably to use the bathroom. I roll onto my back, feeling the cool rush of the air-conditioning hit the sweat lingering on my skin.

The bed dips when he returns. I don't move at first. When I finally look over, he's mirroring my position, on his back with his arms at his sides. His eyes meet mine. It feels *right*, everything between us. Comforting yet thrilling, never uncomfortable or forced. Warmth unfurls in my chest when Gray spreads his arm away from his side in a silent invitation. I take it, resting my head on his chest and tangling my legs with his.

"How did you know I love carrot cake?" I whisper. It's bothered me since he said it, and this feels like one of those rare moments where words can be said without repercussions. They'll drift away into the darkness of the room, forgotten come morning.

"Because that's what you request for your birthday every year. Including when you turned thirteen. Your mom forgot to buy carrots, so she called *my* mom, who thought she had carrots but didn't. Rather than tell your mom that, she sent me to the store. It took me an hour to bike there and back."

I'm silent.

I don't know what to do with all these emotions. So, I shove them down. Far away. As far as they'll go. Because sometimes— always—that's easiest.

CHAPTER NINE

I sign my name with a flourish and hand the chart to Haley, the nurse on shift tonight. "Here's the discharge paperwork for Hopkins in 409."

She nods and takes the binder from me. "I'll get it all entered into the system."

I give her a tired smile, which she mirrors. "Thank you."

"Have a good night. Or morning rather."

The reminder increases the ache of exhaustion. "You too."

I head toward the elevator. The doors open to reveal it's empty, which is a rarity, even at this hour. I press the button for the bottom floor that houses the resident locker rooms and lean back against a poster detailing STD symptoms, closing my eyes. The doors slide closed, then ding open a minute later.

A low male laugh sounds. "Long night?"

I crack my eyes open to see Ben standing before me. "Long night," I confirm.

He yawns as he steps inside the elevator with me. "Me too. Neuro was nuts." He presses the button to close the doors. I've always wondered if anyone actually did that. "Hey, you grew up here, right?"

"Yeah."

"You ever been to Frosted before?"

I laugh. "Been? I'd make my brother stop there every morning on the way to school. Best doughnuts I've ever had."

Ben smiles. He's got a clean-cut, all-American look to him. Not bland, just straightforward. But his smile is lopsided and a little crooked. It adds more character to his face.

"Yeah, I agree. There was a doughnut place right across the street from my apartment in California. I thought theirs was the best there is...but now, I'm reconsidering."

"You're from California?"

"No, I grew up in Cincinnati. I ended up on the West Coast for undergrad and then medical school."

The doors ding open. I take a step forward, only to realize we're on the second floor, not the ground level.

Rose is standing there, yawning. She perks up when she sees me and Ben. "Hey, guys."

I arch a brow as she steps inside. "You're taking the elevator down one floor?"

"Don't judge, Collins. I had to drop something off in the lab. You had the same long-ass night I did. Did you get any sleep?"

I shake my head. "None."

Rose yawns again. "Same. I told Ellie and Sara I'd get brunch with them. Of course, *they* didn't get a single code last night." Another yawn. "You guys are both welcome to come. There will be coffee."

"I'm gonna grab a doughnut and a nap," Ben answers. "My brother is coming into town tonight, and he'll want to go out."

"Is this brother cute and single?" Rose asks, unashamed.

Ben laughs and shakes his head.

Rose makes a face, then looks at me. "Evie?"

"Uh, I can't. I've got plans."

"With the hunky soldier?"

"He's not a soldier, but yes."

"Are things serious between you two?"

"No. We're just…no."

"Uh-huh." Rose gives me a *look* but doesn't say anything else.

When she pressed me for details after Gray showed up in the cafeteria last week, I told her we went to high school together, but I didn't delve into the *brother's best friend, next-door neighbor, chief's son* of it all. I also told her we have a firm expiration date, which Rose seems to have conveniently forgotten. Or maybe she just needs a reminder. I sure do.

When we reach the locker room, I change quickly, swapping out of my scrubs for a sundress. The temperatures are steadily rising as July creeps closer, beginning to regularly reach eighty degrees and occasionally brush ninety. I brush my teeth, wash my face, and say goodbye to the other interns in the locker room before heading out into the parking lot.

Gray's Jeep is pulled up alongside the curb. He climbs out when he sees me approaching. The sight smacks me in the center of my chest. It feels good—right—to leave work and find him waiting for me. A soft, gooey sensation of contentment.

The sun is just beginning to rise in the sky, dappling everything in soft light. I study what he's wearing, searching for clues about our destination. The athletic shorts and faded Colorado Avalanche T-shirt give me none.

When I reach him, he kisses me. I was expecting it. At some point, without me really realizing, it became ordinary. No less thrilling, but normal. Each stretch of time we spend together is bookended by a kiss—one at the start and one at the end. I hate how much I love it.

It turns into more than a hello peck. I haven't seen him in two days, and it's worrying how long a stretch of time that feels like. I thought routines took weeks—months—to form, not days. But he already feels like a permanent piece of my life here rather than a temporary one. My life revolves around work and spending time with him.

I tug Gray's bottom lip between my teeth. He responds by sliding a hand down my back to squeeze my butt.

I start laughing, which effectively ends our kiss. "Are you seriously feeling me up in a hospital?"

"We're not in a hospital," he counters. "We're outside. I'm feeling you up on a sidewalk."

I roll my eyes as he pulls the overnight bag off my shoulder and tosses it in the backseat of his car.

"Get much sleep?"

"None," I admit as I climb in the passenger side, yawning at the reminder of my long night. "I had four patients code."

"Did they pull through?"

"All but one."

Gray gives me a long, searching look from the driver's side. "If you don't want to—"

"I want to go," I assure him.

I could have not slept in days, and I'd still insist on going wherever it is that we're headed. Part of it is curiosity. We know Emmett's and Sloane's schedules. Sneaking around in each other's places hasn't been much of an issue. We don't need to go on a trip to have sex. But still, Gray brought it up, asking if I was free this weekend. I'm pretty sure there's more to the story, especially since he's been less than forthcoming with details, but I haven't pushed. I haven't told him I had to trade three shifts to get today and tomorrow off either. Sloane thinks I'm on call again tonight. I'm not sure what Gray told Emmett about his absence.

"Okay." The car engine rumbles, and we start moving, weaving through the hospital's crowded parking lot.

"So…are you going to tell me where we're going?"

Gray glances at me, then back at the road. "Beaufort."

"Really?"

I figured it wouldn't be far since we're only spending one night. I assumed *not far* would consist of a short drive up or down the coast to one of the many small towns gearing up to be flooded with tourists in the coming months. Not a boat ride.

A noncommittal noise is my only answer. He seemed happy to see me, at ease about this trip. But there's also an undercurrent of something else that's evident in the lingering silence hanging between us. I let it, leaning my head back against the leather seat and looking out at the city slowly waking up.

The drive to the ferry port takes ten minutes. Crowds and activity keep me awake, but as soon as the boat pulls away from the wharf, I start fighting with my eyelids. It's a gorgeous day. If we were flying, there wouldn't be a cloud in sight. The sky is an endless stretch of blue, just like the water we're floating on. The bright sunshine and wind aren't enough to keep me awake, though. I doze off against Gray's shoulder almost immediately.

When I open my eyes again, they're gritty with sleep. The large mass of land that is Port Royal Island hovers in the distance, growing larger and larger with each chug of the massive engine steering the ferry along.

Once we're close to the shore, I raise my head from Gray's shoulder. He looks over at me but doesn't say anything.

"You gonna tell me why we're here?" I ask quietly.

Gray turns his gaze back toward the water. "I promised I'd visit."

"Promised who?"

He doesn't say anything at first. "A few months ago, I lost a good friend. We were at the Academy together. Had some of the same assignments once we graduated. Would go on trips together when we had overlapping leave. And then he was...gone." That final word hovers between us for a minute. "I didn't just go back to Colorado to get promoted. There was a memorial service for Sam as well. His parents were there. They own a bed-and-breakfast here, on the island. When they heard I was spending my leave in Charleston, they asked that I come visit. I was worried I'd just be a...reminder, but they insisted. Sam was stubborn as hell too." One corner of his mouth turns up at some fond recollection.

"I'm so sorry, Gray."

His Adam's apple bobs as he swallows. "I'm sorry too. I should have given you some more warning about what this is. A heads-up about what you're walking into. A chance to back out. I...it's still tough to talk about."

"I would have come anyway."

"I know."

I hesitate. "Noah never mentioned..." My not-very-subtle attempt to ask him if he's confided in anyone else.

"I didn't tell him. I've kept them separate, you know. My life there and my life here."

"How did Sam die?" I whisper.

Gray keeps his gaze forward as he answers, "His plane went down. Engine fire. They crashed...and there were no survivors."

The ferry rocks as the boat aligns with the wharf. The speakers blare to life, spilling out reminders to gather all belongings and times to buy return tickets. Other passengers stand from the bench seats and stretch, eager to return to solid ground after the two-hour trip. Gray and I don't move.

I'm not sure what to say. Despite my proximity to death at work, I'm fortunate enough to have never lost anyone close to me. It's painful to lose a patient, but they're not people I've interacted with outside the four walls of the hospital. The feeling of loss is different. If a stranger's death affected you like a loved one's, no one would ever be able to function. People die every day. Every minute.

Grief takes time to shrink to a manageable size. I know there's nothing I can say to minimize it for Gray. But he could have come alone. He chose to include me in this. So, I reach out and tangle his fingers with mine. We've never held hands before. Touching is usually a prelude to something sexual between us.

I've held hands with other guys. I've kissed other guys. Both actions feel different with Gray. I'm not sure if it's because I'm doing them with the knowledge of what doing more feels like…or if it's because I'm doing them with *him*. Hopefully the former, likely the latter.

Gray squeezes my hand, then stands, slinging our bags over one shoulder and pulling me up with him. "Let's go."

I let him guide me down the stairs and off the ferry.

"You've been here before?"

"Yeah. Noah and I came with our parents when you guys were in…seventh grade, I think? I was ten."

"Right."

I expect to take one of the shuttles lined up on the street, but instead, we start walking along what looks like the main downtown section. My memories of my only other trip to this island are hazy, but I spot a bookstore and an ice cream parlor that both look familiar.

Charleston's colorful charm has always looked like home to me. It's not modern, but it feels fresh. Beaufort feels like stepping back in time. It's overflowing with southern character, natural beauty, and rich heritage. Businesses line the street, separated by striped awning and wooden benches situated on cobblestones.

They taper off into antebellum mansions situated under tall oaks dripping with Spanish moss.

"This is it," Gray states, tugging me to the left toward a sign reading *The Beaufort Bed-and-Breakfast.*

The bed-and-breakfast is a three-story building that's painted a cheery shade of light pink. The first two floors have wraparound porches dotted with hanging plants. Leaves spill over the edges of the pots and brush the railing. A white picket fence surrounds the property, which includes a quaint courtyard with wicker furniture.

I follow Gray through the open gate and up the front stairs. A couple who look to be in their sixties are sitting in two rocking chairs to the left of the front door, sipping from steaming mugs. The woman smiles at me. I give her a small wave with my free hand before we step inside.

The front hallway is cool, with a musty undertone to the air that reminds me of a library or a basement. The walls look like they belong to an art gallery with limited space. Rather than the several feet of typical spacing that separates frames at most museums, mere inches are between the many paintings. The flowered wallpaper beneath is barely visible.

Gray veers to the left of the wooden staircase. I trail after him, taking in the layout of the space. An empty fireplace encompasses most of the opposite wall. To its left is a small sitting area with a couch and two armchairs. To the right is a wide wooden desk. A woman with curly, graying hair is standing behind it, flipping through some papers.

Gray drops my hand and steps forward. "Hi, Marnie."

The woman glances up at the sound of Gray's greeting. Instantly, her face transforms. Creases form in the corners of her mouth, and crow's-feet appear as she steps around the desk and wraps her arms around Gray. She says nothing, just holds him tightly.

Rather than infringe on what feels like a private moment, I look around the room more. Behind the desk is a stack of books, most of them on South Carolina history. A few guidebooks are beside it. Directly below a row of hooks is a picture frame. In uniform and in front of a plane, a handsome blond man stands between Marnie and an older man. Sam and his parents, I'm assuming. I stare at it, taking in his broad smile and twinkling eyes, absorbing the loss of someone I never met and never will.

"And who's this?" Marnie steps away from Gray, discreetly wiping her cheeks as she glances between the two of us.

Gray clears his throat. "Um, this is Evie. My girlfriend. Evie, this is Marnie."

I start at the title. I should have seen it coming, I guess. He obviously isn't going to introduce me as his friend with benefits to a woman he respects.

I hold out a hand and smile. "It's really nice to meet you, Marnie."

Marnie brushes my hand away to give me a warm hug. She smells like vanilla and orange. "The pleasure is all mine, dear." When Marnie pulls back, she looks me over closely. "My goodness, you're gorgeous. You're lucky she ever looked twice at you, Grayson."

Gray rolls his eyes. I laugh.

"You didn't mention you were seeing anyone," Marnie says to Gray. Her voice has turned accusing.

"Yeah, well, it, uh…it didn't seem like the time." Gray fiddles with the strap of his bag.

I recall what he said on the ferry, that the last time he saw Sam's parents was at his memorial.

A flash of sadness crosses Marnie's voice before she recovers. "Celebrating life is part of accepting death. I always want to hear about yours, understand? It's what Sam would have wanted."

Gray nods. "Okay."

"Good." Marnie returns to the desk and pulls a key off the hook. She sets it on the counter and then pulls out a sheet of paper with a map. "You're in room 205. Top of the stairs to the right. And here's a map of the town. I'm sure you can pull up whatever you need on your phone. Scott insists we hand out copies to all the guests anyway." She looks at me. "My husband isn't one for technology."

I smile.

"Dockside has the best food on the island. You should plan to go there for dinner. I'm happy to make you two a reservation."

"You and Scott should join us." I make the offer automatically. I've known Gray's parents for most of my life. Yet oddly, I feel like I'm seeking out parental approval right now. It's obvious how close Gray and Marnie are.

"Oh, no. You kids should enjoy yourselves."

"No, really. We'd love to have the company." I don't look at Gray, but Marnie does.

"Okay," she agrees. "That sounds lovely. I'll make a reservation for seven p.m.?"

I nod. "Perfect."

"All right. Y'all need anything before then, just let me know."

"We will," Gray replies. "Thanks, Marnie."

He heads for the hallway with our bags. With one final smile, I walk out after him. There's a middle-aged couple coming down the stairs. We wait for them to pass and then Gray starts climbing. The stairs creak with each step. The walls on the second floor have no artwork besides the same floral wallpaper. It appears every frame in the place was congregated together for a first impression.

Gray unlocks 205 and pushes the wooden door open. Yellow giraffes cover the walls in here instead of flowers. The sight draws an involuntary smile as I peer at one of the animals repli-cated thousands of times around the room. The furniture is all built from old, dark wood and decorated with elaborate carv-ings. The four-poster bed takes up most of the room. There's also a chest of drawers and a love seat covered with pink upholstery.

He tosses our bags on the blue bedspread.

"You're really close with his parents."

"Yeah. They've got a place in Breckenridge, where they spend most of the winter. We'd travel there a lot from the Academy. And they'd always be at the base when Sam and I got back from a deployment. We'd get burgers and beers."

"That sounds nice." Does that mean Juliet and Henry have never shown up?

"It was. And no." Gray walks over to the bed and unzips his bag.

"No, what?" I ask as I sit down on the love seat.

"No, my parents have never come. I can tell you're wonder-ing. I've never invited them; they've never asked."

I don't reply, just lean back. The cushions are firm, not soft, but I'm tired enough that it feels like lounging on a cloud. Gray watches me as he sifts through his bag. With absolutely no preamble, he drops his shorts and boxers before stepping into swim trunks. He leaves his T-shirt on.

"What are you doing?"

"Changing."

"*Duh.* Why?"

Gray shrugs. "Figured I'd go to the beach."

"While I do…what?"

"I don't know…nap?" He matches my tone exactly.

"I can't sleep now. I'll be up all night."

He smirks. "You'll be up all night anyway."

I try to ignore the way those words heat my blood. "Why don't we go sightseeing?"

"Sightseeing?" he echoes, like the word is a foreign concept.

"Yeah. There are museums and stuff. Shopping."

"You want to go shopping?"

"Yep."

Gray sighs. "Okay…we'll go shopping." He sounds less than enthused about the prospect but doesn't renege his agreement as we head back out onto the street.

It's nearing noon, and the streets are busier than I expected. Maybe it's because I barely do anything besides go to work, but it doesn't feel like summer is in full swing to me yet. The other pedestrians on the crowded sidewalk clearly feel differently. There are kids clutching ice cream cones, teenagers giggling and flirting, older couples ambling along…and then me and Gray. He doesn't reach for my hand the way he did earlier, but he's walking close to me. As we approach the start of Beaufort's downtown, our arms brush a few times, sending a shock to my system each time.

The bookstore I remember from my one and only other trip here appears up on the left side of the street. I head there first, and Gray follows me inside. The cool rush of air-conditioning feels heavenly after the hot glare of the sun.

"Don't you already have enough books?" he asks

"I'm just browsing. I'm not going to buy anything."

"Uh-huh. Sure."

I roll my eyes and continue running my fingers along the spines. "I mean it. You never finished building my bookcase. I don't have anywhere to put them."

"If you want me to finish a project, you can't climb into my lap in the middle of it."

"No straddling. Noted."

"I mean…we could assess on a case-by-case basis moving forward," he says, sending me a smirk that looks decidedly dangerous.

Rather than cause concern, it makes something flutter in my chest. *Not good.* My reaction to Gray is supposed to be dwindling, not strengthening. He leaves in a week.

I should be starting to get sick of him.

I should be tired of sneaking around.

I should be eager to meet a guy I could have a future with.

Those are all the things I *should* be feeling. Instead, I'm dreading June 19—the day he leaves—like it's my own personal doomsday. It feels like it is. Gray hasn't just become a routine; he's an addiction. Instead of weaning myself off, I'm chasing another high—as many hits as I can get before my supply runs dry.

The things you want aren't supposed to be all you hoped and more. People who chase success often end up unsatisfied. People who chase money often end up unhappy. People who chase love often end up heartbroken. I would know. I didn't expect that same guy who barely acknowledged my existence for years would one day make me feel special and seen and sexy. And then say, *See ya.* I thought I knew what Gray Phillips was to me—and what he never would be. That's been rapidly rearranged and forever altered.

"What?"

I blink, and Gray's confused face comes back into focus. I've just been standing here, staring at him. He looks over one shoulder, like there might be something behind him that's more interesting.

Pretending like no staring took place and I didn't hear him, I head toward the back of the store. The rear section houses a wide array of items marketed to capitalize on the tourism industry—T-

145

shirts, hats, booklets, snow globes, key chains, maps, posters, stuffed animals, and an impressive assortment of postcards. Impulsively, I pick up a turtle figurine to stick in my locker at work. At the moment, it holds nothing but my stethoscope and badge. It could use some livening up.

"This stuff is for tourists," Gray complains as he follows me down the aisle toward the postcards.

"We *are* tourists," I remind him.

"We live less than two hours away."

"But we don't live *here*, which makes us tourists." From the carousel, I grab a postcard depicting dolphins and head for the register, holding the turtle figurine I picked out in my other hand so that I'm double-fisting my memorabilia. "I'm finished looking, which means you can stop complaining."

"I'm not complaining."

"Yeah, you are." I sigh. "You know, why don't you just go to the beach? Surf or whatever you were planning to do. I'll meet you back at the bed-and-breakfast by seven for dinner."

"Evie…"

"Do you know when the last time I went on any sort of vacation was? Spring break, freshman year. *Six years*. Since then, I've been nowhere but Boston and Charleston. This is the first time I've had *two straight days off* since I moved back. Excuse me for trying to enjoy it."

Before I can stalk past him, Gray grabs my arm. "I'm sorry, Evie."

"If you don't want me here, then why did you invite me?"

"I *do* want you here. I just … I've been dreading this. I've never spent time with Scott and Marnie without Sam there too. I remind them of him. They remind me of him. It's strange, and I'm on edge about it. But I'm happy you're here. Really. Anything else I'm feeling…it's not because I don't want you here. Okay?"

"Okay," I whisper.

Gray nods and reaches past me to grab a Beaufort ball cap off the rack. "You ready?"

I eye the blue hat. "What is that for?"

"To show every idiot on the street I'm a tourist."

I bite my bottom lip, so I don't laugh. "You don't have to do that."

He gives me a lopsided smile that's half-amused, half-resigned. "Yeah, I do. And I know Sam would have preferred that I wore this around town, having fun and sightseeing with you, than wandering about, wondering if he'd been to a place or not. So…ready?"

I nod, and we head for the checkout.

I smooth down the front of my dress and dab on one final coat of lip gloss. Smack my lips together. Study my appearance in the mirror.

I'm stalling.

I'm nervous.

In my experience, reality rarely lives up to the hype. Adulthood definitely hasn't. I don't have any regrets about pursuing medicine, but it hasn't been what I expected. It's underwhelmed my expectations in some ways, exceeded them in others.

Most of the time, the way you imagine something is far superior to the actual reality.

Gray seems to be my exception.

And I've imagined what it might look like—feel like—to go out on a date with Grayson Phillips many, many times. Swings on the playground in elementary school. Walks on the beach in middle school. Kissing under the bleachers in high school. My expectations were low when it came to activities back then. I was more focused on the company.

That's love, I think. Not caring *what* you're doing, but *who* you're doing it with.

I thought I was in love with Gray Phillips before.

I'm concerned—terrified—that the giddiness I'm experiencing right now is the real deal. Is what my seven-year-old self confused contentment while eating a Popsicle and watching him play basketball from my back stoop for.

"Evie? You've been in there for ten minutes. Are you almost ready?"

I roll my eyes at my reflection. Obviously, Gray has never gotten ready with a woman before. I like to think I'm low maintenance—ten minutes is nothing.

We got back from the beach twenty minutes ago, after spending the afternoon walking through a museum and touring the lighthouse. We got sandwiches and went to the beach for the rest of the day. I napped under an umbrella while Gray played volleyball with a group of college-aged guys. It was...perfect. Fun, easy, lighthearted. And I'm worried it'll be more damaging for my heart than the who knows how many times we've had sex. I've lost track of the exact number, which is concerning as well. That's when things become routine. And now, we're going out to dinner.

I looked up Dockside on my phone while Gray was being athletic. It's fancy—a far cry from the Chinese restaurant where Logan and I went for our six-month anniversary. Middle-aged strangers accompanying us or not, it feels like a *date*, date.

"Yep. Coming!"

I take a deep breath and open the bathroom door to walk out

into the bedroom. I'm wearing the nicest outfit I brought—a royal-blue cotton sundress. It's strapless, showing off the slight tan I've gained from the little time I've spent at the beach so far. I took the time to straighten my wavy hair, so it falls in a sheet of blonde strands.

I spin once I'm back in the room, trying to shake off the nerves. Trying to act like going out to dinner with him is no big deal at all. "What do you think?"

Gray is waiting by the door, wearing a pair of khaki shorts and a light-blue button-down. He has his phone in his hand, like he was in the middle of looking at something, but his gaze doesn't stray from me. Less is more with Gray. He's never the loudest or flashiest guy in the room. He'd rather sit in silence than make forced small talk. I've heard him share more critiques than compliments.

So, when he says, "You always look stunning, Evie," I know he's not just *saying* it. Then, like he said nothing at all, he nods toward the door. "Ready?"

"I, uh, yeah." I grab my clutch off the bed, slip on a pair of wedges, and walk through the door he's holding open. "You look nice." God, I sound awkward. Breathy.

Gray chuckles as we walk down the hallway. "Thanks."

Marnie and her husband are waiting at the bottom of the stairs.

Marnie beams when she sees us. "What a good-looking couple you two are."

Gray smiles as he shakes the man's hand. "Good to see you, Scott."

Scott claps Gray on the back. "I'm so glad you came, son. Means a lot to us."

Both of their expressions turn grim for a moment before the heaviness disappears.

"This is Evie."

Scott turns to me. He has the same genuine friendliness as his wife does—it simply exudes without saying a word. His tan, wrinkled skin suggests he spends plenty of time outdoors. "It's lovely to meet you, Evie."

"You too, Scott. Thank you for hosting us."

He shakes my hand with a weathered palm. "Our pleasure."

The walk from the bed-and-breakfast to the restaurant is only a few blocks. Gray and Marnie walk ahead. Scott and I amble behind. I ask him a few questions about the bed-and-breakfast. His descriptions of the family history behind the business and the upkeep he takes care of on the grounds last the whole walk. He's still talking about the magnolias he's cultivating when we're led to a four-person table overlooking the water. His enthusiasm reminds me of Henry's love for his garden. That's the only similarity I can find between the two men Gray seems to have paternal relationships with.

"Scott!" Marnie scolds as we sit down. "That's enough. The poor girl doesn't want to hear about pruning and mulching."

Scott holds his hands up in acquiescence and leans back in the wicker chair.

"It was interesting," I insist.

Marnie's bracelets jingle as she waves my words away. "No need to be polite, dear. I zone out every time."

I smile at that.

"Now, how did you two meet?" Marnie takes a slice of bread from the basket on the table and spreads butter on it, waiting expectantly.

I glance at Gray, letting him take the lead.

"We've known each other for a long time," he answers. "Evie grew up next door to me."

"My goodness, isn't that sweet?" Marnie smiles as she looks between the two of us. "You just started dating recently?"

"Yep." Gray takes a sip of his water.

"There was always a spark, though?"

"I guess." Another sip.

Marnie doesn't take the hint that this isn't Gray's first choice of conversation topics. "There must have been a moment, right? When you realized there was something there?"

Gray gives me a look that could be loosely translated to, *A little help here?*

I avert my eyes and grab a roll for myself, buttering with slow, deliberate strokes. Not only am I terrible about coming up with lies on short notice, but anything I might say along the lines of love at first sight would also hit embarrassingly close to home.

"Uh, yeah. Probably."

A romantic, Gray is not.

Marnie disagrees.

"How special." She demonstrates an accurate impression of a Victorian era swoon.

I chew my bread and bite back the urge to smile. Honestly, you can't pay for this sort of entertainment. I've never seen Gray put on the spot before. He usually just ignores questions he doesn't want to answer.

"What was it?"

I perk up for a whole new reason. Is he going to make something up? Manufacture some moment where our eyes locked across the middle school cafeteria?

Gray shifts in his seat. Clears his throat. "Oh. Just...you know, lots of little things."

"Like what?" Marnie homes in on Gray's vague response like a human polygraph machine. There's nothing but eagerness in her nosiness. She'll never have the chance to interrogate her son about the woman he's dating.

I never met Sam. His name hasn't even been spoken tonight. But I can feel his presence hovering in her hopeful questions, searching for the light in life rather than its darkness.

I think Gray hears it, too, because he actually answers her. "Well, the neighborhood we live in did all these celebrations growing up. Most of it was stupid. Caroling at Christmas and leprechauns for St. Patrick's Day. The only event I ever enjoyed was the Fourth of July. There would be a big cookout in the afternoon, and then everyone would set up chairs in the street to watch the fireworks. Anyway, one year—I think I was in seventh or eighth grade—they passed out sparklers. Once the fireworks started, that's what everyone was focused on. Everyone except Evie. She ran around the front yard, waving those sticks around the whole time. Every time one ran out, she'd light up a new one right away. I missed the whole show and watched her instead."

This time, when Marnie swoons, I have to resist an urge to do the same.

"Oh my word, isn't that just the sweetest story? I—"

"Can I get you folks any drinks or appetizers?" A waiter appears beside the table, cutting Marnie off.

His timing couldn't have been better. I drop my eyes to my menu, which I haven't even glanced at, and everyone else does the same. The paper gives me a necessary excuse to hide my expression. I don't want anyone at this table scrutinizing my response to Gray's patriotic little anecdote. Now, I wish he *had* spun some ridiculous story—the less believable, the better.

Because that moment he described, about the sparklers? He's not making it up. It happened. I can remember it clearly—the humid air, the fizzle as the coating burned away, the explosions in the sky. But I don't remember him—had no idea he was watching.

Were there other moments I missed?

Was my interest in him not as pathetically one-sided as I thought?

Does it matter either way?

I'm suddenly grateful for Scott's and Marnie's presence. It keeps me from dwelling on those questions—or even worse, *asking* them.

Marnie doesn't ask any more questions about me and Gray. She and Scott converse with the comforting ease of a couple who not only know each other well, but have also lived through the hard times along with the happy. We sip wine, slurp oysters, and savor entrées as Sam's parents share stories about the bed-and-breakfast. They pelt me with plenty of questions as well, asking all about my life in Charleston.

When we finish dinner, Marnie and Scott insist on paying for the meal, then send us to "the best bar in town." Since they were right about Dockside—the food was incredible—I'm inclined to believe them. I'm running on fumes after a long day and limited sleep, but I feel wide awake as we walk along the same street as we did earlier. The only difference is, it's dark now, and the people out and about are almost exclusively our age.

I'm wearing wedges tonight, which are more comfortable than heels. I wince as I watch one woman navigating the cobblestones in stilettos. A sprained ankle would have been a sure outcome if I'd attempted the same. She teeters but stays upright, thanks to the long umbrella she's holding. I glance up at the inky, clear sky in confusion. Maybe she brought it as a walking stick?

There's no question which building is our destination. Noise and music spill out into the street, audible even when we're still half a block away.

Gray rests his hand on my lower back when we walk inside the bar. The possessive touch sinks through the cotton dress I'm wearing and sears my skin, branding the flesh about as subtly as an iron. I've never come to a bar alone with a guy—just me and him. I've had nights out with other women. Logan and I would go for drinks but always with our group of friends.

I catch a few guys glancing at me. No one approaches. Gray's presence by my side is a powerful deterrent from any lewd comments or suggestive offers. He keeps his palm pressed against my back, guiding me through the crowd and over to the tiled counter that spans the bar. Heat spreads from the few inches where he's touching me, dancing along the surface of my skin and sending tingles everywhere. Rather than become accustomed to his proximity, I feel like I've become more attuned to it. I'm always aware of exactly how close he is.

"What do you want?" Gray asks when we reach the counter.

"Tequila shot."

He smirks. "That kind of night, huh?"

"I just want one."

I don't tell him I associate tequila with him—because he tasted like salt and lime the first time we kissed. The white wine we had with dinner is buzzing through my bloodstream. More alcohol is probably a bad idea. But it's too late. We get served immediately—female bartender—and so I follow through. Gray watches with a smirk as I lick the salt, down the shot, and make a face as I bite into the tart wedge. He kisses me as soon as I toss the lime, stealing the last drop of sour juice from my lips.

My feet stumble on absolutely nothing as he pulls me away from the counter, giving me no time at all to recover from that display of oral aptitude.

"Want to play pool?" Gray asks when we reach the corner of the bar, as if he didn't just melt my insides into a puddle of goo.

I strive to match his nonchalance. "I don't really know how to play."

"I'll teach you," he declares, confident as ever.

I watch as he sets a plastic triangle in the center of the green felt and starts filling it with colored balls, then grabs a couple of long wooden sticks.

He takes a sip of the beer he ordered and then beckons me over. "Come here."

Saying *no* never seems to be an option with him. I comply, coming to stand at one end of the table. He moves in behind me, bracketing me between his arms and brushing up against my back. I doubt he can hear my breathing accelerate. "Rocket Man" is blaring in the background, mixing with the loud chatter, but I don't think he's oblivious to how my body is vibrating with awareness. He murmurs instructions in my ear, talking about cues and racking and breaking. I don't absorb a single word. Instead, I memorize how he feels pressed against me and process how he smells like sandalwood and hops—a surprisingly arousing combination. Then again, I'd happily kiss Gray if he'd eaten garlic and I hadn't, so maybe it's not all that surprising.

"Ready?"

My time to daydream is up.

I turn in his arms, so I'm facing him. "If you want me to focus on anything you're saying, you can't stand this close."

"So, of that, you got…"

"Nothing," I finish.

One corner of his mouth rises, forming a lopsided smile. "Maybe that's part of my winning strategy."

"You've played before, and I haven't. I think that's all the strategy you need."

"We'll find out, huh?" He hands me a stick. "Here's your cue."

"What are we playing for?"

One eyebrow rises. "You mean, what am I winning?"

"That's awfully presumptuous."

"Not really—unless you're lying about playing before."

"I'm not," I assure him. "Just trying to keep things interesting."

"Interesting how?"

I pretend to think about it. "If *I* win, I'll give you a blowjob when we get back to the room."

Gray has a hell of a poker face. I make a mental note never to play cards with him. "You realize that will require me to lose?"

"Yep." I pop the *P*. "Gentlemen first."

He narrows his eyes at me, like he's trying to figure out what my end goal is. Good luck to him because I don't know either. I feel light and loose, thanks to the alcohol and easygoing ambiance. Thanks to him. Being around Gray makes me over-think less. Ironic for two reasons.

One, I used to second-guess everything I did around him in hopes of impressing him.

Two, Gray is one of the most serious guys I've ever met. Together, we should be uptight, not playful.

I never find out if my incentive had any effect on Gray's competitive side. One of the rules I should have listened to spelled out which balls I was supposed to send into the pockets and which I wasn't. Gray doubles over, laughing, when I start celebrating as I hit his in instead of mine, thinking I'm winning.

After he officially wins our game, we leave. The bar is becoming rowdier and rowdier as it grows later, and neither of us is in the mood to drink more. I wouldn't mind grinding up against him as payback for the pool lessons, but I'd rather do it in the privacy of our room, followed by sex and sleep.

"Want to walk back along the beach?" Gray suggests as we step outside.

"Yeah."

Rather than head straight along the street, we turn toward the sound of the surf, stepping onto sand after a couple hundred feet. I kick my wedges off and sink my toes into the sand. The waves are twice the size as they were when we were here earlier. They're huge, aggressive. They pound the shore like they're trying to prove a point, sending drops of spray flying. Salty wind swirls my hair and dress. Tiny birds run from each new swell, flying across the wet sand as fast as their little legs will carry them.

I laugh. When I look over, Gray is smiling at me.

"What are you laughing at?"

"I don't really know. I'm just...happy?" I say the statement like a question. Like happiness is a confusing concept.

Isn't it, though? It means something different to everyone. How do you know when you're truly happy?

Is it knowing you wouldn't rather be anywhere else, with anyone else? If so, then, yeah, I'm happy.

"Are *you*?"

"In general, or right now?"

I hope he's happy all the time. But what I *really* want to know is whether he's happy around *me*. "Right now."

"Yeah, I am."

"Good."

"I love storms," Gray says, watching the swell overtake the sand and slide away. "The devastation is terrible, but it's also breathtaking. That sort of power...it's so *raw*. I used to stay up and marvel at it when I was a kid."

I sink down into the sand. He takes a seat beside me.

"I know. You wanted to be a weatherman for a while."

"Right. I did."

"What else do you love?"

Gray glances at me. "What, you want a list?"

"Sure." I lean back on my palms.

"I don't know. Little things, I guess."

Little things. That's what he told Marnie made up our spark.

But the list he rattles off doesn't have anything to do with me.

"Waking up without an alarm. Surfing when the water is flat. Seeing the stars at night. My mom's peach pie. The feeling when I lift off the runway."

"That's a good list." I stare out at the churning sea.

He lets the topic drop. "I'm going to miss this view."

"The water looks different down here. Boston was always bleak and busy, it felt like. Plus, there was never any..." I look over at him and lose my train of thought.

Gray isn't looking at the surf or the palm trees or the white sand. He's looking at me. In an intense, focused way that makes me think that he didn't change his focus when I started talking. In a way that makes me think he might have been already looking at me before I said a word.

I *love* the way he's looking at me. Like, out of everything on this beach, I'm the most beautiful thing he's ever laid eyes on. I want to photograph this moment and tuck it away to pull out when I'm tired and stressed and questioning every decision I've ever made. But right now, I'm suddenly grateful for them all. Every choice that led me to this exact spot, here with him.

He breaks eye contact before I can decide if I'm brave enough to ask. "Did you ever consider staying in Boston?"

"No. Do you ever consider leaving?" It's something I've always wondered about.

His life here feels very temporary. He shares a loft with Emmett. His room sits empty most of the time.

"Yeah."

My heart sinks at his answer.

"I feel stuck in Charleston. I'm disappointed when we hit the runway at the joint base."

"Oh."

"It's always been that way. I love flying. I love my job. I just saw the ugly side—the scary side—of it right before coming back. That can make you question choices."

The sky chooses this moment to suddenly open up. A deluge of water drops, immediately soaking everything in sight.

"I guess this is why people had umbrellas," I shout.

Gray laughs before he grabs my hand and pulls me upright. We start running down the beach in the direction of the bed-and-breakfast. The sand we're kicking up sticks to my calves in wet globs. And the rain keeps falling in thousands of tiny drops that have the effect of an aimed hose. My dress can't absorb any more water. It starts slithering off the fabric in endless rivers, forming tiny valleys in the malleable sand.

The only structure in sight is one of the lifeguard huts they store equipment in. When we reach it, I sigh. The overhang is only enough to shield half my body, and there's a padlock on the door.

Gray fiddles with it, then lets out a grumble of annoyance. "Dammit. Different lock."

I arch an eyebrow. "You break into beach huts on a regular basis?"

He huffs a laugh as he presses his back against the locked door and turns his head, so the runoff from the roof only hits the front of his shorts and shirt. "I worked at that surf shop by Tremont Beach in high school. Those shacks all had faulty locks that would open if you jiggled them right. When we had parties, I would take, well…yeah."

I don't hide my smirk. "Didn't really think that story through, huh?"

Gray rolls his eyes while also managing to appear sheepish.

"It's fine. I know *you* weren't a virgin when we hooked up."

We stare at each other until I become self-conscious.

"We should probably just make a run for it. It doesn't look like this will let up anytime soon."

"Yeah, okay."

I lean down and wring out the hem of my dress. "Ready?"

"Hang on."

He moves out from the shelter of the overhang to press against me, so I'm caged between his wet clothes and the wooden exterior of the hut. Water pours between us like a waterfall until he leans forward and presses his wet lips against mine. His body shields mine from the downpour. He tastes like beer and rain— which I didn't know had a taste until right now.

After a few seconds, he pulls back. "Ready."

We start sprinting down the beach.

CHAPTER TEN

Streaks of pastel are creeping across the sky when I walk out of the sliding doors of Charleston General. I blink at the foreign sight of natural light like a baby bird that's just emerged from the blackout of an egg.

I'm tired. So tired that I'm no longer sleepy. It feels like I'm in a lucid dream, where colors are hazy and nothing feels quite real. I walk across the asphalt toward Sloane's black sedan. My parents are back from their trip, meaning I'm car-less again. I've been taking the bus most of the time, but Sloane insisted I drive her car today, claiming she didn't need it until this afternoon. I need to go see if the MINI I looked at is still available.

I wave goodbye to Rose, who's yawning as she walks toward her own car. I wonder if anyone has ever left a shift at the hospital, only to crash into traffic and return in an ambulance.

Witnessing death can make your thoughts take a turn toward the morbid, I guess.

I'm exhausted, both mentally and emotionally drained. But there's still something I want more than sleep.

I drive to Gray's apartment under the muted light of a new

day. This has become routine, though it won't be for much longer. I park in the garage, take the elevator to his floor, and let myself into the loft, using the key under the mat. My steps are silent as I tiptoe through the living room and past Emmett's bedroom door. The hinges swing without a single creak. I slip into the bedroom and slide off the scrubs I was too lazy to change out of. Gray stirs as I climb into his bed.

Sleepy green eyes meet mine. "Hi."

"Hi."

He reaches for me, letting out an appreciative hum when he realizes I'm already naked. "I wasn't sure if you were coming over. You never texted me back."

"I know. I got a page, and then a patient crashed, and it—" I blow out a breath. "It was just a long night."

"Did they—"

I shake my head. "No. They didn't make it."

"Do you want to talk about it?"

"No."

I lean over and kiss him, sliding one hand down his chest and stroking the length of his hardening cock. His groan vibrates on my tongue.

I've lost count of the number of times we've had sex. Every time feels different. This time, there's a fresh desperation. There are a lot of things I'm trying to forget right now. Being with Gray like this erases everything else from my mind—even when his upcoming departure is one of the weights.

I roll over and sit up so that I'm straddling him. His hands rest on my hips, gripping me tight enough to keep me in place.

"You're upset. We don't have to do—"

"What else would we do, Gray? We fuck, right? That's it."

His jaw tenses. I have the perfect view of the straight line.

"Evie."

"What?" Exhaustion sharpens my tone. "My name isn't an answer. This is just sex to you, right?"

He holds my gaze. I watch regret pass across the eyes that say more than his words, like a cloud covering the sun.

"Right," he finally confirms.

I nod; I expected that answer. I haven't let myself hope for more. He's leaving tomorrow. I just needed a reminder.

I grind against him. Arousal overwhelms annoyance as we both respond to the delicious friction. He slips inside of me, and I start to sink down.

After a few inches, Gray stills. "Condom."

Rather than move away, I hold his gaze. "I'm on birth control. Do you need a condom?"

Gray exhales a sound somewhere between a laugh and a scoff. "I don't know whether to be flattered or offended that you think I have the time or energy to be hooking up with other people." He doesn't appear flattered *or* offended though. He seems mad.

"Is that a no?"

He sighs. "It doesn't matter, Evie."

"It matters to me." I sink down another inch. My body wants to take him.

He hisses as his features tighten. Not with annoyance this time, but with pleasure. "I've never..."

"Does it feel good?" I barely recognize my own voice. This isn't just torture for him.

Gray groans, which is better than a yes. "I'm clean. I had a physical last week."

I don't move.

"Didn't that answer your question?" Challenge flits in his gaze.

He didn't answer what I was really asking, and we both know it. It almost seems like he wants me to push. To admit that him being with someone else would bother me. But other desires are overriding my curiosity. And what does it really matter anyway? Either it will fuel the false hope I've been desperately trying to extinguish or it will break my heart.

I drop my hips, so he's fully seated in me. We both groan. He's chanting my name as I rise and fall and press against him. Gray seems to get sick of the slow pace. He flips me so that I'm under him and slides back inside with a swift invasion I don't see coming. I cry out, and he kisses me, smothering the sound.

"Emmett's home."

"Warn me next time, then."

Gray smirks. Sex seems to have restored his good mood. "Nah."

He starts moving. I hook my ankles behind his back, opening up and allowing him deeper. He sets a brutal pace, pounding into me over and over again. I come quickly, and he follows, spilling a foreign warmth inside me. As soon as he pulls away, I feel the liquid start to slide down my thigh. I lean over to grab tissues from the bedside table and wipe it away. Gray watches me, something unreadable in his gaze.

He stands abruptly and walks over to his dresser, pulling out a pair of navy swim trunks.

I sit up on my elbows. "You're going *surfing*?"

"Yep. Did you want to have sex again first?" His good mood is gone as soon as it appeared. Annoyance rears its ugly head again.

"*Nope*." I climb out of bed and pick my scrubs up off the floor, so I can pull them on. "I've actually never wanted to have sex with you less than I do right now."

He hesitates. "I won't have time to surf before I leave tomorrow. This is my last chance for...months."

"That's not why you're leaving."

"Then, why am I leaving, Evie?"

Anger boils over. "You're running out of here because me asking if you were screwing anyone else freaked you out. Well, guess what. I care! I'd like to know if you're fucking other girls before I get into your bed. Don't act like that's ridiculous; don't forget how our first time ended. Another resident asked me to get coffee with him at the end of our shift. It wouldn't bother *you* if I screwed him in a Starbucks restroom and then came here?"

I don't miss the flare of anger in his eyes. The way his breathing turns deliberately deep for a few seconds.

He doesn't know what to say. I watch him fight back a few retorts. "I'm trying not to hurt you."

"Well, you're doing a shitty job of it. I'm a fly by for you. A temporary distraction, right?" I gather up the rest of my stuff. "If you want a final fuck, you know where to find me. Or call one of the other girls you might or might not be sleeping with." I stride toward the door.

"Where are you going?"

He's angry now too. Good. That will make this easier.

I stare him straight in the eye. "I don't know. Maybe I'll go to Starbucks."

Then, I open the door and slam it behind me.

I also slam the front door for good measure.

It sounds like déjà vu.

The buzzing of my phone wakes me up. I knock over everything on my bedside table in my quest to answer it without opening my eyes. "Hello?"

"Evie?"

I yawn. "Hi, Mom."

"Is something wrong?"

"No, I was just sleeping."

"I didn't think you were working last night."

"I wasn't supposed to. I traded shifts."

"Oh. I'm sorry, sweetie. I wouldn't have called otherwise."

"It's fine." I yawn again. "What's up?"

"I wanted to see if you were free for dinner. I already talked to Noah. We have gifts and photos to show you from our trip."

"Yeah. Sure. What time?"

"Six?"

"Okay. See you then."

"Bye, Evie."

I hang up, set an alarm for five thirty, and promptly fall back asleep.

When my alarm rings again, I don't want to get up. It takes me five minutes to talk my muscles into moving.

By the time I've gotten dressed and fixed my hair into something resembling a ponytail, I'm running late. I take an Uber instead of the bus, pulling up at my parents' house at six fifteen. I don't bother with ringing the doorbell, just walk into the kitchen.

My mom is standing at the stove, stirring a bubbling red sauce. My dad is chopping cucumbers at the kitchen island. Noah is sitting at the kitchen table, contributing nothing.

"Evie!" my mom greets, stepping away from the stove to give me a big hug.

"Hey, Mom," I say, squeezing her back before I'm passed to my dad and then to Noah. I'm the baby of the family, and I get treated like it most of the time.

Dinner turns out to be an authentic family recipe my mom sweet-talked a Michelin-starred chef into sharing with her. As we eat the pasta, maps and ticket stubs are passed around the table along with my mom's phone to show off the slideshow of photos. It looks like an amazing trip. I've never been to Europe before. Annoyingly, the first thought that crosses my mind is whether Gray has. I've never asked where his deployments have been. He's selective about sharing information…and I've also been living under the delusion that I'll have time to get the answers, not that my access to them ends tomorrow.

After dinner, Noah corners me in the living room. "I'm worried about you, Evie."

"What? Why?"

When I shared stories from work at dinner, he said he was impressed.

"I know you said you're fine about Logan, but it seems like you miss him. You work all the time, you never go out, and—"

"It has nothing to do with Logan, Noah. I just started a new job. With long hours and lots of stress. If I show up to work hungover and make a mistake, someone could die. I'm not going to apologize for taking that seriously."

"You shouldn't apologize. I'm so proud of you, Evie."

"Okay…so, what? We've established I work a lot. Why are you worried? You want me to go pick a guy up in a bar?" *Because I already did. Oh, and he happens to be your best friend.*

Noah cringes. "No. I just…do you have to work tomorrow?"

"No…" My answer is hesitant since I'm not sure where he's going with this.

"Perfect. I'm going out with the guys tonight. Come out with us."

"The guys?"

"Yeah. Emmett, Harrison, and Gray. Gray's leaving tomorrow."

I act like the reminder is news to me, not a stab to the gut. "Oh. I'm, uh, I'm not dressed to go out." I gesture to my jeans.

"We're not going to a club. Gray shot that idea down, surprisingly. Just some pub on Pleasant."

"I don't want to intrude—"

"You're not. I'm inviting you."

I have a feeling Gray might feel different, but I can't come up with an excuse Noah's pleading eyes will accept.

"Okay," I relent.

Ten minutes later, we're on our way. Noah talks about work the whole drive to the pub. And he says *I'm* too focused on my job. I *mmhmm* and *uh-huh* along, not really paying attention.

"Gray's leaving tomorrow." Noah stating that fact made it sink in more.

The fist around my heart is tightening. He's leaving, and it makes me want to cry and scream and panic. But I just nod instead.

The pub we walk into is cozy. I've never thought of that adjective to describe a drinking establishment before, but it fits this place. I don't feel the excitement of walking into a club or the exhaustion at making small talk until I can face-plant into bed. It feels comfortable. There's a group of older men seated at the bar, laughing and joking. A few middle-aged couples. And one booth containing two familiar guys and one green-eyed gaze that immediately erases any ease I'm experiencing.

Gray is good at hiding his emotions, but I'm getting better at seeking them out. There's a flicker of surprise that tells me Noah didn't mention me tagging along.

Will he think I'm infringing? Needy? I knew he'd *be here.*

"Hey, guys." Noah plops down in the booth, the picture of ease.

Of course he's relaxed. I would be too. Before. I know these guys. I grew up with them. Despite my crush on Gray, I was never affected by his presence the way I am now.

Consumed.

Engulfed.

The dynamic has changed, and we're the only two who are aware.

"Hey, Collins. Evie." Emmett greets us both with an easy smile. Expected.

So is Harrison's grin. "Not too cool to hang out with us, Evie?"

"Noah called me lame. Apparently, I work too much." I sit down and give my brother a pointed look. "Pot."

"Not to mention, you're saving lives while Noah is…what do you do again, Collins? Draw houses?" Emmett teases.

Noah flips his friend off.

My phone begins buzzing in my pocket. I pull it out to see Sloane is calling. "Hey," I answer.

"Hey. Sorry to call. I'm driving, so I thought it would be easier."

"No worries," I reply. "Is everything okay?"

"Yeah. I'm headed out, and I realized I forgot my house key. You'll be home in the morning to let me in, right?"

"Yeah. I'm off tomorrow."

"Okay, perfect. Bye!"

"Bye," I echo, then end the call and set my phone on the table.

"Sloane?" Noah asks.

"Yeah. She forgot her house key."

"Do you need me to take you home to meet her?"

"No." Leaving is tempting, but so is staying. "She won't be back until the morning."

My phone lights up again. I move to grab it, but Emmett picks it up first.

"Whoa, sick photo."

He's talking about my lock screen. It's one I took of the beach in Beaufort. I watch Gray look at the screen. His face doesn't change.

"By the way, a *Logan* texted you," Emmett says with a smirk, sliding my phone back to me.

Noah looks at me, surprised. "You're texting with Logan?"

"*He* messages me sometimes." I make sure to emphasize the *he*—and not for Noah's benefit. Not that I have anything to feel guilty about. Not that Gray will care. This news might be a relief to him. No one looking for a messy relationship here. Nope. Nada. Not interested.

"Logan is the doctor ex?" Emmett questions.

"Yeah." I'm so, *so* tempted to look at Gray right now, but I don't.

"Texting you on a Friday night instead of out getting laid? Guy wants you back. Bad."

"He's probably at work."

Emmett snorts. "He sounds perfect for you."

"He wasn't. We didn't work. It was a mutual decision."

"So, you both just sat up in bed one day and were like, *This is it. We're done?*"

I wait for Noah to jump in, but he doesn't. Honestly, I didn't tell my parents and Noah much about my breakup with Logan. I could tell they were surprised—and disappointed. I'd barely dated before him, and they all loved him.

"No." That would have required us ever sharing a bed. But I don't say that. "I guess it was more amicable than mutual."

"Can you move, Ledger? I've gotta take a piss."

Harrison rolls his eyes but stands to let Gray out of the booth.

"Hey. Move." Noah nudges me. "I need a drink."

I roll my eyes but oblige.

"What do you want?" he asks me.

"A beer, I guess?"

Noah nods, then walks toward the bar.

"Think he'll notice if I leave?" I sit down and scooch toward the middle of the booth.

Emmett chuckles. "He's just worried about you."

I sigh. "I know. Anything new with you two?"

"Eh, not much," Emmett replies. "I'll miss having Phillips around."

Me too.

I shift my gaze to Harrison.

"Just came from a date," he says.

"Really?! How was it?"

He shrugs. "Fine."

Whoever this girl is, I hope she didn't enjoy the date. It doesn't sound like there will be a second.

Emmett comes to the same conclusion. "Ouch, man. Do you need dating advice?"

Harrison looks like he's majorly regretting bringing this up. "No. It was a casual thing."

"What was a casual thing?"

I startle at the sound of Gray's voice. Stiffen when he decides to slide into my side of the booth, not back next to Harrison.

"Ledger's *date*," Emmett answers.

"Ah." That's all he says.

"No words of wisdom, Phillips?"

"I don't know shit about relationships."

"I think Ledger was more looking to get laid. Although based on the way doors were slamming this morning, you could use some help in that department too."

Where the hell is Noah? I could *really* use a drink right now.

"The door slamming was because she wanted more."

It's a struggle to keep my mouth from gaping open.

"Here you go." Noah sets a bottle of beer in front of me, then takes Gray's former seat beside Harrison. "What'd I miss?"

"Ledger had a bad date and can't get laid," Emmett summarizes, leaning back with a lazy grin as Harrison flips him off.

"I said *none of that*." He glances to me, seemingly for confirmation.

"I have no interest in getting involved," I reply. "Unless you want a female perspective."

"Yes!" Emmett crows. "This is perfect. Try to pick Evie up, and then she can give you pointers."

"Um, no," Harrison replies. "No offense, Evie, but it's too weird. You're like a sister to me."

I startle. Not from the words, which are a relief, but from the hand that's settled on my leg. The heat of Gray's skin sinks through the denim of my jeans. I wish I'd worn a dress. Even more when his hand drifts higher. He teases the seam of my jeans, running a finger up my inner thigh. I take a few hasty gulps of my beer, trying to cool the fire suddenly simmering in my veins. Then, his hand slides back down, stopping on my knee. He grips it like he's adrift in the ocean and it's the one thing that can save him.

And I don't really hear another word of what's said until Noah and I leave an hour later.

My phone buzzes with a call as soon as I walk through the door.

Gray doesn't bother with a hello. "You home?"

"Yes."

"Two minutes."

He was too eager to text. He called. The thought makes me smile—until another one snuffs it out like a candle.

This will be the last time we do this.

I fill a glass with water and lean against the fridge as I sip it. Anticipation simmers in my veins as I wait for the knock on the door.

When I open it, I'm sort of expecting him to attack me. For all his eagerness on the phone, he takes his time walking inside. Doesn't even touch me.

Once we reach the kitchen, he turns to me with a sigh. "Evie, about this morning—"

I press a finger against his lips, silencing him. "I don't want to talk about it. It was stupid. I shouldn't have...you're leaving tomorrow. This is what it is."

"Yeah," he agrees quietly. "It is."

I can feel my heart fissuring, tiny cracks forming that feel audible in the quiet room.

But I paste a smile on my face. "Sorry for crashing your boys' night earlier. Noah didn't really give me much of a choice."

"It's fine. It was nice, actually, having you there."

"Oh. Good."

"Worth it to see Ledger squirm about picking you up."

I seize the opportunity to lighten the mood. "Why? You think you could do better?" I cock my head in a clear challenge.

Gray smirks, slow and delicious. "Could? I *did*."

"*Do you want to get out of here?*" I quote. "*That's* your big pick up line?"

He rolls his eyes, then nods toward one of the kitchen stools. "Take a seat."

I listen and look at him expectantly. He sidles around the edge of the island and takes a seat on the stool next to me with a serious expression that makes me want to laugh.

"This seat taken?"

I make a show of looking him up and down. "Now, it is."

"So, aside from being sexy, what do you do for a living?"

I snort before I lean forward. "What's your name?" I lower my voice. "So I know what to scream later."

He's shocked. Of the two of us, he's always been the dirty talker. "Fuck, Evie."

"I didn't tell you my name," I tease, staying in character.

Gray smiles. "Lucky guess. If you're feeling down, I'd love to feel you up."

I laugh. "You'd better do more than that."

He stands and steps closer. I wind my legs around him as he jerks my shirt up and over my head.

"I changed my mind. I don't want to pretend like this is our first time. I like that I know when I do this"—he lowers his mouth and sucks on the curve where my neck meets my shoulder, and I moan—"you moan. And that when I take these off"—he tugs at my jeans—"you'll be dripping for me. Right, baby?"

"Right," I gasp.

And then he's kissing me, and neither of us is doing any talking at all. Joking or serious. Sweet or dirty. Familiar or foreign.

We stumble into my room and onto my bed. His eyes heat when I pull his shirt off, but his smile is still playful. He rains kisses over my temple and jaw. Even once he finds my lips, they're light pecks. I squirm, and he laughs before our mouths fuse together.

Gray continues teasing me with his tongue. Then, slowly, the mood shifts. It turns serious. Hands linger and kisses deepen.

His right hand slides up my left calf and hooks my knee. "You

174

have a big smile. It takes over your whole face, and it's impossible to look at anything else." He pulls my legs apart before moving over me. His hand keeps moving upward, cupping my butt. "You have an amazing ass." He flicks my bra open. "You're the hardest worker I know."

I swallow a couple of times. Otherwise, I'm worried I might start crying. Compliments don't have to be sweeping declarations. They can be simple and matter-of-fact. And coming from Gray, who doesn't compliment anyone about anything, it means a lot.

He keeps talking and touching me, and there's a voice telling me that this won't end well. That I might have *thought* I fell in love with Gray a long time ago—that was child's play compared to this. That I fell when I kissed him. When he kissed me back. That every moment we've spent together, I've sunk deeper. That moving on before—as pitiful an attempt as it apparently was, since it didn't exactly take me long to warm back up to the idea— might have been easy in comparison to this.

After we both come, he's the one who tugs me to his chest.

We lie like that. He traces circles on my skin. I listen to his heartbeat.

And I know it with complete certainty.

I love you, Gray.

I just don't know what to do about it.

I'm already awake when he starts to move. I keep my eyes closed because I know what I'll have to face when I open them. Gray climbs out of bed. I hear the rustle of fabric as he starts pulling on his clothes. I never knew how final getting dressed could sound.

You can do this, Evie.

I scrunch my eyes as tightly as I can in protest, then open them. I sit up slowly.

Gray finishes pulling his T-shirt on before he glances over. "Morning."

"Morning." My voice comes out scratchy, so I clear my throat. Once. Twice. Three times. The ball of emotion doesn't go anywhere.

He walks over and takes a seat on the edge of the mattress. "I've got to go."

"Yeah. I know."

"Evie…"

"Be careful. Don't do anything stupid. Okay?"

"I'm good at my job, Evie."

"Modest too."

A smirk flashes across his face.

"Promise me you'll be careful, Gray."

"I promise."

I lean forward and wrap my arms around him, inhaling his scent and soaking in his presence for the few more seconds I have it.

He kisses the top of my head. "You're not a fly by, Evie."

Then, he pulls back and walks away. In seconds, he's gone from my life without a backward glance.

When I finally climb out of bed, there's a set of Jeep keys on the kitchen counter with a note that says, *You'd better use these.*

CHAPTER ELEVEN

Two weeks go by. Some days drag, other pass fast. I work. I go to the beach with Sloane. I go to my parents' house for a Fourth of July barbeque. I have brunch with Noah. I even get a drink with Miranda Hendrix after she texts me an invitation to.

None of it distracts me from the Gray-shaped hole in my life.

It's a Tuesday. I'm sprawled out on the couch, surrounded by an array of food meant to ensure I won't need to get up for a few hours. Sloane is at work, so I revel in my messy tendencies. I'm binging some high school television drama and crunching corn chips when my phone rings. *Unknown Caller* flashes across the screen.

It's likely spam, but I answer anyway. "Hello?"

"Evie?"

I sit straight up, pillows falling and chips flying. For a second, I can't speak. Then questions rush out in a torrent. "Gray? Oh my God, is everything okay? Are you hurt? Did something—"

"I'm fine." There's a smile in his voice. He's pleased by my panic—that I was worried about him. He clears his throat. "I didn't mean to freak you out. I just had some time. So, I thought I'd call."

"Oh." That's all I say. All I *can* say. My mind is spinning too fast to formulate sentences. Words. I need words.

Seconds pass before he says my name again. It's another question. This time, there's an uncomfortable edge. Of uncertainty. Maybe even some nerves. Nothing like the assurance I expect from him.

"Yeah, I'm here. Sorry. I'm just…shocked, I guess. I didn't think you would call. I didn't even know if you could."

"I wanted to hear your voice."

I tuck away the sound of those six words in *his* voice. To the special spot where I store moments I know I never want to forget. "You're okay, right?"

"Yeah. Just…tell me about your day."

"I woke up two hours ago and have been watching teen televisions dramas while eating junk for the past hour and fifty-five minutes, give or take."

He chuckles, and my chest warms like I downed a cup of cocoa. "What did you do yesterday, then?

I lie back down on the couch and tell him everything I can think of. Starting with the line out the door of Charleston Coffee Traders first thing in the morning. Then about how Rose was running so late that she did rounds in scrubs pulled over penguin-patterned pajamas. About the baby with a murmur, whose life I helped save. The questionable turkey sandwich I had for lunch. I talk and talk and talk. More than I ever have, possibly. I pause a few times, self-conscious. But then he asks what happened next or laughs, and I keep talking.

I don't stop until I hear commotion on his end that grows louder instead of quieter.

We're both silent for a minute.

FLY BYE

"Thank you for the car," I blurt. "Not that you're, like, giving it to me. I don't mean that. But thank you for letting me use it. It was really...sweet of you." I'm not sure I could sound any less eloquent. Like lots of things, a simple *thank you* is more complicated with him than it would be with anyone else. I don't want him to think I'm reading into the gesture. I'm also wondering if I *should.*

Rather than provide any insight, he asks, "Have you had any problems with it?"

"None. The thing runs great. And I haven't gotten into any accidents, so don't worry about the paint job."

He's silent for a beat. "If you were in an accident, I wouldn't give a fuck about the paint job, Evie. Just *you.*"

I'm glad he can't see my face because I'm certain it's showing everything I never told him.

"I've gotta go." There's regret in his voice, and it makes my heart race.

Hope. That's what this giddy emotion is called, I think.

Whatever it is, it makes me bold. "Are you going to call again?"

"Do you want me to?"

"Yes." That's my answer when it comes to him. Do I need him? Will he break my heart? Am I stupid for enabling this? All yeses.

"Okay. Bye, Evie."

"Bye, Gray."

I let my phone drop and then stare up at my ceiling with a stupid smile on my face.

A week later, he calls again. I'm in his Jeep, on my way to work. When I admit that, I can hear the smile in his voice. For the whole drive to work, we talk about nothing meaningful. I don't ask what these calls mean, and he doesn't offer up any explanation.

Despite that, I'm in a good mood all morning. Rose regales me with a dramatic retelling of her date last night over Caesar salad. When she's finished making fun of the way he ordered wine in a French accent, she shifts her attention to me.

"What about you?"

"What about me?" I ask, playing dumb.

Rose's expression tells me she doesn't buy it. "Are things with Gray…"

"Over," I reply. "He left."

"Have you heard from him at all?"

"Yeah. He's called a couple of times."

"That's good, right?"

"I guess."

"Why don't you sound sure?"

"I just…I don't think anything has changed. He said from the start that this wasn't anything serious, that he's not looking for a relationship. And I agreed. Dragging things out now that he's gone, well, it'll just hurt even more in the end."

"Did you tell him that?"

I play with a crouton. "No. *I* want him to call. I want to know he's okay, and I want to hear his voice. That's the problem."

"Yeah. That would be tricky." Rose plays with her fork. "You know Ben has a thing for you, right?"

"He's friendly with everyone."

"True. But he's friendliest with you. He's never invited me to Starbucks."

"You're always talking about guys you're seeing."

The fork gets pointed right at me. "*You* get hearts in your eyes every time Gray gets mentioned. Yet Ben still asked me if I knew whether you were single."

"He did?"

"Uh-huh." Rose studies me closely, obviously attempting to determine my reaction to that news.

"What did you tell him?"

"That I wasn't sure. I don't stick my nose in other people's love lives unless they ask me to."

"Hmm."

I take a bite of salad, testing out the idea of me and Ben in my head. I'm not sure I can picture it—kissing him. More than kissing him. Then again, I can't seem to picture doing either of those things with anyone who's not Gray. So much for using him as a transition to one-night stands with strangers—or whatever the hell I told myself when we first started hooking up.

"So…what are you going to tell him?"

I laugh. "Where's your nose right now?"

Rose rolls her eyes. "I'm not telling you what to do. Just curious what you're thinking."

I play with a piece of lettuce. "I don't know what I'd say. I should give it a try. He's a great guy."

"But…" she prompts knowingly.

"But I'll probably tell him I'm still hung up on someone else. Because…I am."

"Yeah, that's what I thought you'd say." Rose's pager goes off, vibrating against the table. She groans. "Crap. I gotta take this one. See you later?"

I nod. "Yeah."

Once Rose disappears, I stand and toss the remains of my salad in the trash. It's late for lunch, nearing two, so the cafeteria is mostly empty. I only have to wait in line for a couple of minutes before buying an iced tea to wash away the aftertaste of anchovies. It was slim pickings by the time I had a chance to take my lunch break.

Rather than sit down at one of the tables that makes me feel like I'm in a high school lunchroom, I head outside. There's an attached courtyard with winding paths and neat landscaping. I take a seat on one of the curved metal benches flanking the fountain in the center, watching some of the more mobile patients visit with their families.

It's a warm, sunny day. A perfect day, really. The sky is a bright, vibrant blue, the hue only interrupted by the occasional fluffy white cloud. The sun beams down in bright rays, dappling the leaves of the trees and the blooms of the flowers. I focus on the fountain, watching the soothing trickles of clear water spill over the edge and then disappear, only to be recycled.

The rumble of a distant engine draws my gaze back up to the sky. A plane flies by, its speed and size deceptively slow and small against the vast backdrop.

Gray's parting words echo in my mind. *"You're not a fly by, Evie."*

I haven't asked him what that means. It implies we aren't temporary, but he said them right before walking out the door, with no other assurances or declarations. Technically, we're both single. We never made any commitments. He could be involved with other people. I could go on a date with Ben.

Would he care?

Should I ask?

"Beautiful day, isn't it?"

I glance to my left to see Henry Phillips approaching. He sits down on the bench beside me. "Picture-perfect," I agree.

"How have you been doing, Evie?" he asks me kindly.

"All right," I respond. "Busy."

"So I've heard. You've made quite the first impression here." He gives me a proud smile. "Not that I expected anything less."

I smile back. "Thank you."

"Made it to the beach much?"

"Twice. You?"

Henry dons a sheepish expression. "Not once. Easy to say, *I'll just go tomorrow*. Hasn't happened yet."

We sit in companionable silence for a few minutes.

"How is Noah doing?"

"Good. He loves it at his new firm. And he's talked about a coworker named Megan a few times, so he might have managed to find a woman who can put up with his annoying tendencies."

He chuckles. "Good. And how about you? Anyone special?"

Opened myself *right* up for that one. "Um, no. There was a guy in Boston, but that ended when I moved back. I'm just focusing on work for right now."

"I was the same way—until I met Juliet."

Another plane passes overhead.

I look up at it. "Good flying conditions today."

Henry follows my gaze. "Yes, they are." A pause follows. "Gray left a couple of weeks ago."

"Yeah, I know. Uh, Noah mentioned it."

He nods, eyes still on the few fluffy clouds drifting by, covering the white trail left by the engines.

"Have you—have you talked to him?"

"No." Henry shakes his head. "No. I—to be honest, I wouldn't even know how to go about it. He barely answers the phone when he's on leave. I have no idea how to reach him while he's deployed."

Honestly, I don't either. He always calls me.

When I look at Henry's expression—holding a hint of stoicism and a lot of sadness—there is a long list of things I'd like to say. Condemnation, for letting his relationship with Gray deteriorate to the point it has. Admiration of who Gray is. I want to tell his dad everything—how he feels about storms and how he lost Sam and what it's like to be up in a plane with him.

"Maybe you should try to find out," I suggest softly.

It takes a minute for him to reply. "Maybe." He stands, straightening his white coat. "Have a good rest of your day, Evie."

"Yeah, you too," I reply.

Henry disappears, and I raise my gaze back to the sky.

CHAPTER TWELVE

When I walk outside at the end of my shift a week and a half later, a familiar figure is leaning against one of the planters that lines the entrance to the hospital. I freeze, take a step, and then freeze again. It's been a typical Friday. I'm not expecting anything out of the ordinary.

Gray watches my stilted approach. A slow smile unfurls on his face, and if I was managing to play it cool at all, I abandon it entirely. I don't let myself think; I react, flinging my body at his. He's either expecting it or he has really good reflexes because he doesn't even stumble as we collide.

I tighten my arms and legs around him, breathing deeply. He smells like soap and leather and something uniquely Gray I couldn't put a name to. He feels solid and firm and alive.

Something brushes my hair as I cling to him. His hand, or maybe his lips.

We stand still for a minute. Me clutching him and Gray tolerating it. He's holding me loosely, but I'm the one pressing us together. Finally, I relax my grip enough that I can tilt my head back and look up at his face. His expression is smooth, but emotions are dancing in his eyes.

I do the most embarrassing thing possible. I burst into tears.

That takes care of the indifference he was sporting.

Gray's face turns wary, then concerned. "Bad surprise?"

Pull it together, I scold myself. I'm normally skilled at harnessing my emotions, both at work and outside of it. I didn't even cry at the end of *The Notebook.*

Apparently, I overestimated my ability to school my emotions in certain situations. I underestimated how much I care about Gray, which was not a low bar to begin with. Time and distance haven't changed its height. I didn't realize just how heavy and tightly knotted the ball of worry in my stomach was until it lightened and slackened.

"No. It's a great surprise. I'm sorry. Long day."

Gray's face says he knows my waterworks have more to do with him than my job, but he doesn't press the topic.

"What are you *doing here*? Did something happen?" Visions of engines on fire and twisted metal flash through my mind. *He's here. He's fine*, I tell myself.

"Nothing happened. Everything is fine. One of the guys in my unit had to fly back for a family emergency. I volunteered to copilot. It's a long trip to make by yourself, and I passed all my duties off to a first lieutenant."

"How long are you back for?"

"I've got to be back on base by noon tomorrow."

Less than twenty-four hours. "Short trip."

"Yeah."

But he made it. He *volunteered* for it even. What does that mean? Was it out of friendship and loyalty to whoever had the emergency? Or is he here for me?

"Uh, today is Noah's birthday…"

Gray's eyes briefly close. "Dammit."

"Sloane has spent the past week decorating our backyard. There's a patio…and stuff. She wants to show it off, so she had me invite Noah, Harrison, and Emmett over. They're supposed to be there"—I check my phone—"really soon. And then we're going to Malone's."

He gives me a wry smile. "I didn't check the date. Not exactly how I pictured this evening going."

"We can…after. You know, if you want to. I'm not assuming anything. I just—" *Smooth as molasses, Evie.*

He bends down and kisses me. It's not a peck. There's heat and tongue and urgency. And a promise of more when we're not in public and fully clothed.

"I didn't fly five thousand miles *not* to fuck you, Evie. I want to."

Five thousand *miles?* "Okay." I think my giddy smile counteracts the nonchalance of that single word.

Gray smirks. "So…are you going to invite me to your party?"

"Do you want to come?"

"Beats sitting around, waiting for you to come over."

"Okay, well, you know where I live, right?"

The smirk deepens, both dimples punctuating his cheeks. "Right."

"Okay, well I—*oh!*" I realize. "I, uh, have your car."

"I know."

The more frazzled I become, the more relaxed Gray appears.

"I'll catch a car back to my place and then get a ride with Emmett to yours."

"Are you sure? It's *your* car, and I can—"

"I'm sure." He bends down and gives me a quick kiss. "I'll see you soon."

A wide, silly smile stretches across my face. It lingers the whole drive back to my house and is still firmly in place when I walk in the front door. Sloane is flitting around, straightening magazines and arranging flowers. She cut back on her hours at the law firm and is now working part-time at an interior decorating company as well. It shows in our house, and I'm definitely not complaining.

"Hey!" I greet.

Sloane studies me. "Are you drunk?"

"What? No. I just left work."

"You're never this cheery when you get home from work."

"Well, I'm excited about the party," I lie.

She buys that excuse. It's not a total fib, just a small stretch of the truth. I'm *especially* excited now that I know we'll have an unexpected guest.

"They'll be here soon. Better go get changed."

I hang my bag up on one of the empty hooks by the door. "Okay. You need help with anything first?"

"Nope. Everything's ready."

"Okay."

I shower, then head into my bedroom to get ready. I take longer with my appearance than usual, sorting through several outfits, applying more than just mascara, and taking extra care in selecting my underwear.

The whole process takes a while. I realize how long when I leave my room, walk out onto the patio, and discover that Noah, Emmett, Harrison, and *Gray* have all arrived.

I hug Noah, wish him a happy birthday and then greet the rest of the guys. My voice comes out higher than usual when I express surprise at Gray's appearance, but no one seems to notice.

I can't stop stealing looks at Gray. He was wearing his uniform when he showed up at the hospital, but he's showered and changed since. I greedily absorb every detail I can, knowing what a limited time I'll have to stare before he's gone again. He's so handsome; it hurts. I don't know how to act around him. What we are. It doesn't help that we're surrounded by friends who know us only as separate people. Who *don't know* how well we know each other.

When the bowl of hummus empties, I stand and offer to refill it, mostly under the guise of getting my libido under control. It's not even that warm out tonight, yet I can feel my skin radiating with heat. I can't look at him without imagining all the things I'd like to be doing right now instead of making small talk in front of my brother.

The barista at Charleston Coffee Traders flirted with me this morning, and I barely batted an eye. He was cute. But attraction is one thing, chemistry is another. Gray and I have buckets of both, and it feels combustible.

I'm rooting through the fridge for the container of hummus when I hear the door open again, and footsteps near.

Was I hoping he'd follow me inside? Yes.

I don't turn to confirm it's him, but no one else would approach me silently. Big, masculine hands settle on my hips. I sway, resisting the urge to melt back against him. The pink wrap dress I settled on shifts as his hands move to my waist. Pulsing tingles of heat shoot through me. Goose bumps pebble on my skin, both from his light touch and the cold air emanating from the fridge. I should probably shut the door, but I can't seem to move.

"You took a long time to get ready." His warm breath skates across my skin.

"I had trouble deciding what to wear," I admit.

"I like the dress."

I don't know if it's part of his compliment game, but I no

longer need a shovel or an exploding agent to unearth one—it appears.

"I meant, underneath."

He chuckles, but it comes out more pained than amused. "*Fuck*, Evie."

I want to ask if it's been as long for him as it's been for me, but that's not really a conversation I want to get into with our friends and my brother right outside.

"You didn't call this week," I whisper instead.

"I know. I was trying…not to make this harder."

I turn to face him, finally shutting the fridge. "What does that mean?"

"You know what."

I shake my head. "You—"

The door to the backyard opens, and Sloane steps inside. "Evie?"

There's something off in her tone, something hesitant.

I tear my gaze from Gray's and glance at her. "Yeah?"

"Uh, Logan is here to see you."

"What?" I blink at her blankly, like I've never heard the name before.

Sloane is still talking, mumbling something about a medical conference and knowing an address, but I'm no longer listening. I leave the hummus on the counter and head outside. Sure enough, Logan Fitzgerald is standing in my backyard, shooting the shit with my brother. His blond hair has grown from the crew cut length he kept it at throughout our relationship. Aside from that, he looks the exact same as he did at our med school graduation— the last time I saw him. The last time I thought I'd *ever* see him.

"Logan." I approach them. "Um, wow. Hi."

"Hey, Evie." He gives me a warm smile and a hug. "It's so good to see you."

"You too," I reply automatically. "Uh, what are you doing here?"

His expression grows sheepish and a little uncertain. I mentally kick myself.

"I mean, I just wasn't expecting you. Here."

"I know." He scratches the back of his neck. "I was in the neighborhood, actually. Professor Benson—you remember her?"

I nod.

"Well, we worked on the proposal for that research grant together. We got a meeting with a medical device company that's headquartered in Charlotte. Founder lives here though. Since I was here, I thought…" His voice trails off. "I should have texted or called, I know. But there's some stuff I'd like to talk to you about in person, and I had your address. I heard the commotion in the back and came around here. I shouldn't have intruded. I'll just head out. If you have time tomorrow, you can give me a call."

"You're not intruding. Evie has been wanting to talk to you too." Sloane doesn't hesitate to throw me under the bus—and *this* is why you should never lie to your best friend. All my words about needing time and not being ready to move on taunt me.

Noah jumps right on the *rekindle the relationship* train with her. "Yeah. It's great that you're here, man. We were about to head downtown anyhow. You guys can stay and talk."

I love how no one—besides Logan—seems to have taken into account how *I* feel about this. But it's a conversation we need to have. "Okay."

"Gray! Ready to go?"

I don't turn around to see how Gray is reacting to my ex's appearance. Knowing him, he'll look indifferent.

"Ready."

I still don't look, but I feel his presence near.

"Hey. I'm Logan. Nice to meet you." Logan introduces himself to the only person in the backyard he hasn't met.

I hold my breath.

Gray gives him a long stare before shaking the offered hand. Tension thickens the air like a rubber band pulling taut. "Gray."

Logan looks at me. I don't need to be a mind reader to know what he's thinking. I mentioned Gray's name once. *Years* ago. He hasn't forgotten, though.

"Nice to meet you."

"Let's talk inside, huh?" I suggest, heading for the door.

"Sure," Logan agrees. He smiles at Noah. "Happy birthday, man. Sorry again to interrupt the party."

"No worries." Noah smiles back.

I give Noah a quick hug. "Sorry about this," I whisper.

"Don't apologize, Leigh-Leigh. I'm happy for you."

Tears threaten to burn my eyes. I don't want to have this conversation. There's only one thing Logan could possibly want to talk about, and I won't be able to give him the answer he wants. I'll have to break his heart again. And while I do, precious minutes I could be spending with Gray before he's five thousand miles away again will slip through my fingers.

I pull away and force a smile. "Have fun tonight."

Logan follows me inside, into the kitchen and down the hall to the living room. "Warmer here than I was expecting," he comments as the air conditioner hums in the background.

"That's the South for you," I say as I take a seat on the couch.

"Yeah, I guess." He settles down beside me.

"So…"

Logan rests his elbows on his thighs and looks at the floor. "This is…well, I…" He shakes his head and chuckles. "Damn, this is harder than I thought it would be."

"It's just me, Logan."

192

He looks up. "I miss you, Evie. Everything you said when we broke up made sense. I wanted to stay in Boston, and you wanted to move back here. We both knew our schedules would be crazy. But… I miss you so damn much. I work insane hours, but when I'm not working—hell, even when I am—all I think about is you." He smiles. "I know nothing has changed with work. But… I guess…I'm asking if you want to figure it out."

"I… I thought you were dating someone else." It feels cruel to shoot him down immediately, but I can't put it off. It's everything I was worried about.

"It didn't work out. I want to be with someone who understands what it's like to have a demanding career, not someone who resents it. People think they want to date a doctor until they actually do, you know?"

I don't. Because the only guy I've done anything with that even came close to resembling dating was Gray, and he never once made me feel like I needed to put my career second. If he texted and I was busy with work, he'd just suggest a new time to meet up. Was that because it was just sex? He asked about my job, acted interested when I told him about my patients.

And the fact that all I'm doing is thinking about Gray says a lot as well.

"I haven't done much dating," I reply.

Logan smiles, and I belatedly realize that sounded more encouraging than I meant for it to.

"I know this is a lot and out of nowhere, and it's your brother's birthday. Think about it, okay? I've looked into some programs down here, but I haven't applied or let Mass General know. I will though, if I should. And we can take things slow."

Sex. He's talking about sex. About the fact that in ten months, we never made it past third base. Because I hesitated and was embarrassed and it became routine not to talk about it—let alone have it. A problem I never had with Gray.

When I saw Gray, my heart flew. When I saw Logan, it sank. My answer isn't uncertain.

"I don't need to think about it, Logan. I'm sorry. I admire you, and I respect you...but I'm not in love with you."

He sighs but doesn't seem surprised. "I had a feeling—when I saw him here."

"It's not just that. I'm just..." I give up. "I think we're best off as friends."

"Okay."

"I'm sorry. I wish—"

"Don't apologize. I needed to say this in person, and now I can move on for real."

He leans over and kisses my cheek.

No tingles. No butterflies.

"Goodbye, Evie."

"Bye, Logan."

I stay seated on the couch, even after I hear his steps recede and the door click shut. We broke up months ago, but this felt like finality. I doubt I'll receive any more gifts and probably fewer texts.

I should go to Malone's. Noah and Sloane will be wondering what happened with Logan. But I don't feel like answering any questions. I don't want to watch women hit on Gray and pretend I'm not staring at him.

Fifteen minutes later, I park in the garage of his loft. Déjà vu hits as I take the elevator and walk down the sweet-smelling hall. I haven't been here since he left. Muscle memory kicks in as I unlock the door and weave through the mess in the living room to get to Gray's bedroom. I open the door and stall in place.

He's here. On his bed, fully clothed and staring at the ceiling.

My heart pounds so loudly that I'm amazed everyone within a mile can't hear it. With anticipation and anxiety. I close the door behind me. When I turn back toward the bed, his eyes are on me.

He says nothing. Neither do I. I kick off my shoes and peel the pink dress over my head. Leaving me in a matching set of blue lingerie.

He doesn't move. I do. I approach the bed and climb on it beside him. I align my body with his and settle my head on his chest, just below his chin. We lie still for a few minutes before his hand moves. Fingers weave through my hair, pulling my head back. Moonlight streams through the window, casting shadows across his face.

"What are you doing here?"

"You're here."

"Did you talk to Logan?"

"Yes."

"Are you moving back to Boston?"

"He offered to move here."

"Wow. He must be confident you'll put out this time."

I exhale. "Don't do that, Gray."

"Don't do what?" he challenges.

"Do you want me here?" I ask.

"I want to know why you're here."

"You know why I'm here. But *you*? You told me that this— that I—didn't mean anything and then you left. I don't know *anything*, Gray."

I stare, and he stares back. I let it all bleed across my face. All the hope and the worry and the relief and the giddiness.

"Why did you come back, Gray?"

Gray sighs. "Because I can't do this when I'm five thousand miles away."

He kisses me, and I'm swept up in sensation. I didn't forget

195

what it felt like to be kissed by him, but I forgot what it was like to experience it firsthand. To not recall a single fear or thought or dream and simply sink into a cloud of bliss.

We kiss and kiss. Until I'm out of breath and my lips feel swollen. I expect him to escalate things. When he doesn't, I do. But he keeps his hands on my waist, up until I move my own downward. He snags my wrist before I make it halfway down his chest.

"I don't—this isn't—I just…" He groans and closes his eyes for a second. "You deserve better than this, Evie."

"Better than what?"

"Me."

"I want *you*."

I reach for his jeans. This time, he doesn't stop me. I unzip the denim and pull his cock out of his boxers, gripping the length in teasing strokes. He thrusts in my hand.

"Someone's eager."

"It's been a while."

"Has it?" I keep my tone detached even though I'm anything but. A while as in days? Weeks? The length of time we've been separated?

Rather than answer, Gray finally decides to become a willing participant. He flicks a strap off my shoulder so that the lace of the bra droops. His gaze turns hungry—predatory—as he studies my chest. But there's also something tender and familiar and dangerous. He's looking at me like he cares. Like this means something.

His right hand dips downward, pulling my underwear to the side, not even bothering to pull it off. He lines the head of his cock up with my entrance, then pauses. "Do I need…"

And…we're back to the *dancing around if we've been with other people* game.

FLY BYE

"You tell me."

"I haven't been with anyone else, Evie."

I do an atrocious job of keeping the shock off my face. I convinced myself he would have. Conditioned myself to nod and smile in response to the admission. "Since you left?"

"Since we first hooked up."

I suspected, but the confirmation still comes as a surprise. "Why?"

He doesn't answer. He teases my entrance with his hard length, and I can no longer think straight. "You didn't answer my question."

"You think *I've* been with anyone else?"

"It's fine. If you have."

The words say one thing. His face says another. Still, the two sentences royally piss me off.

"Oh, it's *fine*, is it?"

His face tenses. We hold a silent stare-off, desire and stubbornness mixing in the air. He starts to move away, but I grab the front of his shirt, holding him in place. He could break out of my grip easily, but he doesn't.

"Do I need to put on a condom, Evie?"

"No," I mutter.

He slams into me in one powerful thrust. I have to bite on my bottom lip—hard—to keep from crying out. It's better than I remember—the full sensation and the rush of arousal. From the way Gray growls, it feels pretty damn good for him too. He's still fully dressed. I have to yank the cotton of his T-shirt up, so I can touch the powerful slab of muscle that forms his back.

Gray sets a brutal pace. He's been rough before, but I've never felt like he was *fucking* me. Not this primal, desperate pounding. He's mad. At me. Maybe himself too.

I'm annoyed with him, but it doesn't slow the build of pres-

197

sure as he fills me again and again. The explosive pleasure of my orgasm takes me off guard. Gray groans as I start spasming around him, pressing his palms on either side of my open thighs as he ruts into me twice more. The foreign, warm sensation of his release catches me off guard.

He pulls out and yanks a few tissues out of the box beside his bed, handing them to me. "Here."

"Thanks."

Gray doesn't move. Doesn't react as I wipe myself and lie back down beside him. I'm the one who breaches the distance between us. His hand fists my hair. For a moment, I think we'll start all over again. But his grip relaxes. He runs his fingers through the strands rather than just holding them.

I close my eyes and melt against him. Muscle by muscle, the tension seeps away. I feel his chest rise and fall. I listen to the rhythmic pound of his heart. I memorize the temperature and texture of the firm skin I'm resting on.

When he speaks, I'm half-asleep. "I lied earlier."

"What?" I try to sort through everything that's happened today, try to find a fib, but my brain trails off mid-process, too exhausted by the prospect.

"When I said it would be fine if you—when I acted like I wouldn't care if you'd been with another guy. I would care. Can't think of anything that would piss me off more, actually."

That permeates the fog in my brain. "Is that what you meant when you said I'm not just a fly by?"

"Hmm?"

"You said our flight was a fly by. That it would be quick. That they don't stay for long."

"My job isn't to stay. It's to go where I'm needed."

"I'm not talking about your job, Gray."

"You're not a fly by because I know you only get hot coffee

around the holidays, when it's gingerbread-flavored or pepper-mint-flavored or has eggnog added."

"I—what?" That answer throws me for such a loop that I'm dizzy.

"You have a strange obsession with colored Post-it Notes. When you haven't washed your hair, you wear it up in a bun. You ask your dad about the weather and pretend like you care because you know he does. You can't drive anywhere until you've picked the perfect song. You have a dimple on your left cheek, but not your right one. And you deserve everything, Evie. A hell of a lot more than I can ever give you."

"You *can't*, or you *won't?*"

"Both."

I expected the answer. It still stings. "You know a lot about me."

"I guess that's what happens when you've known someone for twenty years."

"Yeah, I guess so."

I twist my head so my lips can reach his. He kisses me back. Sweetly. Softly. And it *hurts*. I seek out more pleasure to counteract the pain, sliding my hand down his chest. I tug at his shirt, wanting it off, and he complies, finally shedding his jeans as well so we're skin-to-skin. My fingers trace the valleys of his abs before fisting his cock. He groans into my mouth. One palm slides down my ribs, passing the small of my back, gliding over the curve of my ass. He hooks his hand around my knee and pulls it upward, opening my thighs. I'm right atop his erection, and I rub against his length. I could come from this alone, but I don't want to. Especially since I think this might be goodbye.

He slides into me slowly, inch by inch. I memorize each piece of this moment.

The slight curve of his lips.

The expression on his face—half-awed and half-cocky.

The way he smells like soap and salt.

Gray rolls us, so he's hovering above me. He kisses me in time with his thrusts. It's a gradual build, like climbing a peak you can see in the distance. You want to reach it, but you're trying to enjoy the climb. Prolong the journey.

I twine my fingers in his hair, wishing I possessed the strength to keep him here.

The rest of the world fades away. It's just me and him and the languid way he's moving.

I feel happy. Protected. Cherished.

I'm also battling the urge to cry. Because he said he can't give me everything, but this *is* everything. All I've ever wanted—all I couldn't obtain by myself—was for this boy to love me. And it feels closer than ever and also so far away. I couldn't move on before. How am I supposed to now? When I have all these memories to supplant the fantasies and feelings I've held on to for years? I've come so far and fallen so short. Both are debilitating in their own ways. It's hard knowing I've fought for nothing. Harder to stop fighting.

Ecstasy explodes, and I'm granted a temporary respite from worrying about those answers. I moan against his lips as tremors radiate through me. As I feel his release spill inside me. It feels so right, and I hate how much I love it.

I bury my face in the crook of his neck, not caring about the sticky mess. That he's about to pull away. I focus on the whoosh of his heart and the smell of his skin and the fact that he's *here*. Above me. In me. Surrounding me.

"Evie."

"What?"

"I missed you."

I don't realize moisture is spilling out of my eyes until some detached part of my brain starts to wonder why his neck is damp.

With a muttered curse, he slips out of me and away. But then his arms scoop me up, one under my knees and the other behind my back. He cradles me against his chest and walks into the adjoining bathroom, setting me down inside of the shower. My legs feel wobbly, but I stay upright.

Gray turns the water to full blast, then steps under it next to me. The water is cold. It hits my bare skin like icy knives. But I don't move, embracing the chill and then the numbness.

"What time are you leaving again?"

"I've got to be at the base by noon."

"Where are you going?"

Something shimmers in his gaze. "You know I can't tell you that."

"Then, tell me the last time you had sex with someone else."

His gaze flicks away, toward the neat line of soap bottles, then back to me. "The night before your parents' anniversary party."

"The *threesome*?"

He coughs. "I mean, if we're getting technical, I only had sex with one of them. The other just sucked me off."

I nod, then look away. The tears sliding down my cheeks mix with the water pounding over us that's turned tepid. "I can't picture it. Having sex with someone else. With Logan, there were moments we got close. I always found some excuse."

Gray steps closer.

"I didn't tell him no because of you. I told him no because it's never felt this way with anyone else—with him—and it wouldn't have been fair. Asking him to measure up when I already knew he'd fall short."

I tilt my head up. He looks down at me. Water falls over us. I watch droplets roll down his face and shoulders. Feel it plaster my hair to my neck and my forehead. It's warm now, turning hot. Steam starts to swirl. He leans one forearm above my head. Reaches for a bottle with his other hand. He drips some clear liquid onto my chest, then returns the bottle to its original spot. His palm lands between my breasts, catching the soap and spreading it. Over my shoulders and along my arms. Around my breasts, down my stomach, and between my legs. I arch against his touch.

"So fucking responsive," he murmurs.

"I've never had shower sex," I inform him.

"Never?"

"Everything I've done...it's been with you," I remind him.

Something flashes across his face, but he crushes his lips to mine before I can get a good read on it. In minutes, we're both coming again. We rinse, towel off, and end up back in bed.

"I can go," I offer.

"You should stay," he replies.

"I should?"

He rolls, so he's spooning me. I feel the brush of his breaths on my shoulder. But he doesn't say a word. He holds me and lies here.

I'm not sure if I can say anything past the lump in my throat. If I should. I lose track of time as I study the shadows cast by the moonlight.

I fight my heavy eyelids. I don't want to miss a moment. It's not until I feel exhaustion start to spread that I speak the words that have been sitting on my tongue ever since he told me I deserve more.

"This *is* everything."

He says nothing. But the arm splayed across my stomach tenses for a second, and I know he heard me.

I close my eyes and let sleep pull me all the way under.

CHAPTER THIRTEEN

In the morning, we both pretend like last night never happened. Emmett has to be at the gym early on Saturdays, so the coast is clear to wander around the loft. I pull on one of Gray's T-shirts, and he puts on a pair of boxer briefs.

The smell of pancakes and sizzling bacon soon fills the apartment. Gray can cook—better than I can. He made the same breakfast our first morning together, back in my parents' house after the disastrous dinner with his. The memory tugs at something in my chest.

I take a seat on the kitchen counter and drum my heels against the lower cabinets, watching him work.

"You could contribute, you know," Gray teases me as he measures flour.

"I'm good here," I reply. "Just enjoying the view." I make a show of looking him over, my eyes lingering on the bulge between his legs. I'm sore from last night, but I'm also hoping for a final round before he has to leave.

Gray rolls his eyes, but he's smiling. I grab the television remote and tap the power button, making myself right at home. Maybe there are cartoons on. Gray makes me feel like a kid again, so might as well embrace it. When the screen flickers to life, it's displaying a video game screen. I hit the home button, but nothing happens. I shake the remote, then try hitting it against the counter.

"What the hell are you doing?"

"Your remote is broken."

Gray abandons the stove and comes over to me. He peers at the remote, then hits one button once. A guide listing all the channels appears on the screen. "Beyond repair, obviously," he drawls.

I hook my ankles behind his waist before he can move away. "Thanks."

"Mmhmm." Rather than break my hold, he moves closer. His hands drift under the T-shirt I'm wearing. His chest vibrates with an approving growl when he realizes it's all I put on.

I'm lost in a heady haze of him. I don't hear the door until it's too late.

"*Holy fucking shit.*" Emmett's voice.

Gray's hands disappear. My knees close. It doesn't matter. His voice is nearby, and anyone with eyes would know what they just walked in on. Emmett has two of them.

I pull in a deep breath before I turn around. Will he lie to Noah for us? But when I look over my shoulder, I realize that's not a necessary question. Emmett isn't the only one who just walked in. Harrison is behind him. Closely followed by my brother.

The only sound is the sizzle of our breakfast and the hum of the television. Following Emmett's profanity-ridden reaction, no one speaks.

I have no idea what to say. *It's not what it looks like*? It's *exactly* what it looks like, and everyone here knows it.

"Can I talk to you, Evie?" Noah's voice is even and calm, but I can hear the anger and betrayal lurking underneath. "Alone."

I risk a glance at Gray. He's stoic.

"Um, yeah. Sure." I slide off the counter. Slowly, so I don't flash anyone. Once I'm standing, I hesitate. "Where did you want to talk?"

"Outsi…" His voice trails when he fully registers what little I'm wearing. It's barely appropriate to wear inside, let alone outside.

"You can use my room," Emmett offers, shattering the increasingly awkward silence and solving our dilemma.

I shoot Emmett a grateful look. The only other option is Gray's room, and I have a feeling that standing in the room where I've had sex with his best friend while we talk about me having sex with his best friend won't exactly smooth over the moment.

There's a long pause before Noah starts walking toward Emmett's bedroom. I take a deep breath and follow him. I've never been in here before. The layout is identical to Gray's room, but the space is cleaner and with more decorations.

We face each other in silence.

"I'm sorry you found out about it this way. You weren't *ever* supposed to find out about it, honestly."

It's clearly the wrong thing to say because Noah's expression turns furious.

"Are you kidding me, Evie? I find out you're *sleeping with* one of my oldest friends, and all you have to say is sorry I found out? You missed most of my birthday to talk to your ex. How the hell did you get from there to here?"

"I don't make judgments about *your* sex life, Noah. It's none of your business. I'm an adult, and I can make my own decisions."

"I'm not fucking *your* best friend."

"I wouldn't want to know if you were."

Noah runs both hands over his face and into his hair. "What the *hell* are you doing with him, Evie?"

"I just told you, my sex life is—"

"None of my business. Yeah, I know. He's my oldest—my closest friend."

"I know."

"You had a crush on him forever."

My cheeks burn. "So?"

"So? You're telling me you don't care about him at all? That it's just sex?"

I hold his gaze. "Right. I got over that crush a long time ago."

Noah snorts, then crosses his arms. "How long has it been going on for?"

"A while. Ish."

"*A while-ish? Dates*, Evie."

I sigh. I can't lie to his face. "Since Mom and Dad's anniversary."

"Almost *two months?!*"

"He's been gone for one of them."

Noah shakes his head. "What's the point, Evie?"

"What?"

"You and Gray. What's the point? You've seen how he is with girls. You could get with any guy you want. You could probably be engaged to Logan right now. Mom and Dad might have bought that mutual breakup bullshit, but I saw how he looked at you. Then. Last night. He's a good guy who wanted to settle down, and you ended it. For what? To have sex with a guy who's slept with half of Charleston?"

I wince at the blatant scorn. "They're *my* choices, Noah."

"And you're *my* sister. You seriously think I'll be able to stay friends with the guy who broke your heart?"

"He's not going to break my heart. I knew exactly what this was when it started."

"You think having sex with the only guy I've ever seen you go starry-eyed over is going to end any other way?"

I stare at him, defiant.

Noah shakes his head and scoffs. "Dammit, Evie." He turns to leave the room.

"Wait." I take a step closer to him. "Just…don't be mad at Gray, okay? *Please.* I wanted this. I instigated it. You mean a lot to him. Don't let this change anything between you two."

Noah studies me for a minute. Something akin to a smile ghosts across his lips. "Yeah, you clearly couldn't give a shit about him."

I open my mouth, then shut it again.

Noah walks out of the room. I stay behind until I hear the murmur of voices, followed by the front door closing. When I walk back into the common space, Noah, Emmett, and Harrison are all gone. Gray is standing at the counter, eating bacon.

I approach him hesitantly, unsure of what to expect. Wordlessly, he moves a plate of pancakes and bacon toward me.

We eat in silence until I muster the courage to speak. "Did Noah say anything to you?"

"Told me to fly safe."

"Oh. That was…nice?"

"The tone was more *hope you crash.*"

"Right. I think he'll come around. He was just shocked."

Gray makes a sound that could be an agreement or a disagreement before he continues eating. I glance at the clock on the stove. My stomach sinks when I see it's already almost eleven thirty. What little food I've eaten sours.

"I've got to get some stuff together." Gray disappears into his bedroom.

I continue to pick at my breakfast. This part would have sucked no matter what, but it feels especially fraught now. *Did he hear my conversation with Noah?*

When his bedroom door closes, I know it's time. My steps from the kitchen to the front door are hesitant, weighted with dread.

"Got everything?" I paste a smile on.

"Yeah." He's gotten dressed in a T-shirt the same color as his name and a pair of black basketball shorts. A small duffel bag is slung over one shoulder.

"That's good." I fidget with the hem of his shirt until he makes a small sound. My cheeks burn as I let the material drop. "Sorry. I, um, forgot."

For the first time since Noah's surprise visit, he smiles. "Sure."

"Fly safe—for real."

The smile stays. "Thanks. I'll call you."

"You don't have to keep calling. If—if you don't want to."

"I wouldn't be calling if I didn't want to, Evie."

"Okay." I sniff, starting to lose the battle with my emotions. "It's, uh, nice hearing from you. I…worry."

He sighs. I think he's going to reassure me that planes are safe and chances are high he'll return to Charleston perfectly fine. "There's a list. Of people who get notified—if something happens. I added you to it when I left for this deployment. If anything ever does happen, someone will let you know."

Tears start to slide down my cheeks. I swipe at them angrily. I've watched lots of people lose loved ones. Husbands. Wives. Children. Grandparents. Friends. It always hurts. Some hit harder than others, but I always keep my emotions under control. Except around Gray, I can't seem to keep a damn thing contained.

"Okay."

His thumbs brush my cheeks, catching the tears that are still falling. "Evie."

"It's fine. I'm fine."

"I didn't mean to make you cry. I just hated the idea of you waiting for me to call if I couldn't. And not knowing why."

"Yep. Great. Thanks." I hiccup.

He stares at me.

I blink rapidly, trying to keep more tears at bay. "It's getting close to noon. You'd better go." The other airman he flew back with is supposed to be picking him up.

He nods. "Right." Then, he steps forward.

This is it. I pull in a deep breath as I feel his lips brush my hair.

"Bye, Evie."

"Bye," I whisper.

"No one else has ever measured up for me either." He pulls back, face sober and serious. "Just for the record."

He turns and walks out. And then he's just…gone. Again. For another month, at least.

I make it to his room before I collapse, curling on my side and shoving my face against a pillow to muffle my sobs. They rack my body like the tremors of an earthquake. It takes a long time for me to become aware of anything else. A male voice is talking somewhere, but I can't summon it in me to care about who it is or what he's saying.

It's not the voice I want to hear. The one saying, "*No one else has ever measured up for me either,*" over and over in my head.

I hate him a little for saying that to me.

More time passes before I hear a voice that cuts through some of the pain and confusion. "Evie."

I raise my head from the wet pillow to meet Noah's gaze. He's standing in the open doorway.

"Fuck," he swears. "I'm going to fucking kill him."

"No. He didn't do anything."

Noah takes a seat on the end of the bed. I scramble to sit up, trying to appear a little less pathetic. I never wanted my brother to see me like this. Emmett must have come home and called him. I should have held it together until I got home. Or at least until I made it to the car. He left me his Jeep—again.

"I don't want to ruin your friendship."

"You just produced ten gallons' worth of tears, and you think that's what I'm worried about?"

I bite my bottom lip. "It's his job. He had to go. I just…miss him."

"Just sex, huh?" Noah's voice is wry.

I sigh. Something clatters in the kitchen.

"All good out here!" Emmett's voice calls.

It's weird, being in Gray's bedroom with Noah and Emmett nearby. A collision of two worlds that were held separate.

More tears fall.

"Oh, Leigh-Leigh."

"I'm sorry, Noah. I never wanted…I'm sorry."

"He won't commit?" The sympathy in his voice is shifting toward anger.

"It's complicated."

"It's *not*, Evie. Either he loves you or he doesn't."

"If he does, I don't want him to say it just because I asked him. And if he doesn't…well, I'd rather have that conversation over the phone than in person."

"On the phone?"

"Yeah. He calls me from the base. Don't you guys talk?"

"While he's deployed? No, never."

"Oh. I just assumed..." I let my voice trail off.

Knowing Gray, I'm not totally shocked. I thought he'd at least call other people occasionally. I know he doesn't call his parents, but I assumed I wasn't the only one. It adds more weight to the fact that he does, and I almost wish it didn't.

"Um, I should go." I stand and start picking my clothes up off the floor, hiding the blue lace under the pink material of my dress from last night. "Do you mind..."

"Oh. Yeah. Sure." Noah rises and heads into the hallway, closing the door behind him.

I change back into my clothes. I debate on tossing the T-shirt I was wearing in the hamper, but I carry it with me instead.

"Hey, Emmett," I greet.

He's sprawled on the couch, holding a video game controller.

"Hey, Evie." For the first time ever, Emmett appears somber. I must look really terrible.

"Sorry about, uh, earlier." I wave my arm vaguely in the direction of the kitchen.

"No worries. The kitchen counter has seen worse."

I hope he's kidding. "Okay. Great. I'm going to go."

"Do you need a ride?" Noah asks.

"No. Thanks. I have Gray's Jeep, remember?"

"Oh. Right." Noah's brow creases, like he's just now putting that together.

I'm surprised no one else asked questions when I started driving it. Maybe we're *that* unlikely of a couple.

"Okay. Bye." I head out the door and drive home.

One look in the mirror of the Jeep confirms I do, in fact, look terrible. The omnipresent circles under my eyes are exacerbated by my puffy eyes and tearstained cheeks. I rub at my face with a napkin I found in the center console, then head inside.

Sloane is sitting at the kitchen counter, sipping from a mug of what smells like coffee. She takes in my appearance silently. "No Logan?"

I shake my head, almost tempted to laugh. Last night's drama feels like a lifetime ago after this morning.

"You never showed up last night. And *Gray* left without flirting with a single girl on his one night back."

I lift one shoulder, then finally drop it. I'm too drained to deny it or share details.

Sloane smirks. "I knew you were full of shit when you said you were over him."

I laugh, then sigh. "He's...he makes me forget there are other people walking around in the world, you know?"

She shakes her head. "No, I don't. I've never been in love."

"He's going to break my heart." I sound confident—because I am. Things between me and Gray have a high percentage of not working out the way I want them to.

Sloane gives me a small, knowing smile, recognizing the same truth. "I'll help you pick up the pieces."

I hug her. "Thank you."

"Is he huge?" she asks. "I mean, he seems like he would be huge."

I chuckle before I pull away. "I don't have anything to compare it to."

Sloane's eyes widen. "You and Logan never..."

I shake my head.

"Wow. I just assumed..."

"I know. But, no, we didn't. I just didn't—"

"You didn't forget there were other people on the planet."

"I didn't forget about anything."

"He left?"

"Yeah." My voice is quiet. "I'm sorry about not telling you."

"It's okay. I get it. Frankly, I'm shocked. And proud."

I offer a small smile. "Yeah, I kind of figured you would be. I'll tell you everything later, I promise."

Sloane nods. "I'm holding you to that."

I fill a glass with water to rehydrate after my crying jag and then I head to shower and sleep.

CHAPTER FOURTEEN

I don't hear from Gray for a full week after his departure. I spend the stretch of time stressing and second-guessing. Working and worrying. By the time he finally calls, I've worked myself up into a mess. I'm in my bedroom, getting ready for bed, when the phone rings. I fall onto my bed and babble for the first ten minutes, barely letting him get a word in.

Everything I can think of to say, I say it. The recent rain and work and updates on Charlotte's sports team, which I only know about thanks to Noah. He just listens. Yet, somehow, I can *hear* him in the silence. I can tell that he's content to listen—that he wants to. He's at ease as I desperately scramble to make it feel normal. To spout off whatever nonsense comes to mind.

When I run out of topics—and air—he takes over, telling me about the card game he played last night and what he ate for breakfast. Without prompting and without me asking. It feels like we're a normal couple, each coming home from work and filling each other in about our days. I hoped I would one day have a relationship like this, where even the boring and mundane seem important and exciting. I fantasized that Grayson

Phillips might one day treat me like an important part of his world.

Listening to the familiar cadence and rasp of his voice, I'm hit with a wave of longing powerful enough to knock me over. It's not just that we're separated. It's that we *feel* separated. There's a big wall between me and the happy ending he never promised— the happy ending he told me not to expect. A translucent one, so I can *see* everything I want, I just can't reach it.

I'm not sure where we stand. He's given me more mixed signals than a malfunctioning stoplight. And I suddenly *need* to know. This is torture, made all the more painful because parts of it are pleasure. I've laughed and smiled more on this call than I have in the last week. The high makes the low feel like rock bottom.

So when he announces he has to go, I call on the same reckless abandonment that made me kiss him in that hallway at Malone's. The moment that sent this all into motion.

"Gray?"

He hesitates before clearing his throat, like he can sense the importance of what I'm about to say in the single syllable of his name. Know what I'm about to say will change us. "Yeah?"

"When we were in Beaufort, on the beach before the storm… you told me a list, remember?"

Silence, then he repeats, "Yeah."

"Am—am *I* on that list? Is there a chance I will be, one day? Are you…open to adding to it?" I feel moderately ridiculous, talking in metaphorical circles. But bravery has bounds—mine, at least. I can't force the words *Do you love me?* out of my mouth.

More silence. *Foreboding* silence. I'm grateful I can't see his expression; the pause is painful enough. It's not a question you should need to think through, and if you do, that says a lot in itself.

"If I'm not, if I won't be, can you stop calling? Because it…" The white plaster of my ceiling swims before my eyes. "God, it *hurts*, Gray. I don't know what we are or where we stand. I don't know if I should hold on or let go or move on. And I *need* to know. I know where we're *supposed* to stand, but not where we really do. You've said things…I've said things…" I bite down on the inside of my cheek until I taste metal. "I want this—*us*—for real, Gray," I admit. "I need to know if you do too."

It's quiet for so long that I think we've been disconnected and I've been pouring my heart out to open air this whole time.

Then, he finally responds, in a way that makes me wish the phone lines had been snipped after all. "I have to go, Evie."

The next two weeks pass slowly…and silently.

Gray never calls.

Day by day, I give up on the hope that he will a little more. Until there's none of the pesky emotion left. If I'd never let myself hope, this would be easier. I know Gray cares about me. You can't share moments like we have and walk away completely unaffected. But there's a long leap from care to love. One I apparently made solo.

Maybe I should have waited to ask him in person.

Maybe I pushed too fast.

Maybe he just needed more time.

But in the meantime, I was falling and falling and falling. Better to start pulling myself up now than tumble any further.

Even my mother notices my depression and forces me to come over for dinner. We've always been close, but she's never asked me about boys or relationships or love unless I broached the subject first. She's not the touchy-feely sort, and neither am I.

Henry and Juliet Phillips join us for dinner, which makes it extra challenging for me. Not only are they a potent reminder of Gray, but Henry's presence makes me feel like I can't blame the dark circles under my eyes and my pale skin on the insane hours I've been working lately. I'm covering twice as many shifts as the next intern. Third-year residents know my name. Every nurse on staff has my pager number memorized.

Professionally, I'm killing it.

My personal life is another story. I've barely seen Sloane as of late, and I know she's worried about me. On the rare occasions I'm home, I'm sleeping. Work and sleep are my two respites. When I'm dashing around the hospital, I'm too busy to think. When I'm home, I'm too tired to do anything but embrace the blissful oblivion of sleep.

The worst part is the anticipation. I didn't fall for any random guy. When Gray returns to Charleston, there's an excellent chance I'll have to see him. Interact with him. I'm not confident I can handle it without throwing something at him or crying. Or both.

He said he'd be gone "at least another month." I probably should have clarified before asking for a live love declaration. There's no way I'll end up in this situation again—I hope—but lesson learned. Ask basic questions before big ones.

Noah is chattier at dinner than normal, and I know it's his attempt at drawing attention away from me. I should be grateful, instead it makes me feel worse. He's helping me, protecting me, even after I showed no regard for *his* feelings. Pursuing something with Gray was entirely selfish. It would be one thing if it had a point. If I went into it with the possibility we might end up together and it would all be worth it in the end.

Instead of thinking with my head, I acted with my heart and

my hormones. I told myself I would act normally around him after we ended, that Noah would never know, much less suspect. Maybe that was a lie all along. It's *definitely* a lie now. I've forever changed the dynamic between my brother and his oldest, closest friend.

The knowledge Gray broke my heart will always be there between them, whether I'm around or not.

And it breaks my heart all over again.

After dinner ends, I say goodbye to my parents and the Phillipses and head to the hospital for the graveyard shift. Noah insists on driving me. I stopped using Gray's Jeep to get around two days after our final conversation. Parked it in the loft's garage and took an Uber to the hospital. I've been taking the bus ever since because I have been working nonstop and haven't even had the time to go look at a car. It's an outing I'm avoiding because I know I'll be plagued by memories of my last trip to a car dealership the next time I return.

Noah makes small talk on the drive. He hasn't asked about Gray since he comforted me in his bedroom, after finding out about us. There's really nothing left to say. I know he hasn't taken my recent behavior as a sign things are going well between us. He never mentions Gray, but there's worry etched on his face as he drops me off. I'm tempted to normalize things some, to ask if he's still seeing the woman from his architecture firm, Megan, that he mentioned to me weeks ago. But I don't. I'm worried it will lead to the inevitable question of when I'll start dating, the one I have no answer for. Maybe I already should be. Simply pretending I'm fine hasn't healed my heart much.

I should be exhausted when my shift ends at seven a.m. There was a five car pile-up on I-26 that kept me and the rest of the staff on call busy for most of the night. I'm not tired, though; I'm wired with restless energy. My feet drag as I cross the parking lot toward the bus stop, dreading returning home to Sloane's sympathetic stares and a restless day's sleep.

"Evie!" I focus my tired eyes on a black Volvo. The driver's side window is down, and Ben is waving at me.

I walk over to him. "Hey."

"You waiting for the bus?" He glances at the stop behind me.

"Yep."

"Want a ride?" When I hesitate, he adds, "I was planning to stop at Frosted..."

Since an iced coffee and sugary doughnut sound like heaven right now, I agree. "That sounds great. Thanks."

I round the front of the car and climb into the passenger seat. The air-conditioning feels heavenly. Summer's full wrath is upon us. Even at this early hour, the heat is intense.

"Something wrong with your car?" Ben asks as he starts driving.

"More the lack of one that's an issue," I reply.

"Weren't you driving that Jeep?" As if realizing how that sounded, he quickly adds, "Not a stalker. I promise."

I laugh. "Um, yeah. I was. The Jeep's owner and I have... parted ways."

"Oh. I'm sorry."

"Thanks."

We chat idly after that, Ben making an obvious effort to lighten the mood following my admission. He also holds the door for me and pays for my breakfast, reminding me of Rose's comments a few weeks ago.

When we climb back into his car, I suggest we eat back at his place. The insinuation hangs between us in the chilled air inside the car as he agrees and starts driving in the opposite direction from my house. I finish my doughnut on the short drive, mostly as a way to keep my hands and mouth occupied. Without meaning to, my mind wanders to a different, yet similar, trip. In a Subaru, not a Volvo. Feeling equally nervous.

Ben lives in a nice complex just outside of downtown. It's comprised of individual townhouses, so it doesn't feel like you're in the middle of a city, just a small community like at the base I visited with Gray.

I smile when I see the bowls set out on his front porch. Ben does too.

"Darn cat won't leave me alone."

"Not feeding it would probably help," I point out.

He chuckles. "Yeah. It probably would."

I follow Ben into his kitchen, taking in the shiny appliances and new furniture. The decorating makes me feel like I'm in a furniture showroom. There's nothing wrong with it; it's just all perfectly matched, coordinated in dark wood and shades of green.

"Nice place."

"Thanks. My mom picked all the furniture out." Ben makes a face, like the matching set might not have been his first choice either.

"You're close with her?"

"Very. My dad passed away a few years ago. It was tough when I was out on the West Coast, but my brother lives close by her. He stayed in Ohio for college, and since."

"That's nice." I'm having trouble focusing on the polite conversation. Nerves are percolating in my stomach and prickling at my skin.

I feel like a virgin again. This all feels new. Different. Strange.

An awkward silence falls, and I channel my nervous energy into action before it can turn into babbling or fidgeting instead. I walk right up to Ben and kiss him. He wasn't expecting it—at all. He stumbles back a step before resting his hands on my waist and steadying us both. As the surprise fades, he starts to kiss me back.

His tongue teases the seam of my lips. I part them. He tastes like coffee and sugar. I probably do too.

We start to move. I keep my eyes closed, trying to shut off my brain and just relax into the moment. Something soft hits the backs of my legs. A bed. I'm horizontal now, pressed against a downy comforter that smells freshly washed.

I kiss Ben harder, trying to force some sort of reaction. Any sort of reaction. All I feel is the pressure as Ben responds to my urgency. It's eliciting the amount of passion that pressing my lips against the edge of a glass would. Worse is the nausea swirling in my stomach and crawling up my throat. It tastes like betrayal. Like I'm being unfaithful to a man who doesn't want my loyalty.

I lied earlier. When I said it would be fine if you—when I acted like I wouldn't care if you'd been with another guy. I would care.

Gray's voice echoes in my mind, reminding me of words I unintentionally memorized and moments I'm trying to forget.

Can't think of anything that would piss me off more, actually.

I can't shut my brain off, no matter how hard I try. Can't do *this*. Having sex with Ben won't change how I feel about Gray.

I stiffen before I pull away and flop onto my back, panting. It feels hot in here—suffocating. With guilt and with annoyance over that guilt. I don't owe Gray Phillips a damn thing. I should take back everything I've ever given him.

He has it all anyway. My fidelity. My trust. My body. My love.

"I'm sorry," I say to the ceiling.

This won't be progressing any further, and I can tell Ben realizes it. I don't owe him anything, but I definitely led him on. Led him here.

Ben shifts beside me, accepting the literal distance I put between us. "Don't apologize, Evie."

"I know I made it seem like—"

"Evie. It's fine. Really."

We lie in silence. I'm also sweating. "I swear, it's *me*, not you."

"You mean, it's *him*. Gray, right? The guy Rose asks about?"

His name douses me like cold water. It's unexpected, leaving me no time to school my reaction—my surprise—at hearing that one syllable in a dark bedroom, spoken by a guy I was just kissing. On the plus side, the resulting chill means I'm no longer overheating. On the downside, Ben catches my wince.

"You're in love with him."

My first instinct is to shrug like that observation means nothing to me. But it's difficult to shrug while lying down, and Ben is staring at the ceiling the same way I am, so he likely wouldn't even see it.

"Probably." I suck my bottom lip between my teeth.

Gray and *love* aren't words I've used in the same sentence before outside my own head. I don't know how else to describe everything I felt when we were together, though. Everything I feel when he's gone.

"I thought I was making progress. I thought I could do *this*... so that's a minor setback."

Ben snorts a laugh.

"Sorry."

"Don't apologize, Evie. I should have made a better first impression at the bar."

It takes me a few seconds to figure out what he's talking about. "Oh. That's not when I met him. He, uh, grew up next door to me. I've known him since I was five."

Ben whistles. "Wow. When did you start having feelings for him?"

"The day he moved in."

"Nothing ever happened between you two until now?"

"I was interested. He wasn't." My cheeks burn at the confession. "We don't need to talk about this. I'm sure you don't—"

"We're friends, Evie."

"You kiss all your friends?" I tease.

Ben turns his head to smirk at me. "Only the ones in love with another man."

I let out some unattractive mixture of a snort and a scoff. "Right."

We're both quiet again. I should leave, but I kind of like lying here in the dark with him. His curtains are drawn, probably because he sleeps during plenty of daylight hours, like me. The guilt and anxiety have dissipated. I feel empty again. It's nice not to be alone when you feel empty.

"Did you tell him? How you feel?"

"No," I admit.

Ben hums a disapproval.

"That would have been…a bad idea. We agreed it was just sex." I can only imagine how our last conversation would have gone if I'd preluded my list question with those three words. Pity probably would have permeated the long pause. I'm sure Gray has an accurate sense of how I feel about him. It's simmered in the subtext of every encounter we've ever had. I wouldn't have asked him if he loved *me* if I didn't love him. That's different from outright saying it, though.

"And you didn't think it might end poorly? Sleeping with a guy you've had feelings for since you were five?" There's no judgment in Ben's question, just naked curiosity. Maybe a hint of amusement too. As far as failed hook up partners go, I chose well.

"I figured it would, actually. I just…wanted him more than I cared about the consequences."

"And he didn't?"

I sigh. "I have no idea. I asked how he felt the last time he called, and he hasn't called since. It's been two weeks."

"Maybe you should call him," Ben suggests.

"I can't."

"Of course you can. From what I've seen, you're fearless."

I only manage to tamp down the snort because I can tell he's being genuine and sweet. When it comes to Gray, I'm mostly a complete coward. "I mean, I literally *can't*. I have no idea how to reach him while he's deployed. He calls me from a private number."

"Oh. What if you contacted the base? They must have some way to reach him?"

"And say what? *I'm trying to reach an airman who doesn't want to talk to me*?" I scoff. "No, it's better this way. Cleaner. No temptation at all. I'll just move on."

I make it sound easy.

I know it'll be anything but.

CHAPTER FIFTEEN

There's a teenage couple waiting to cross the street we're stalled at. The stoplight turned red and the walk sign appeared, but they're still standing there, too caught up in each other to notice. I'm jealous of two strangers years younger than me. Because I know what that feels like, and I'm worried I'll never find it again.

I look away from them, catching Sloane's concerned gaze in the backseat beside me.

"You okay?" she asks.

"Of course. Why wouldn't I be?"

"Um...do you *really* want me to say it?"

No. "Say what?" Denial has been a close friend the past few weeks. I'm not ready to part ways with it yet.

"He broke your heart, Evie."

The light turns green and the car we're in starts to move again. I look out the window at the darkened street. "It was always going to end...whatever we were."

"It was a relationship that you were too scared to call one and he was too idiotic to acknowledge was one."

I never told Sloane about our final phone call. Never told

anyone besides Ben. The short list of people who knew we were ever connected by anything more than my brother and his parents' choice of home when they moved to Charleston two decades ago —Sloane, Noah, Harrison, and Emmett—all think things are unresolved between us. Tense, but unresolved. They're not. I don't need Gray to tell me to my face he'll never give me what I need. His silence has said enough.

"Sloane, please. I can't talk about this right now. Not when I'm about to..." See him. Two days ago, I found out from Noah that Gray was back from his deployment.

He's here.

Home.

Alive.

Silent.

And tonight is Emmett's birthday party. The timing could have definitely been better. I *think* he'll be there, but I'm not certain. My heart is split on what it's hoping for.

Sloane gives up on conversation with me and starts chatting with the Uber driver instead. I watch the downtown lights continue to flash by, a mixture of apprehension and excitement swirling in my stomach.

I spot him as soon as we walk into Malone's. Other emotions temporarily drift away as relief smothers me. Part of me didn't believe it, not until I saw him with my own eyes. I soak in the sight of him greedily, feeling the familiar awareness enter my system like a drug. No matter how I feel *toward* him, how I feel *around* him hasn't changed.

Colors seem brighter.

Sounds sharper.

Even the scents swirling in the air—cologne, liquor, and leather—hit me harder.

Gray has trimmed his hair since I last saw him and grown out a light layer of stubble. In his standard uniform of jeans and a faded T-shirt, he manages to make my heart skip a beat. He doesn't seem to notice—or care—that I'm here as he continues chatting with Harrison.

The uncertainty and trepidation that I've been grappling with for the past forty-eight hours since I learned he was back is completely absent on Gray's face. He's sporting an easy smile and sipping a beer.

It makes me want to scream. Cry. Kiss someone right in front of him.

Instead, I paste a smile on my face.

Emmett is acting like twenty-seven is a substantial milestone. It's not just Noah, Gray, and Harrison here. Guys he knows from high school, college, and work are all gathered around the corner table. Most of them I've met before.

Sloane and I are greeted enthusiastically—that might have a little something to do with the fact that we're the only two females in attendance—by the group. Gray is standing on the left side of the table, so I veer toward the right.

I greet Noah first with a hug and a whispered, "Hey, big brother."

He smiles, then gives me the concerned look he always seems to wear around me now. I move on quickly.

I don't have many close friends in Charleston. Noah has always been more social than me. Most of my childhood friends moved elsewhere, and none of my friends from college or medical school live here. I work an insane amount of hours. It feels nice to be enveloped in a group of warm, familiar people. Noah's friends have always treated me like an honorary little sister, for the most part.

Sloane's phone rings. "Ugh, I have to take this. I'll be right back."

227

I nod as she heads for the door, then allow my eyes to dart where they want to. I look at Gray. He glances over at the same moment. Our eyes lock. I'm not sure if I have a right to be mad at him for not loving me, but I sure as hell am hurt. The emotion exacerbates when he turns back toward Harrison after a few seconds.

I approach Emmett, not allowing my smile to wobble. "Happy birthday!"

"Evie!" He gives me a warm hug. "I've barely seen you."

"Work has been busy."

I've also avoided him since he saw me crying in his apartment. Things with Noah have returned to normal—or at least we act like they are—but I haven't been able to shake the awkwardness I feel around Emmett and Harrison. I'm worried they might resent me for causing conflict. Or even worse, pity me. Plus, they walked in on me about to have sex on a kitchen counter. So there's that.

"Uh-huh. Come on." He flings an arm around my shoulders and starts guiding me toward the bar. "Let's get you a drink."

"I can get my own," I tell him. "This is your party."

"Exactly. I can do whatever I want."

He puts his hand on the small of my back and guides me toward the bar top.

I sigh. "I'm *fine*, Emmett. This is sweet, but I swear I'm not going to start crying. That was a onetime thing."

Emmett studies me for a minute. "He hasn't brought anyone home."

I look away. "He can do whatever the hell he wants. *Whoever* the hell he wants." Not to mention, he could easily go elsewhere to have sex. He even told me that was his preference.

"He can—does," Emmett agrees. "But he's spent the past couple of days in his room. Alone."

"The two of us are done, Emmett. We had our fun. It's over."
Fun feels like a misnomer for what took place, but heartbreak hits too close to home.

Emmett sighs as the bartender appears.

"What can I get you guys?"

"Uh, Moscow mule, please."

The bartender nods, then glances at Emmett.

"I'm good, man, thanks."

"Now, you really didn't need to come," I grumble.

"Do you remember Iris Jones?" Emmett asks.

"Um, your high school girlfriend?"

"Yep, exactly. My senior year, she broke up with me right before homecoming."

I raise a brow. "Is there a point to this stroll down memory lane?"

Emmett chuckles. "I didn't want to go alone, and sure, I wanted to make her jealous. So, I asked Gray if he thought Noah would flip if I asked *you*."

I tilt my head, hanging on to his every word.

He smirks, sensing he's caught my interest. "He said, 'No guy is good enough for Evie Collins,' and then barely spoke to me for a week."

"You never asked me."

"I know. Iris and I got back together a few days later." He smiles. "Look, I don't know what went down between you and Phillips. I think of you like a little sister, so I don't actually *want* to know any details. But...just because he *acts* indifferent doesn't mean he is. I'm pretty sure he's had plenty of practice."

"I'm done waiting for him to decide if I'm worth it."

Emmett nods slowly. "Good for you. But...for what it's worth, I don't think that's what he's trying to figure out."

"Here you go." The bartender sets my drink down in front

of me.

"Thanks," I reply, digging through my clutch for my credit card.

"Put it on the Baker tab," Emmett tells him.

The bartender nods. "Sure thing."

"Emmett, you don't need to—"

He grabs my hand and pulls me back toward the table. "I did."

"Thank you."

Right as we reach the table, I hear my name being called. I turn to see Chris approaching. Everyone at the table looks at him as he walks over. Sloane's returned from her phone call. She makes an appreciative sound in her throat.

"Hey!" Chris gives me a hug, which I wasn't expecting. Although I probably should have, based on the smell of alcohol coming off him. "Fancy running into you here. Small world, huh?"

"Small town, for sure."

"Ben is on call tonight. He'll be bummed you were here. I swear, all the guy does is talk about you."

Does it make me a terrible, vindictive person that I'm glad Gray heard that?

"He and I are just friends."

"You should give him a chance, Evie. He's a good guy. Not like the asshole who broke your heart."

Emmett coughs a laugh. "Sure hope you don't have to go to the hospital, Phillips. You might get denied care."

"Stay the fuck out of it, Baker."

Chris looks between Emmett and Gray. I watch his drunk brain put the two pieces together. "*Oh.*"

An awkward silence stretches. Anyone here who wasn't aware of what happened between me and Gray is now caught up on my train wreck of a love life.

"I'm here with Drew and Jessie. If you want to come say hi…"

"Yeah. Sure." I set my drink down on the table, then follow Chris over to his table and spend a while talking with him and two of my other coworkers. It feels nice to be amid people who are *my* friends, not tied to Gray in any way.

There's no sign of Gray when I return to my original table. I'm relieved as I settle on a seat and sip on my drink, half-listening as Noah and Emmett discuss the Sharks' chances of having a decent season now that they've lost Jace Dawson.

I'm relieved when Harrison announces it's time for the next stop. My cue to leave for the night. Proving I'm able to be around Gray is different from prolonging it, especially in a situation where he could easily entertain female attention.

"Hey." Sloane reappears at my side as our group gathers up our belongings and begins to migrate toward the exit. "I think I'm going to go home with Jackson."

"Yeah?" I glance at her, then at the guy who co-owns the gym with Emmett.

"Yeah. He's nice. We'll see where it goes. We're just going to get another drink."

"Okay." I give her a hug. "I'll see you later."

"You're sure you're good?" she asks as we walk outside.

"I'm sure. Go!"

"Okay." She smiles, then walks off with Jackson.

Emmett, Harrison, and Noah are all standing to the left outside the bar. I flash a small smile in their general direction, then head right. Everyone else seems to have already left. There's no sign of anyone else from our group lingering outside. I dig my phone out of my bag to call an Uber.

"You good, Evie?"

I glance at Noah, who's walked over to me. "Yeah. Just heading home."

"Want me to go with you?"

"No, of course not. I'm fine. Great." I smile and hope it comes across as genuine.

Noah hesitates. "I know we never really talked about…"

"We don't need to, Noah. Just because…I just…" I sigh. "I'm sorry. You shouldn't feel like…" God, I can't even get a full sentence out.

I know Noah feels torn between loyalty to me and his friendship with Gray, even though I've told him not to take sides. I feel terrible for putting him in this position. And I hate myself for ever expecting more from Gray.

"I'm just going to go home and pass out. Go have fun with your friends, okay?" I want to ask where Gray is. So badly. But I refrain.

Noah nods slowly, then leans forward and hugs me. "Love you, sis."

I smile. "Love you too."

Noah walks away. I turn back toward the street, and then I get the answer to the question I couldn't voice. Gray exits the bar.

Rather than head for his friends, Gray walks straight toward me. He stops a few feet from me and shoves his hands into his pockets. He's not relaxed or at ease now. His jaw is clenched and his shoulders are tight. "Hi."

"For the record, I didn't call you an asshole." I figure there's no point in acting like this is a casual catch-up.

"You should've."

I don't dispute it; I cut to the chase. "You didn't call."

Can you hate someone for not loving you? For confirming something you already should have known? Right now, I do. I hate him. I hate all the other emotions that are flooding me right now. How he still looks like the person I'd forget to cross the road with. I've had plenty of time to accept that he's not.

"I know." He stares at me.

I stare back.

"Evie." He says my name like it's breaking in two, like there's a big crack between the *Ev* and the *ie*, where all the things he's not saying are lodged.

"You didn't call," I repeat, this time with more emotion.

More conviction.

More pain.

More love.

More, more, more.

He doesn't agree with me this time. He just looks at me, and I get mad. So, so mad. I'm mad at him for not loving me. I'm mad at myself for hoping he would. I'm mad at him for giving me hope.

And all that anger mixes with relief that he's here—home—and spills out in streams of liquid that dribble down my cheeks. *Dammit.* I swipe at the tears angrily—harshly.

"Fuck." The rough edge to the word tells me he cares—just not enough.

He takes a step forward.

I hold a hand out. "Go."

"Or you'll tell Noah?" There's a glint to his eyes that's a new arrival to this conversation.

He knows everyone knows. I can't tell if he's annoyed or relieved or just letting me know I'm fresh out of blackmail.

That glint makes me madder. I want to scream and throw something heavy at him. But Gray doesn't make promises he won't keep. And he never promised to love me. Never promised me anything at all.

I turn and walk away. People say *walk away* like it's a good thing. Like it's a strong choice—to not engage in conflict. I've never felt weaker.

I kissed Gray inside this bar that night to prove to myself I'd changed. That I *was* the girl who pursued what she wanted. Didn't let doubt hold her back. There were moments with Gray where I felt like that girl. Right now, she's nowhere to be found. I feel like a younger version of myself, coming to the painful realization that just because you develop feelings for someone, it doesn't mean they will feel them back. That they're wasted and bottled up with no place to go.

Footsteps sound behind me, but I know they're not his. Things between us are messy. Gray doesn't do messy. When he said Charleston is boring, I think he really meant messy. I've made it messier.

Noah's voice murmurs, "Let me take you home."

I nod. I don't fight it or pretend I'm okay—because I'm not. I hid a lot from him—I didn't realize how much until right now, when it's all spilling out into the open. Things that have nothing to do with Gray—aside from the fact that they're things I told him and no one else. I hid how lonely I was in Boston. How draining school was. How my friends were all as driven as I was, so no one was ever telling me to take a break. How things with Logan never felt right.

I'm in a daze that makes mundane things disappear. Like how I get from the sidewalk to the car to being halfway home.

It's a sigh that pulls me out of the fog. That makes me realize he's about to speak. "Leigh-Le—"

"Can you take me to Mom and Dad's, please?"

"Yeah. Sure."

Noah doesn't attempt to make conversation again. I'm the one who breaks the quiet when he pulls into our parents' driveway.

"I need you to promise me something."

He searches my face, then nods.

"I need you to promise you won't let this affect your friendship with him."

Noah starts shaking his head before I finish the sentence. "Evie, I can't just—"

"You *can*. Me and him? It was me. All me. You've been best friends since you were seven. That means something."

"You're my sister. He can't expect—"

I cut him off again. "It was sex, Noah. That's it. We both agreed."

He winces, then scoffs. "You think I don't know how you feel about him? How you've always felt about him?"

"I hoped I wasn't quite that transparent, yeah."

He bangs his palm against the steering wheel. "Dammit, Evie."

"I'm sorry," I whisper.

"You don't have anything to apologize for." His tone makes it clear he holds someone responsible. And as much as it means to me, I know it's wrong.

"Neither does *he*, Noah. He never lied to me. Never. He was thoughtful and sweet, and that was most of the problem. The reality was better than the fantasy."

Noah sighs. "He's…different with you. I've—I've seen him with plenty of other girls. Maybe you should talk to him."

I shake my head. Not even the slightest twinge of hope appears. "I can't. I'm *so* mad at him. And I don't have any right to be, which just makes me madder. If we talk and he says he's sorry and asks to be friends…I can't do it."

Noah sighs. "Okay. I'll stay out of it. I won't say anything to him. But he won't be getting a *welcome home* party either."

I breathe out a laugh. "Sounds fair." I lean over and hug him before climbing out of the car and walking inside.

My mom is curled up on the couch, watching a movie, while my dad snores in an armchair. She startles when she sees me standing in the doorway, pressing a hand to her chest.

"My goodness, Evie. You startled me." Her expression creases with concern as she stands and studies me. "You all right, sweetheart?"

I nod and walk over to the couch, sinking into the soft cushions that have seen me through other hard days. "Well, I will be."

"Do you want to talk about it?"

"Is there more wine?"

My mom smiles before heading into the kitchen and returning with a glass that matches the one on the coffee table.

I thank her and take a long sip, letting the tartness sink in before I swallow. "It's good."

"One we tried in Italy. We went to the vineyard and met the sommelier."

"That's nice." I look down and swirl my glass, watching the liquid spin round and round for a few seconds. "I'm in love with Gray Phillips. It started when I first moved back, and it ended, well, I'm not sure when exactly. But it did. End."

"Oh, Evie. I'm sorry, sweetheart. I know—"

"That it was a long time coming?" I give her a wry smile before drinking more wine.

"I had a feeling you felt that way about him, yes."

I exhale and relax into the couch. "Yeah, we were heartbreak waiting to happen, I guess. I just felt like being home tonight. I hope that's okay."

"Of course. This will always be your home, Evie."

I smile at my mom. "Thanks."

She pats my arm before turning back to the television. We watch the show and drink wine in silence. Familiarity—reminders of the past—can destroy you. Right now, it's soothing.

CHAPTER SIXTEEN

The following morning is one of the best I've had in a while. I wake up to the smell of fresh bagels and frying eggs. My dad analyzes the coming week's weather while my mom works on the daily crossword. I soak in their quiet contentment. I'll find this. Someday. Somewhere. With someone.

After breakfast, I change into the one-piece from high school still sitting in my drawer and head into the backyard to swim laps. It's hot, clear, and humid out. The cool water feels like heaven when I jump in. I float for a while, staring up at the blue sky and the fluffy clouds and the sunbeams filtering down before rolling onto my stomach and starting to exercise. My arms churn the clear water in rhythmic motions. My heart rate rises and lactic acid builds as I count each stroke. By the time I pull myself out of the pool, I feel tired and relaxed.

Rather than take a towel from the stack, I lie down on the sun-warmed stones surrounding the chlorinated water, absorbing the bright sunshine like a lizard. Birds call in the distance. The scent of freshly cut grass wafts by. Warmth soaks my damp skin. It's been a while since I allowed myself to slow down long enough to do anything but sleep. My skin is dry and my mind empty by the time I rise and start to take lazy steps toward the deck.

Then, I freeze. "I don't want to talk to you."

Gray exhales as he approaches. "I know."

"Then, why are you here?"

"Because *I* want to talk to *you*."

"You could have called. Or texted," I add quickly. Calling means something different between us now. Something different than what I meant. He made his choice about *calling* and I don't want to discuss it.

Gray doesn't answer. He continues walking toward me until he's only a couple of feet away. He sinks his hands into the pockets of his shorts and studies me. I wish I had more clothing on.

"We don't have to do this."

"Do what?" He passes me and takes a seat by the pool.

I follow and sink down beside him with a sigh. Looks like... we'll be having this conversation.

"*This*. The whole *smoothing things over, let's go back to normal* thing. I'm fine. We're fine. I'm, you know, basically over you."

That last sentence amuses him. "You are, huh?"

"Yep. Figured it was...time."

He smiles, but it fades fast. He leans back on his hands, then sits up straight.

He's nervous. "Look, I—"

"*Gray?*"

We both look to the left. Juliet Phillips is standing on the other side of the landscaping that separates their property from my parents', holding a watering can and wearing a shocked expression. She obviously had no idea he was home.

There's a pause as she absorbs his presence and we absorb

hers. I wasn't expecting this to take place at all—for him to come here. He wasn't expecting Juliet to appear.

"Hi, Mom." Gray stands and traipses through mulch to give his mother a hug.

"You said you wouldn't be back until tomorrow," she says.

"I know. My schedule changed last minute."

I glance away at the pool, because I have a feeling the conversation is about to shift to me.

Sure enough, she says, "What are you doing in the Collins' backyard?"

"Asking Evie out." He says it so casually, so easily, that I'm certain I misheard him.

He *didn't* say that, right?

Juliet's shocked gasp makes me think he actually did.

"Your timing sucks, Mom. I'll come over in a bit and we can talk, okay?"

"I—okay."

Juliet says something else to him I can't hear before Gray's legs reappear beside me. Then his torso as he sits back down again.

"Are we about done here?" I ask pointedly.

"You don't have to pretend you didn't hear what I said."

"You should work on your communication skills. I get why you didn't tell me you were coming back, but you should have told your parents."

"That wasn't the part I was talking about." He blows out a sigh. "I didn't call you because I didn't—I wanted to talk to you in person."

"There's nothing left to say."

"*I* have things to say."

"You said everything you needed to say when you never called again." I stand and kick a stray pebble into the bushes.

There's too much simmering inside for me to sit still and discuss this calmly.

He stands too. "It wasn't that simple, Evie!"

I step forward and shove his chest. It feels good, so I shove him again. "It was exactly that simple! It's a fucking yes or no question, Gray! You don't sort of love someone. Maybe love someone. Consider loving someone. Either you *do* or you *don't*. And I should have known your answer. I should have seen it coming. I *would have*, if you hadn't blurred the lines right alongside me. You said it was sex, and that was fine. But you knew. You knew I had feelings for you! I thought I knew what I was getting into. And I *would have* if you hadn't taken me to Beaufort with you and called me and made it seem like it all meant something to you. Like *I* meant something to you."

He takes a step closer. "Evie, I—"

"No. I'm done. I can't *do* this, Gray. Please. If you—if you ever actually cared at all, then just go." I turn away. "Just go do whatever the hell you want to do until you leave again."

"I'm not leaving."

My muscles freeze so I'm physically incapable of moving any farther away. "What?"

"I'm not leaving Charleston. I'm back to stay. I asked to be permanently assigned to the base here. I'll have to take some shorter trips, but ninety percent of the year, I'll be here."

I look back at him. "What?" I repeat, disbelieving. "Why—why would you do that?"

Gray holds my gaze. "Because you're here."

It takes me a solid twenty seconds to speak after that. "But you didn't..." I'm worried those three words will be hard to recover from. And then he keeps talking.

"You're on my list, Evie. You're at the very top. You have been for a while. I used to be disappointed when I landed in

Charleston. It was an ending. The end of a flight. End of a mission. But now? I'm so damn excited for those wheels to hit the runway here. Because once they do, I'm that much closer to seeing you."

I open my mouth, but no sound comes out. I'm sufficiently stunned silent. He's saying everything I've ever wanted to hear, but I've had the rug pulled out from under me by him too many times before. I can't allow myself to trust it, to absorb what he's telling me.

"I didn't call…" He runs a hand through his hair, which is barely long enough for him to grip. "I didn't know what to say to you, Evie. I'd put in for the transfer, but I hadn't heard back. I didn't want to…I needed you to know I was serious."

I scoff at that. "You being on the other side of the world was not the fucking problem, Gray! All I needed from you was for you to tell me how you felt about me. I needed you to call. I needed to talk to you. That's what I *needed* from you."

"You're right," he agrees. "I should have said it when you asked. I should have said it before. But I'm saying it *now*. I love you, Evie. I'm in love with you. And if we're laying it all out here…you've *never* said it."

I'm the furthest thing from amused right now. But I laugh—I can't help it. "You honestly think there's a chance I'm *not* in love with you?"

He stares at me.

I stare back.

"Will you go out with me?"

What? "What?"

"Will you go out with me? Tonight, if you're free." He says the two sentences completely matter-of-fact. Like he's a guy and I'm a girl and we met for the first time not too long ago. Like there's no history or fights or unresolved feelings stacked up between us.

"On a *date*?"

That damn smirk appears, dimple and all. "Yeah. On a *date*."

"I..." God, I'm considering it. Ten minutes of talking after weeks of stark silence, and I'm considering it. I *want* to tell him yes.

He reads my hesitation. "It's just dinner, Evie. We'll talk. You can ask me anything, and I'll answer it. I promise."

That's the word that gets me.

Promise.

Here's the thing about promises: they're just words. You might promise to *do* something, but there's no action associated with the promise itself.

They're easy to make.

Easy to break.

But Gray has never broken a promise he's made to me.

So, I find myself agreeing.

"Okay."

Sloane shakes her head. "No. The black was better."

I yank the purple top over my head and scramble to pull the black tank back on.

"Actually, I think you should wear the white."

I might strangle her.

Sloane loves imparting fashion wisdom on others. She's mostly given up on me as a lost cause. Twenty-plus years of friendship, and I mostly wear sweatshirts and leggings, especially in the winter. Or scrubs now.

It says a lot about my level of nerves that I asked her to help me pick out an outfit for tonight. And it's a decision I'm regretting.

I sigh as I swap the black shirt for the white one. The sun I got this morning offsets the pale color.

Sloane smiles. "Perfect."

The doorbell rings. Anxiety explodes in my stomach like a firework. Why did I agree to this? I must be a masochist.

I smooth down the gauzy material of my shirt and take a deep breath before I pick up my purse.

"Have fun. Let me know if I should make myself scarce later." Sloane waggles her brows in a poor imitation of a pervert, as if I could have possibly missed the insinuation behind her words.

"You won't need to."

"Uh-huh. You're barely attracted to the guy."

I hesitate. "Am I being stupid, agreeing to this? It hurt so much before, and that wasn't anything like this. If it ends this time, I can't even…"

Sloane slides off the bed and stands in front of me. "You're not stupid, Evie. It takes courage to try something that failed before. You're not weak; you're brave. And we both know that if you don't do this, you'll always regret it. So, go."

She smacks my butt, which she declared looks "damn good" in these skinny jeans, which were an *endeavor* to get into. If anything does happen between me and Gray tonight, he's going to have to literally peel them off me.

"Go!"

I spin and give her a hug before heading for the front door.

When I open it, all I can see is a bouquet of pink peonies. It lowers to reveal Gray's smirk.

"Did you get lost on the way to the door?"

I hate that he's making this easy. It's a struggle to hold my glower in place as I take the flowers from him. "Thank you," I say grudgingly, ignoring his comment about how long I took to appear.

"You're welcome."

"Stay here." I shut the door in his face, then release a shaky breath. Two minutes, and my resolve is cut in half. I want to kiss him.

Sloane walks into the kitchen as I'm sorting through a cabinet, looking for a vase to put the flowers in.

"What's going on?"

"He brought flowers." I point to the offending, beautiful blooms.

"Ooh. Nice." She picks one up and smells it, then looks around. "Where's Gray?"

"Out on the front porch."

Her lips quirk. "Why? Worried about being too close to a bed?"

I don't deign that with a response, just a *look*. Although that is kind of what I'm worried about.

Sloane laughs. "Go, Evie. I'll put these in water."

I sigh and step down from the stool I was using to go through the cabinets. "Okay. Thanks."

When I open the door for a second time, Gray is standing right where I left him. He's silent as I step outside and as we walk toward his Jeep, parked along the curb.

"You look nice," he says, halfway across the grass.

A pulse pounds between my legs. I might be angry and hurt and experiencing a million other emotions right now, but I'm also in love with the guy. And he looks almost as good in his jeans and a button-down as he looks wearing nothing at all.

"Thanks," I reply.

He looks at the house for a minute before pulling away from the curb. When he speaks, I realize he was looking at the driveway, not the house.

"You get a car?"

He obviously noticed his was returned.

I shake my head. "No."

"How have you been getting to work?"

I bite back the *none of your business* that wants to spill out. "The bus."

A muscle in his jaw tics, but he says nothing, which is a wise choice, considering the state of things between us.

Based on the flowers and the very *date* vibe of this date, I expect us to head to The Boathouse or Florentini's—two of Charleston's more upscale restaurants. Instead, Gray parks outside a small Mediterranean restaurant I've only been to once before with Sloane. It makes me wonder if she did more than pick out my clothes in preparation for this evening.

"I'll be right back," Gray tells me, then heads inside.

I fiddle with my fingers on my lap, trying to expel some nervous energy.

Minutes later, he's back, holding a large paper bag. It gets set in the backseat, and then we're driving again. This time, our destination is obvious. The long stretch of sand that comprises Folly Beach is mostly empty, with only the occasional person in sight and a few cars in the lot. The sun is sinking in the sky, coating everything in golden light.

Gray turns off the Jeep and then grabs the bag of food from the backseat along with two beach towels I didn't notice until now. He doesn't say a word as he heads for the sand. I trail behind him, suppressing the urge to ask questions and babble. Which he knows I have a tendency to do. He knows *me*, and that puts me at a disadvantage in the ice-queen routine. Each second, I thaw a little more.

Especially when I watch him spread the towels and start to pull out containers of food.

I take a seat on the striped terry cloth, cross-legged. "This is nice," I admit, picking up a grape leaf and taking a bite. The flavor of spiced rice explodes across my tongue, and I almost groan out loud. "Sloane tell you about this place?"

"No. I just know you like hummus."

I laugh. He smirks, his expression triumphant.

Fuck. He's winning in our battle of wills—because I want him to.

We eat mostly in silence after that. This time, it's not forced. I'm not schooling my reactions and responses. It's just comfortable. I'm happy sitting here with him, and I don't need to put it into words. He's relaxed as well.

"Want to walk?" he asks once we've finished dinner.

"Yeah. Sure."

He shoves himself upright from the sand and holds out a hand. I let him pull me up, and I stay in place when momentum causes us to collide. I missed touching him. The heat of his skin and his smell.

I don't move away. He doesn't either.

One hand tangles in my hair, pulling it back and away from my face. I close my eyes and lean into his touch, feeling the warmth of his skin seep into mine. I fall forward, knowing he'll be there to keep me from landing flat on my face.

We stand like that—with me pressed against his chest.

"I'm sorry," he whispers into my hair. "Sorry I hurt you. Sorry it took me so long to figure my shit out."

I don't say it's okay because it's not. Not yet, at least. The pain is too fresh, too visceral. But I lift my hands and wrap them around his waist, shrinking the gap between us down to nothing.

I'm not sure how long we stand there for, but my chest feels lighter when I step back. He takes my hand, and our fingers tangle as we walk down the beach, closer and closer to the white foam that approaches and retreats.

Gray pauses to roll up the bottoms of his jeans, then walks into the water. I attempt to do the same, then quickly remember that my pants are practically painted to my skin. The only way they'll be harder to get off is if they're wet, so I stay on the sand.

"Why aren't you coming in?" Gray asks.

"I can't roll my jeans up," I admit.

As expected, he laughs before wading back onto the shore. "Is this like the television remote?"

"No!" I scoff.

"On your butt," he demands. In the same tone as he's demanded other positions.

I complied then, and I do the same now. He kneels before me and starts tugging on the denim around my ankles, trying to force the material upward.

After a minute, he huffs. "Jesus. You weren't kidding."

"Told ya." My voice is smug.

"Who designed these?"

I push his hands away and take over. "They're supposed to make my butt look good. They're not meant for wading in the ocean."

He sits back on his heels, a secret smile spreading across his face. "Well, in that case, you'd better stand up, so I can judge them on that."

"I saw you get a good look earlier."

247

"You did, huh? Wouldn't you have had to be looking at me to catch me looking at you?"

"I guess I get how you got there."

Gray laughs before his gaze settles back on my ankles. "How long is it going to take you to get those all the way off later?"

"Don't assume you'll find out."

"I'm not even expecting a goodnight kiss," he assures me.

"You'll get one," I confide. I might make him wait for sex, but there's no way I'll get through this whole night without reuniting with his mouth.

His eyes dance as he pulls me upright. I use our joined hands to pull him back toward the water, no longer caring if my jeans get wet. Some moments are too special for practical matters.

Gray raises a brow as the denim below my knees gets soaked, but he says nothing. When he does speak, it's unrelated to wading while fully clothed.

"You know," he says as the salty water swirls around our calves, "there was a moment."

A gust of wind blows half my hair in front of my face. I brush it away so I can see him without the blonde curtain. "A moment?" Another breeze, and he's half-hidden again.

"When I realized I was in love with you."

I forget about my hair. "Oh?"

Amusement lights up his face in response to however I'm looking at him. "That day we went to the base? I wasn't supposed to fly that day. I hadn't flown—not since Sam had died. He was a damn good pilot, as good as me. What happened to him humbled me, I guess. Before that, I'd thought I was invincible. Sam's death reminded me there's always something bigger at play up there."

He sucks in a long breath between his teeth. His eyes wander to the endless stretch of water we're standing in before returning to my face.

"As soon as I invited you in that Raptor, I knew. I knew if you were up there with me, I'd be fine. Knew I would never—*could* never—let anything happen to you. Knew I loved you."

"But…that was a long time ago. We'd only slept together a few times."

"It wasn't about sex, Evie. I've known you most of my life. I've known there was the possibility for"—his hands squeeze my waist—"*this* for a long time."

I'm stunned. "You never said anything. *Did* anything. I had a crush on you forever." Something I never imagined I'd admit so freely to him.

"Yeah." A smirk flashes across his face. "I know. Part of it was Noah. I knew he'd be pissed. Not that we were dating, but I knew he'd be worried I wouldn't treat you right. And he would have had reason to. I wasn't ready for a serious relationship then. Look at how much I've fucked this up now. Me in high school? College?" He shakes his head. "It would've ended badly. But it doesn't mean I didn't think about it then. Doesn't mean I'm not ready for it now. And it definitely doesn't mean I didn't mean everything I told you this morning. I did. I *do*. I love you, Evie."

It feels like a moment where there should be a Polaroid snapped and a favorite song playing and a distant *pop* of champagne. All of those things take place in my head, but what's happening here, now, right in front of me isn't. Gray is really standing in front of me, saying all the things I've ever wanted to hear from him.

There are lots of emotions bubbling in my chest and thoughts flying through my head. But in the end, it all boils down to four words that fall off my tongue like I've said them a thousand times before. That I hope to say a thousand times more.

"I love you, Gray."

EPILOGUE
GRAY

A blue jersey runs into the end zone, and Emmett almost upends the entire table. Beer, peanuts, and all. I can't stand watching sports with him. There's a reason our living room is minimally decorated—because Emmett likes to celebrate or bemoan each play like he's one of the players on the field. Unfortunately, there is plenty of furniture to knock over in this sports bar.

"Jesus, Baker! Watch it!" Harrison grabs his beer and sets it between his legs, obviously deciding that's the safer spot for it. Noah does the same.

I check my phone. Nothing from Evie. I'm anxious to get out of here. I've been gone for the past week, and listening to Emmett cuss out the Bears defensive line is much less enjoyable than other things I'd prefer to be doing as soon as she's off work.

The television flips to commercials—probably the fiftieth ad break since we started watching. Noah and Emmett start discussing offensive strategies. Harrison looks at me and rolls his eyes. He's not a big sports fan in general, and I've never followed any besides basketball that closely.

"Your trip go okay?" Harrison asks. There's some hesitancy in the question that's my fault. I took my friends' surprise at my career choice as personally as I took my father's disapproval and made my job a topic we didn't discuss.

"Yeah, fine," I reply. "Long."

"Long? You used to be gone for months."

"I know." I can't imagine it now. The weeks I spent away from Evie were hard enough.

"Hey!" Suddenly, she's here, sinking down in the booth beside me and sliding over so she's almost in my lap.

I give her a quick kiss and a pointed look. "Tell me you didn't take the bus here, Evie."

"I didn't take the bus here," she parrots.

"I told you to text me!"

She rolls her eyes. "I knew you were already here. You can get up at four thirty and drive me to work in the morning, if you want to be my chauffeur that badly."

"No news on your car?"

"Nope. The garage left a message earlier. It won't be ready till Tuesday now."

I push my half-full beer away. "Looks like I'll be getting up at four thirty, then."

Evie's expression softens. "You don't have to do that."

"You're *not* taking the bus, Evie."

"Fine." She caves. "Only so you stop making that face."

"What face?"

"That pouting puppy-dog face."

"I do not have a pouting puppy-dog face."

"Yes, you do. I look at your face more than you do."

I smirk before I lean down and graze my lips against her ear. "You're usually looking lower, baby."

She lets out a breathy, small gasp that immediately has me hardening.

Noah makes a gagging sound from across the table. I forgot he was here, honestly. Evie captures every ounce of my attention. "Seriously, you two?"

I don't think he could actually hear what we were saying, but I'm guessing our body language didn't leave a whole lot to the imagination.

"Calm down, Noah. We were talking." I squeeze Evie's thigh as she reaches out and takes a sip from my beer.

Noah has been far more accepting of our relationship than I ever expected he might be. I try not to push him.

She glances at me, smirks, and then takes another sip of my beer.

"You can order a drink," I tell her when she settles back against the back of the booth.

"I have to work tomorrow."

"I know." I trail my fingers along her leg.

Evie usually stays at her place—alone—on nights when she has to work the next day. Both because her place is closer to Charleston General and because neither of us gets much sleep when we're in bed together.

It's part of the reason I'm so eager to move in with her. Not only is the house I found five minutes from the hospital and ten minutes from the base, but it'll also mean we'll be able to spend a lot more time together.

"I saw your dad today," she tells me, tilting her head back to meet my gaze. The end of her blonde ponytail brushes my arm.

My parents are happy Evie and I are dating. Actually, that's a massive understatement. They're ecstatic.

It hasn't thawed my relationship with them much, though. We went over there for dinner last month, and Evie did most of the talking. I like that she gets along with my parents—especially my father, who can find fault with practically anyone—but it also throws my dysfunctional relationship with them into sharper contrast. I didn't realize quite how strained things had become between us until I watched them laughing and joking with Evie.

I knew my decision to join the Air Force would piss off my father. I underestimated how much—how it would become the defining characteristic of our relationship. How it would bleed into every conversation with my mother as well—become the burden that none of us could escape.

"Gray?"

I meet Evie's blue gaze. "Yeah?"

"Did you hear me? About your dad?"

"Yeah. I heard you."

"About dinner?"

"Dinner?" I echo.

"We're having dinner over there tomorrow night. I told you last week."

"When?"

Evie bites her bottom lip. "When you were in the mood to say yes." She shifts, giving me the real answer. "He's your dad. And my boss's boss's—"

"Boss's boss's boss's boss. Yeah, I know."

"You added too many."

I roll my eyes at that. "You're lucky I love you."

"You're lucky I love *you*."

Something about this moment—the blonde hair spilling over her shoulder, the dark wood backdrop of the bar, the happy gleam in her eyes—makes my chest tighten with the realization that losing Evie is not an option. Ever.

"Yeah, I am."

Emmett sets his empty bottle of beer down. Loudly. "Yep. I'm calling it a night. Happy for you two, but *wow*, is this hard to stomach."

253

"Try being related to her," Noah says dryly.

Harrison snorts before draining his own beer. "I'm ready to go too."

"I'm going to run to the restroom," Evie tells me. "I'll meet you outside."

I nod, and the rest of us head outside.

"Twenty-five-minute wait," Harrison grumbles as we wait out on the sidewalk, checking for nearby cars on his phone. "Is there a concert or something happening tonight?"

"No idea," Emmett replies. "Too bad we know no one who *has a car* and, in my case, happens to be headed to the *exact same place*."

"I can't give you guys a ride."

Emmett groans. "Are you kidding me? You can't wait an extra fifteen minutes to get laid?" He glances at Noah. "Sorry, Collins."

Noah grumbles a response.

"That's not why. I just—"

Evie reappears by my side. "Ready?"

"You don't mind if we ride with you guys, right, Evie?" Emmett asks. "Rideshares are crazy busy tonight."

"You could take the bus," I suggest.

Evie elbows my side. "Of course not."

I sigh. The temperature is hovering in the low fifties—chilly for Charleston. After living in Boston for four years, I doubt Evie is actually all that cold, but she snuggles against my side as we walk to the Jeep, and I'm sure as hell not complaining.

Emmett, Harrison, and Noah are all in high spirits as they climb into the back, happy to have a ride. But if they thought the bar was awkward...

It takes about ten minutes for the guys to realize we're not headed to a destination where any of us currently live. Evie is oblivious, scrolling through social media on her phone. I watch them exchange looks in the rearview mirror as we stop outside the yellow bungalow with a *For Sale* sign out front, finally figuring out this was *not* the night to carpool.

"Ah fuck," Emmett groans from the backseat. "Is this what I think it is? Am I going to have to find a new roommate?"

I ignore his griping and focus on the reason we're here. Evie is staring at the house, saying nothing. "We already went car shopping together—twice—so...I sort of figured this is the next step." *Is it common for couples to go car shopping together?* Is that a step? I have no idea. No sense of what I'm saying. I'm just trying to gauge her reaction to this.

I see the moment she spots the sign. Her phone drops into her lap, and her mouth follows suit.

"What do you think?" I ask nervously.

"Of the *house*?"

"Yeah. It's close to the hospital than your place right now is, and—"

Evie cuts me off. "You want to *live together*?" She's surprised, definitely. I can't tell if it's in a good way or a bad way. If she thinks it's too soon or too fast. Maybe I should have broached this topic before bringing her to look a place.

I'm a lot of things, but I'm not a coward. I don't shy away from the thick disbelief in her tone. "Yeah."

"You want to buy a house together and live together?"

"Yes," I confirm. "But it's okay if you're not—"

She cuts me off. "Can we look inside?"

"Uh, yeah." I wave at the realtor patiently waiting in the driveway. "I made an appointment to tour it. But we don't have to—"

"Gray?"

"Yeah?"

"Shut up." She unbuckles her seat belt and climbs out of the car.

Emmett snorts in the backseat.

I turn and toss him the keys. "Here. Take the car. We'll Uber home."

"You sure?"

"Yeah."

I catch Noah's gaze before I close the Jeep's door. This was a conversation I was planning to have with him, but not now, like this. Before I know if she wants this and in front of two of our other friends. I'm guessing Noah saw this coming, to an extent. I've made it clear how serious I am about her. Reality is different from expectation. Sometimes better, sometimes worse. There was a recent time I couldn't imagine settling down and buying a house here—tying myself to Charleston in any permanent way. Now I'm doing so willingly. Happily.

He nods. "I'm happy for you guys."

I nod back. "Thanks, man."

Evie is standing on the sidewalk, looking at the house.

"When I saw the listing, it reminded me of your parents' place," I tell her.

"You don't want something...bigger?" she asks. "Like *your* parents' place?"

"For the two of us?" I shake my head. "We can get something bigger when we have kids."

Evie looks stunned. "*When* we have kids?"

"Yeah, I figured you'd want to finish your residency and fellowship first."

"You want that? Marriage, kids, all of it?"

"With you? Yes." I look at her as I say the last word, letting her see how much I mean it.

"Okay." Evie says a lot more than that single word, holding

my gaze for a minute before she turns back to look at the house. "Let's go look inside."

We head up the driveway to talk with the real estate agent. She lets us into the house, then begins spouting facts about the property and the surrounding neighborhood as we walk from room to room. I'm not absorbing much of what she's saying. I'm more focused on Evie's expressions as she takes in the honey wood floors and the big windows and the tile backsplash in the kitchen. The bedrooms and the bathrooms.

"I'll give you two a few minutes to look around on your own," the realtor tells us. "If you have any questions, I'll be right outside."

I nod and Evie thanks her.

"What do you think?" I whisper once we're alone, resting my chin on the top of her head and wrapping my arms around her waist.

"I think it's perfect," she replies. "And that you'll need to contribute more than a toaster this time."

I chuckle and tighten my grip. "Deal."

We stand that way for a few more minutes, soaking in our new home.

Fifteen minutes at my parents' house, and I'm already past ready to leave. Outside of medicine, my dad's main interests are golf and his garden. None of those three subjects are ones that interest me in the least. Pair that with years of animosity, and pleasant conversation is hard to come by between me and my dad. I nod along as he goes on about his hole in one earlier, paying more attention to the bird flitting past the living room window and resisting the urge to check my phone. We put an offer in on the yellow bungalow last night. If we don't get it, there will be other houses. But I want this one. I'm ready to take the *moving in together* step now.

When I tune back into the conversation, my father brings up a topic that usually has me tensing.

He leans forward in his favorite armchair, abandoning his relaxed pose. "One of my department heads, Dr. Murphy, his son is applying to the Air Force Academy. He's a close friend outside of work. I know his family well. I thought you might be willing to put him in touch with someone who might be able to put in a good word. If you are, well, I'd appreciate it." My father has to force those last three words out. He hates asking for help or favors from anyone—especially from me.

The first time my father has ever brought up the Air Force without a lecture, and it's to ask for a favor on behalf of someone else. He doesn't seem upset by his *close friend's* son's career choice. I grit my teeth. "You can give him my number."

"I meant—"

"I know what you *meant*, Dad. But you don't know anything about my job. To beat around any bullshit, I'm damn good at it. I'm the youngest commissioned captain in my class. If I recommend this kid, it'll carry weight with Admissions."

I take a long sip of my beer, stand, and then turn to head back out onto the porch. I was sitting out there, waiting for Evie, when my dad lured me in under the pretense of a beer. To ask for a favor.

My mom's chopping away in the kitchen, trying to stay oblivious to the tension. As always.

"Grayson. Wait."

I pause, sigh, and look back at my dad. "What?"

"I'm sorry, son. You're right. I don't know anything about the Air Force, about your work, and that's all on me."

"Yeah, it is."

He sighs. "I was disappointed, Gray."

"I'm aware."

"You've always been stubborn. Contrarian. I thought it was just a phase, that you would try it out and then come back. Stay close to us. Go to Duke."

I feel eighteen again. "Most parents would be proud."

"I was proud. I *am* proud. I just…it took some getting used to. And then you shut us out. Barely came home, never talked about work. I had no idea you were a captain. For all I knew, you sat around and tinkered with planes all day."

"You could have *asked*, Dad. I'll be outside."

I'm still sitting out on the porch when a silver sedan pulls up a few minutes later. I watch Evie climb out of the car and bend down to say something to her friend Rose. After talking for a couple of minutes, she turns and starts up my parents' front walk. I watch whatever is on my face register on hers. Evie drops her bag at the top of the stairs and plops down into my lap. I wrap my arms around her, pulling her flush against me.

She turns to look at me, skimming one hand along my jaw. "That bad, huh?"

I sigh and look at her. "I got into it with my dad."

"Wanna talk about it?"

"There's not much to say. He asked me if I knew anyone in the Air Force who could recommend the kid of one of his coworkers for the Academy."

"Not if you would recommend?" She gets it right away, and it makes me want to abandon this conversation and kiss her senseless. It might show in my expression because she smiles a little, knowingly.

259

"Right. I said if I did, it would carry weight. I'm not sure if he believed me. He didn't ask me to."

She exhales. "He's your dad, Gray. He's best friends with my dad and I have to see him for my job. If you want, it can end there. We don't have to do any more of these dinners or invite him over to our place. Or…"

"Or what?"

"You can be the bigger person," she says softly. "He has regrets. I know he does. He asks about you every time I see him. Your dad wants things to be different, but he doesn't know how to change them. You're the most intimidating person I know, your dad included. You could go golf with him. Or invite him to the base with you and show him around. It's pretty impressive. I'm not saying you need to show off, or that you should have to, but you could just show him. I hope he'll surprise you. If he doesn't…that's on him. Not you." Evie sits up and reaches down into her bag. "I was going to save these for after dinner, but it's already getting dark out. And maybe it will make dinner more bearable."

"Unless you pull a blowjob out of there, I doubt it."

She smacks me on the chest, then places a long, thin box in my hand. "Here."

I tilt the box, so I can read the letters on the side. "Sparklers?"

Evie nods. "Unless you made up the story you told Marnie and Scott…"

"I didn't." I could have listed lots more moments I've watched Evie Collins when she wasn't looking.

She stands and takes the box from me. "Come on."

I follow her down the stairs and onto the grass of my parents' front yard. She pulls a lighter out of her bag, thinking of every-thing, like always. I slide two sparklers out of the box and hold them out for her to light. They take the flame instantly, burning bright and sending flares flying.

Evie takes one from me and leans against my side. We stand in silence, in the same spot I watched her all those years ago, as the sparks we're holding burn down and fizzle out.

I know we'll never do the same.

THE END

ACKNOWLEDGMENTS

Book *eleven*! There was a very recent time when I wasn't sure if I could finish one book...and here we are. So, to start, I'd like to thank everyone who has read, reviewed, sent me a message, shared news about my books, or supported my writing in any way. I've said it before and I'll say it many more times, but you all are the reason these books exist. I have a lot of stories in my head and I hope I will have a chance to publish each and every one of them. But the support and encouragement from people who have read and *enjoyed* my books is truly what keeps me typing into the early hours of the morning. Thank you doesn't seem like enough, but *thank you*.

Jovana, this book was infinitely improved by your edits. Thank you for caring about Gray and Evie's story so much. Your comments made me smile and your thoroughness strengthened every word. It's always a pleasure to work with you and I hope to do so on many more books!

Tiffany, I hope you know you were already mentioned above. Thank you for not only being an amazing proofreader and editor but also an incredible supporter and cheerleader. I'm grateful for the many, *many* ways you've improved my writing throughout all the books of mine you've worked on. Indie publishing can feel like being stranded on an island and I know I can always rely on you for a lifeboat. That means more than words can convey, but I tried!

Kim, thank you for this beautiful cover. I don't think I could pick favorites among the ones you've designed for me—let alone *a* favorite—but I couldn't love the way this one turned out any more and it's perfect for this book. Cover design is the part of the publishing process I look forward to the most. You make it such a smooth and collaborative effort and I'm so grateful.

Jessica and the team at Inkslinger PR, thanks for all your hard work getting this book out into the world!

And finally, to Farley. You were the only one still awake when I finished this book at four a.m. Thanks for celebrating with me. You're the best, buddy.

ABOUT THE AUTHOR

C.W. Farnsworth is the author of numerous adult and young adult romance novels featuring sports, strong female leads, and happy endings.

Charlotte lives in Rhode Island and when she isn't writing spends her free time reading, at the beach, or snuggling with her Australian Shepard.

Find her on Facebook (@cwfarnsworth), Twitter (@cw_farnsworth), Instagram (@authorcwfarnsworth) and check out her website www.authorcwfarnsworth.com for news about upcoming releases!